THE ORDER

BY

MARSHA MEGAN STOKES

Copyright © 2020 Marsha Megan Stokes
All rights reserved.
Published in the United States of America
Kindle Direct Publishing

Stokes, Marsha Megan
The Order; novel/Marsha Megan Stokes
ISBN-13: 978-1477467930
ISBN-10: 1477467939

"Who Knows What" Edition

Cover Design by Kindle Direct Publishing
Cover image RF from Dreamstime

https://sites.google.com/site/theordersaga/

For Chris.

You are my perfect Gift.

CONTENTS

NAMES AND MEANINGS:

Rachel—is pronounced *RAY-chel*, meaning "innocence of a lamb, one with purity".

Peter—is pronounced *PEE-ter*, meaning "rock".

Donavon—is pronounced *DAH-na-vun,* meaning "dark, brown-haired chieftain".

Beth— is pronounced *beth*, short for Elizabeth, meaning "consecrated to God".

Robert—is pronounced *RAH-bert*, meaning "bright fame".

Blake—is pronounced *blayk*, meaning "black/pale, white". Originally a nickname for someone with hair or skin that was either very dark or very light.

Nancy—is pronounced *NAN-cee*, meaning "grace".

Stewart—is pronounced *STOO-ert*, meaning a steward.

Amy—is pronounced *AY-mee*, meaning "beloved".

PROLOGUE: LATER

The cave was unfamiliar. The earthy path was hard-packed and well-used, twisting down through the darkness. The air was crisp, dank, and stale. She wondered how many had come this way before. And how many had never returned.

The Evil was in her mind causing pain—excruciating pain—while it whispered words dripping with foul sweetness.

Come to me… I am here waiting for you. I will have you. I need you. I can make the pain stop, but only if you learn. Only if you surrender.

The voice in her head was stronger now. With every passing minute, every passing step, it grew stronger.

You are mine. No one else can save you. Come to me…

She could feel her eyes glossing over as the Evil cooed inside her brain.

Perceptive, Donavon glanced back, a crease of worry on his brow as if he could hear the voice too. His dark hair was damp from the moisture in the air. A sheen of water glistened on his skin. While others would be uncomfortable in the moist underground tunnel, Donavon didn't even seem to notice—his worried thoughts consumed with the task ahead.

The footsteps of the group echoed off the walls with a steady beat that felt like a funeral procession. The dark path wound down for an eternity. The two women on either side of her supported her body when the Evil would strike.

Finally… mercifully… they reached the end, arriving at a spacious cavern that housed a small beach and a large underground pool. Off in the distance, she could make out the sounds of water trickling down the rock face.

Illuminated by the lantern in his hand, Donavon strode over to the large man-made circle of rocks in the dirt. The women gently guided her to the center and helped her to kneel.

"We need to begin soon. There isn't much time left. Where *is* Peter?" Donavon, usually so calm and cool, had to stop for a moment to contain his rising agitation. His eyes narrowed dangerously as he scanned the dim cavern for the Locator.

Off to the side in the shadows, a slight movement caught her eye. It looked as if Peter was slowly rising from his seated position. He began an unhurried tread over to the group. To the Order.

With equal hostility in his voice Peter sarcastically sneered, "Sorry to keep you waiting." Anger, frustrations, and possibly even hatred burned like embers in Peter's eyes. A dark, sick terror crept into her heart, as she wondered if he would rather let her die than try to save her.

The voice spoke again.

Peter is with me… You know it… You can SEE IT! Come to me. Be with Peter. Wouldn't that make him happy? You want Peter to be happy. No pain. No fear. Look in Peter's eyes. I am there.

The voice mimicked a soothing quality, yet bile rose up in her throat as she felt dark fingers twisting inside her brain, manipulating her thoughts. Reaching up, she absentmindedly rubbed her temples. The throbbing in her skull began to be overwhelming. She mumbled, "Get out, get out…" Unconsciously, her voice grew louder and more desperate. "Get out, get out… GET OUT!" Her screams echoed off the surface of the water before coming back to the quiet crowd.

She crumpled to the ground holding her head. Rocking back and forth, she weakly moaned, "Out, out, out, out…"

Peter glanced at her aching form. Sympathy and tenderness overshadowed the fury in his eyes for just a moment. Then, stone-faced, he took his place in the Order.

Robert took out the Life Box and set it in front of him. Donavon, being the most powerful of the group, would take the lead and begin the ceremony to Cleanse her.

With a savage intensity, he turned to Peter and spat, "Can you do this?" Donavon's face was tormented, but he spoke softer as he added, "I know you are upset with me. But I *need* to know if you can put your feelings aside." His voice waivered with emotion. "Help us save her."

She watched as Peter glared back—the fervor in his eyes intensifying. He stated simply, "Time is running out." His face was torn with anger. Hurt. Possibly jealousy. Or betrayal? Her heart wanted to break.

Her whole body shuddered violently, but not from the cold of the cave or the agony in her mind.

From fear.

Her fate rested in Peter's hands, and she was helpless except to wait and watch.

Marsha Megan Stokes

CHAPTER 1: FIRST DAY

The cool air was crisp and invigorating. Fall was Peter's favorite time of the year, and it was especially stunning in Golden Colorado. Leaning against the rough bark of a shade tree, he ran a hand through his wavy blonde hair, admiring the vibrant changing colors of the season. It was the first day of the semester and campus was coming alive. A hum of excitement permeated everything and everyone.

Students once again sat on the grass smiling, laughing, and catching up with old friends they hadn't seen all summer. Others walked along paths, backpacks slung over shoulders and class schedules in hand. Excitement came with the promise of a new year.

Smiling, Peter's blue eyes twinkled with delight and his heart sped up with a slight sense of anticipation. Surrounded by people, he honed his attention in on one student in particular. This student, this young woman, was special. She was Gifted, just as Peter was also Gifted.

Only, she likely didn't even know it… yet.

"I recognize that look." Donavon's brown eyes were intense, as usual. He studied his best friend's face and then followed the path of Peter's gaze to see what, or rather whom, had caught his attention.

At a glance, it would have been easy to mistake Peter and Donavon for brothers. They both shared a tall, lean, muscular build. When together, they exuded an ease, humor, and familiarity that was perfectly in lockstep. However, Donavon's dark eyes and hair contrasted starkly with Peter's more fair features. While Peter was open, inviting and friendly, Donavon was calm, serious, and loyal. Yin and yang. The perfect balance of friends, each possessing the opposite yet best qualities.

Peter laughed at Donavon's comment, "Look over by the big spruce tree. Do you see the girl standing with the schedule?" He inclined his head in the direction of the dorm rooms. A mischievous smile crept onto his face as he added playfully, "Do you want me to introduce you? I know you like brunettes."

Sighing good naturedly, Donavon quipped, "Just stick to the business at hand. I'll worry about my personal life." He reached over and slapped Peter on the back. "Besides," with equal mischief in his eyes he added, "I've never needed help before."

That was true. Donavon was the epitome of "tall, dark and handsome."

Pushing himself away from the tree, Peter left Donavon to approach the new girl on campus.

It was time.

This was his job—his skill—to find people like her. People with the Gift. Being a Locator was something he had been born with. While he couldn't explain how it all worked, Peter just *knew* when he was around someone who was different—someone who could do things that no one else could, even if they themselves were unaware of their abilities.

This particular girl looked like many of the new students on campus today. Not surrounded by friends, her backpack leaned against her leg as she stared first at the paper schedule in her hand and then intently at her surroundings to get her bearings. Her shoulders slumped slightly as she avoided eye contact with others walking past her. She gave off the uncertain air of someone trying not to draw attention to themselves while simultaneously being lost.

"What she needs," Peter thought to himself, "is someone to show her around."

As he drew nearer, Peter had the strange feeling that he had already seen her that day. The thought was a little disconcerting. He typically spotted people with the Gift instantly. Like a sixth sense or a guiding hand, he would be unknowingly drawn to the right place at the right time to cross paths. Once in their proximity, his skin would tingle and it felt like his hair was standing on end. There was an energy—a power—in their presence.

But something today just felt… off.

Trying to shake the feeling, Peter inhaled deeply to clear his head. His adrenaline was up and his blood was pumping. For him, finding someone Gifted was like finding a long-lost friend or a new member of the family. He felt excited and on high-alert.

Walking slowly, Peter could feel the hum of her aura that marked the girl as Gifted. It was slight, but grew steadily as he got closer. She didn't appear to have noticed his approach, so Peter cleared his throat and asked, "I couldn't help but notice, do you need some help?" Turning up the charm a bit, Peter flashed his most endearing smile and waited for her to look up.

"Turning up the charm" was a literal thing for Peter. Part of being a Locater included the ability to enhance the natural perception of a situation—to make reactions more potent. While he couldn't create a feeling that didn't already exist, he could make true emotions stronger.

And first impressions could be very important.

Startled, the young woman looked up suddenly and met his eyes. A tentative smile worked at the corners of her mouth. It was a good sign and Peter started to relax. She seemed to be responding well to his initial contact.

"Oh…" Her voice was soft and gentle, "I was just looking for my next class." She immediately glued her eyes to her schedule and map of campus, a slight flush now on her cheeks. A lock of hair escaped from her ponytail in the breeze and she absentmindedly tucked it behind her ear.

Gently reaching out to touch the map, Peter commented. "Well, in that case, I bet I can help you. Why don't we start out with turning your map right-side up, eh?" The humor in his voice must have begun to win her over, as the girl looked up and met his gaze with a bit more confidence. "I'm Peter, by the way... Peter Bennett."

"I'm Beth... Beth Andrews." Her blush deepened ever so slightly as she looked at the tenderness in his eyes. Waving a hand around to indicate her surroundings, she continued, "I'm new here... obviously." She gave a self-depreciating laugh as she righted her map. With a wrinkle of concentration on her forehead, she unknowingly chewed on her lower lip while she studied.

Peter thought the whole experience was adorable. She was so shy. Sweet and innocent. Kind and completely unaware of her potential.

"Okay, let's see...this way is north," Peter indicated with a brush of his hand across the map. "I assume this big circled building is where you are headed?" At her shy nod, he went on, "So, you'll follow this sidewalk right next to us all the way around that bend," he pointed, "and it should take you right there." He continued to search her face, "So, are you taking music classes? If I'm not mistaken, that building is the Fine Arts Center."

"Yup. Music 1010. It's just a gen ed requirement." Nervously laughing, she added, "I am hopelessly nonmusical, so I hope I can make heads or tails of what they are talking about." Beth bent over and picked up her backpack. "Thanks for your help."

Feeling like he hadn't made a deep enough impression yet, Peter put his hands in his jacket pockets and started to follow. "I'm headed that way. Why don't I walk with you?" Again, flashing his best smile, Peter used his Gift to help make her feel as comfortable as he could. He had the distinct impression that she was naturally very timid and might normally refuse such a request.

Not really waiting for Beth to agree, Peter began to casually walk alongside her as they made their way down the path. The hum in her aura seemed to dim as they continued.

That didn't normally happen.

Internally, Peter frowned, but on the outside, he remained smiling and upbeat. Usually someone's aura would only change gradually—imperceptibly over the course of a long period of time. Even then, it almost never got weaker, but instead grew stronger as they developed their skills. Maybe Beth's power was unstable. Peter had never personally encountered such a thing before, but it was possible. This new discovery made him a little nervous and uncomfortable.

Trying to mask his uncertainty, he asked, "So... what brought you to Grayson?"

She responded after a moment's thought, "I don't know. I just felt like this was the college for me. I visited campus once during high school, and I really felt at home here. I didn't really think about going anywhere else after that." She shrugged, like it was no big deal, but Peter made a mark on his mental checklist. "It feels good to finally be here."

"You know," he said, trying to sound casual, "I felt that way too when I first started here. It's a nice place. I sure hope you like it." Again, he smiled a little smile, which thankfully received a little smile in return.

She nodded, "It seems nice." Peter hoped that also mean that *he* seemed nice.

Suddenly they were at the Fine Arts Center. With a quick thank you, Beth made her way up the stairs into the building.

Peter turned back towards Donavon. Now that he had made his initial contact with her, using his Gift as Locator it would be much easier to find Beth again. In fact, he would likely be unconsciously drawn to wherever she was. For now, the day was still young and there was plenty of time for him to bump into her again. In the meantime, others needed to know about his discovery.

As he walked, Peter thought it was probably just déjà vu, but he could have sworn that he felt his skin tingle again as he rounded the bend where he initially made contact with Beth. Sometimes, the energies of a person's Gift could momentarily linger, marking where they had been and leaving unseen clues for Locators to follow.

Finally, Peter saw Donavon right where he had left him, lounging against the tree. He wore perfectly tailored clothes and had exactly styled hair. His good looks were drawing all kinds of attention, whether Donavon wanted it or not. A couple of girls across the way were staring, but he didn't seem to notice—or at least he didn't acknowledge that he knew. He simply watched Peter approach.

Peter could sense Donavon's aura long before he was standing right beside him. It was actually incredibly easy because Donavon was one of the most powerfully Gifted people he had ever known. To any Locator, Donavon's aura was like a white-hot beacon on the horizon that could be sensed from miles away. It was so powerful in fact, that Peter often had to build a mental wall around it to block it out so he could focus on other things.

Thankfully, part of Peter's talent was the ability to block out the specific auras of those he was most familiar with. After all, he did live in an entire house full of the Gifted and feeling like his skin was crawling all the time would drive him crazy.

Occasionally though, Peter would drop his walls and allow himself to seek out a particular aura in his home—his Order. Donavon was so incredibly strong that it was almost a high to focus on his power. He felt more alive when he was around Donavon—always had. Peter was sure he could recognize and find his friend anywhere.

But it went deeper than that. Peter could trust Donavon completely. The years of friendship they built together made them as close as blood brothers. They could almost finish each other's sentences. In fact, many times no words or explanations were needed. They just... knew.

When Peter thought about it, it seemed like a nice twist of fate that he and his best friend had both turned out to be Gifted. Otherwise, Peter would have been forced to keep the most important part of himself a secret. Often, once a Gifted became aware of their abilities, they would be drawn to others like themselves. Peter and Donavon's friendship inevitably would have faded.

But as fate would have it, Donavon was extremely Gifted. That allowed Peter to mutually and unconditionally share everything with his friend. There was no need for secrets between members of the Order.

Donavon stared intently as Peter approached. "How'd it goes Casanova?" he teased. "Was she eating out of your hand?"

Peter smiled, "Not like she would have been if you had turned your charm on her." He continued, "I'm going to hang around for a bit and see if I can bump into her again. I'd like to watch her more before we report back to everyone. I'm one hundred percent sure that she is one of us."

A small crease appeared between Donavon's eyebrows. "Is she in danger yet?"

Like a heavy blanket, the seriousness of the situation settled over Peter. Unknown to Beth, danger waited.

Being Gifted was both a blessing and curse. Without the help of an Order, it would be impossible for someone who was unprepared to be able to fight the Evil that would eventually start to take hold in their minds.

Peter replied to Donavon's question, "She didn't have a slip for the twenty minutes or so that I was with her. You know that's not long enough to know for sure, but it's encouraging."

Giving one brisk nod and seeming satisfied for the moment, Donavon tried to turn the tone of the conversation back to something light-hearted. "Well, let me know if you need any help getting her—" he paused, a teasing gleam entering his eyes, "—attention."

Firing back as he strode away, Peter tossed over his shoulder, "You just leave the heavy lifting to me."

***

At about noon Peter entered the student union building carrying an apple. He began making his way to the food court area. Navigating through the river of students was almost a subconscious skill—slightly dodge this person, slip into that open space— gracefully Peter made his way down the hallway. He was being drawn by the call of Beth's aura.

The food court was particularly crowded. So many students were coming and going with business to take care of—registration, fees, and new friends. Peter had seen this same thing over and over each year. This would be his fourth at Grayson—his seventh semester, not counting summers. When he had originally arrived, he had been eighteen. Now twenty-two, he was a seasoned veteran.

With so many semesters under his belt, other students in Peter's place would be finishing up their bachelor's degrees and moving on to the "real world". However, Peter was much more fixated on his inherently private calling. His "real world" was hidden, exotic and dangerous. And he had already been living it for years.

Peter's Gift had come through his family line. His father was a Locator, and then his grandmother before that. The nice thing about having this bit of dirty laundry in the family was that they completely understood what life was going to be like for Peter and didn't ask too many questions or interfere. They could also be a great source of knowledge for him. There weren't many places that Peter could go with questions about his talent, but he could always go to his family.

Of course, in other Orders, there were people who thought they knew all about what Peter was, what he could do, and what it must feel like, but only his family *really* understood.

The emotional life of a Locator was complex by its very nature. A surprising, yet deeply instinctive doubt filled Peter's

8

personal life. His ability to enhance a person's feelings blurred the line between what was genuine and what was manipulated. Long after Peter ceased to alter a situation, what residual effects did that leave on a relationship?

For a Locator, these alterations, these enhancements of emotions were critical to saving someone's life. Peter's job—his purpose—included convincing a stranger to leave their old lives behind. To come with him and enter a new secret world that they never knew existed. Doing so was the only way an Order knew to fight off the Evil.

The Gifted can sense things in the world around them in a way that Non-Gifted are immune to. Flows of energy. The pull of both good and evil. Their perceptions are heightened—enhanced—giving them the ability to manipulate those currents. And with that increased sensitivity, they become more in tune with the good... but also more vulnerable to the bad—the Evil.

Regular people might walk down a street and get the impression to not turn a certain way—a tingling at the back of their necks, or the overwhelming desire to get away and go somewhere else. They don't know why. They don't understand it. Maybe they call it a sixth sense or dumb luck. However, untold dangers are avoided simply because someone has the feeling that they are in the wrong place at the wrong time.

Someone with a Gift can sense these things as well, but it goes one step further than that. They can also hear the Evil calling to them, like a voice in their head saying, *"Come this way. Come closer. Let me wrap my arms around you and keep you here in the darkness with me."*

Seductive.
Alluring.
Mesmerizing.
Deadly.

As time passes and their abilities get stronger, the power of the darkness also increases. Without help, a Gifted can become overwhelmed—a broken mind, shattered by the things that a sweet Voice, dripping in poison, whispers in their ear. It slowly controls them, making them do things they never imagined they were capable of—horrible and sickening things.

But there is hope.

The Evil could be contained with the help of an Order, and the Gifted who was just discovering their talent could go on to live without the darkness threatening to consume them. They simply had to be discovered by a Locator before it was too late.

Like Beth.

Peter quickly scanned the food court, looking for her. He could tell she was near, but her exact location was harder to pinpoint. His sharp eyes swept over the crowd of students waiting in lines at the various counters.

Finally, at a small table where he thought he had already looked, he found her. No longer studying her map or class schedule, she appeared absorbed in a novel. Absentmindedly, she played with the food on her tray.

Peter put on his best smile and approached the table. "Fancy meeting you again!" He didn't want to scare her by appearing overly interested, so he casually added, "Beth, was it?"

Surprised, she looked up from her book. Shock crossed her face, but that quickly melted into a small smile as she said, "Peter? I'm surprised you noticed me in this huge crowd."

"I hope I'm not disturbing you. You seem pretty involved in your book."

She took a small scrap of paper from the table and placed it between the pages. "Reading assignment. No big deal." She indicated the chair across from her. "Are you looking for a place to sit? It's pretty crazy in here."

"Are you sure you don't mind?" At her smile, Peter pulled out a chair and sat down. He placed his apple between them and folded his hands on the table. "So, did you enjoy your music class?"

She groaned and dramatically dropped her head into her hands. "I am so totally hopeless! You've heard about people who are tone-deaf, right? Well, I am one step worse. I am music-deaf. Gen ed requirements suck."

Peter chuckled and picked up his apple, "Yeah. Some of them are a pain." Taking a bite, he added, "You know, I took that class a couple of semesters ago and did pretty well. I could probably help you if you want." Some people might be put off by such a generous offer from someone they just met, but with Peter and his talent, it should come across as the most natural thing in the world.

However, Beth seemed hesitant to accept what he was offering at face value.

"Umm…that's really nice of you, but..." She shyly glanced up at him through her lashes, her face a bright shade of red as she tried to think of a polite way to refuse.

Using the full force of his eyes and all the persuasion he could muster, Peter tried again, but with humor this time. "But… you just met me." Holding up his hands in a placating gesture he continued, "I get it. I get it. Stranger danger and all that. But it's really no trouble."

Peter held her gaze with his.

"All right." Shock filled her face. It looked like one of those moments where someone wished they could snatch the words right out of the air. Clearing her throat and brushing that same loose hair back behind her ear, she immediately looked away.

Not wanting to give her a chance to change her mind, he began to make his exit. Standing, he borrowed the napkin and pen she had by her book and quickly jotted down his information. Taking his apple with him, he hurried on, "Great! We'll turn you into Mozart in no time. Here's my address. Stop by tonight and we'll get started."

Another panicked look crossed her face. "Your place? I don't know…"

Peter was being clumsy. In a matter of seconds, the entire conversation had gotten more and more awkward. Immediately seeing how being invited to the room of a guy you just met sounded rather stalker-ish, he panicked a bit himself.

Was he coming on too strong? Had his Gift made him overly cocky. How had he so seriously misjudging the situation?

Peter was sweating.

It was just that Beth was so incredibly shy! Compared to his previous experiences, Peter felt unprepared for her level of resistance. Usually people responded so well to him, but this was not going according to plan.

He made eye contact with her one last time, trying to ease her fears with his Gift. "You'll love it. I live in a house with a bunch of guys *and* girls. Perfectly safe. Eight o'clock, k?"

At her barely perceptible nod, he left, dodging the crowd of students to make his way to the bus stop.

Beth's resistance—her hesitation—placed a cold, dark seed in Peter's gut. His emotional doubts about his manipulative ability fought to resurface. With Beth, he felt more like a fraud than he had ever felt in his entire life.

Peter could feel his anxiety rise, and he couldn't help but wonder what he had just gotten himself into. Tonight needed to go well or he wasn't sure what he was going to do. Beth was in danger and Peter wasn't exactly helping the situation.

CHAPTER 2: HOME

Strolling up the sidewalk, Peter felt for his key to the house. Every resident carefully kept the front door locked, even during the high traffic hours. They could not afford to have unannounced visitors, even innocent ones.

As the bolt in the door slid aside, Peter stepped into the front entryway to the familiar sounds of his housemates. Robert was in the front room playing a loud racing game on the flat screen. Someone else was banging around in the kitchen, undoubtedly making an afternoon snack. A loud, rhythmic thumping shook the chandelier as someone else was listening to music upstairs.

Amy came bounding down the curved, elegant staircase that dominated the entryway. Her curly brown hair bounced and twisted with her movements, echoing the endless energy she seemed to embody. Amy always smiled brightly, radiating happiness and encouragement.

"Hey Pete!" She was the only one who ever called him "Pete." "Busy first day?" She gave a knowing glance. As a Locator, the first day of school held the most potential for finding the Gifted. Not needing an answer, Amy enthusiastically plowed ahead, "Nancy's in the kitchen making grilled cheese. Want some?"

"Nancy, huh?" Remembering some of Nancy's other culinary creations, he replied, "You go and enjoy for me, okay?"

"Sure thing." And with a giggle, she disappeared into the kitchen.

Calling after her, Peter added, "Meeting today at three in the living room." Taking a quick sniff of the air, he could detect the faint stench of scorched bread and burnt cheese. A small smile played at the corners of his mouth.

This was home.

Peter jogged up the stairs, taking two at a time. Several of the bedrooms were on the second floor, including his own. Entering, he tossed his backpack on the bed, sat down at the oak desk that dominated the far wall and pulled out his phone.

Thanks to Robert's Gift, everyone in the house enjoyed the latest technology. Within seconds, Peter had messaged everyone in the Order about the meeting. Given what day it was and that the message was being sent by Peter, everyone could probably guess that a new Gifted had been found.

Leaning back in his chair, Peter luxuriously stretched out his legs. He loved it here. The house had enough rooms for eight people without having to double up anywhere. Currently, only six of those rooms were filled—there was Peter, Donavon, Robert, Amy, Nancy and Blake.

Peter heard a gentle chime come from his phone and knew that someone had already sent a reply. It was from Blake "Fresh meat! M or F?"

Peter smiled and shot back his reply: "Female."

Instantly another message popped up. "Sweet! It's about time."

Peter chuckled.

Of course, Blake would be excited to have another female around. The men were outnumbering the women, and in Blake's mind, that was totally unacceptable.

Tossing his phone aside, Peter walked over and flopped down on his bed, trying to clear his thoughts. So far, he felt like he had botched things with Beth. Peter had felt incompetent, like a brand-new Locator all over again. Usually, his job came smoothly. Naturally. Effortless even.

But today things had felt strained. Awkward and uncomfortable. Try as he might, Peter had felt anything but in control.

And tonight, one of the hardest parts of his job was about to take place. Peter needed to gauge everything perfectly. He needed to know exactly what to say and how much to push. How much was Beth ready to handle?

For the second time today, Peter's anxiety began to rise.

How do you convince someone that they might have a special ability that they are totally unaware of? And then, even more difficult, how do you convince them that they could be in great danger unless they allow you to pretty much totally take over their lives?

At least for this next step in the process Peter would have the help of the entire household. In the past, he had experienced several different outcomes to helping someone new. For Amy, it had been so simple. She was the newest member of the Order and had already known that there was something special about herself.

Her boundless energy was not some sort of an illusion. She literally had more energy than those around her. Not only that, but she could affect the energy of others. She could make others feel tired or exhilarated. Emotionally, if she was happy then those emotions and energies could bleed into those around her, impacting their mood.

But every Gift has a cost. Nature demands balance. Too much sleep and the body can become dependent—catatonic—eventually, shutting down. Similarly, too much energy and the body will hit a wall—drained—sometimes for days at a time, sometimes ending in a coma, and even sometimes in death.

Initially when Peter found her, Amy had felt so alone, fearing that she was going insane. She had been relieved to discover that there were others like her. Eagerly, she had accepted the Order and instantly felt at home.

In most of the Gifted, abilities would begin to manifest around college-age. For a rare few, like Amy, they manifested earlier. Her Gift began to emerge during her last year of high school, long before the Order had a chance to find her.

That year had been hard for her, but her Gift was also slow in coming, which meant that she was still mostly safe from the Evil by the time she came to Grayson College. Her parents had started to worry that she was becoming depressed and that perhaps she was not handling the transition to college well. They almost decided to force her to return home, which would have been the worst thing they could have done.

Peter had found her the second week of school in his chemistry class. Up until that point, Amy had not felt well enough to attend but decided to make a halfhearted attempt that day just to make her parents happy. The moment Peter stepped into the classroom the hair on the back of his neck had stood on end and every nerve in his body had become a livewire. He immediately honed in on this adorable petite girl with masses of curly brown hair.

She had been painfully thin—wasting away. Frowning, she rubbed her temples while staring down at her desk. Peter recognized the signs immediately and sat in the empty seat next to her. The two of them exclusively shared a black lab table between them.

With sympathetic eyes, Peter asked, "Headache? I've got some ibuprofen."

Amy looked up, grateful but reluctant, "Thanks, but nothing seems to really help."

Going through his Locator's mental checklist, Peter felt himself ticking off the boxes. Headaches? Check! Reaching into his bag, he offered the bottle of pain reliever to her. Weakly smiling, she reached out to accept it.

Just barely… but it was enough… the tips of her fingers brushed his own, sending pins and needles racing up and down his arm. Peter was one hundred percent sure she was Gifted.

Not only that, but the headaches were proof that the Evil had begun to work on her. How much, Peter was unsure, but his level of urgency continued to climb with each passing second. Her obvious pain and the frail state of her body indicated that she had been suffering for some time.

That day in class, the teacher announced that the person you sat next to would be your lab partner for the entire semester and required that you get to know them better. Class was dismissed early, and Peter offered to get a head start on their assignment. Heading out to sit on the grass, Amy was more than willing to come along.

Peter never could tell if it was because Amy's Gift was already strong enough that she could sense that she was safe with Peter—that she belonged—or maybe she just thought Peter was cute and unthreatening. Either way, getting close to Amy had proven much easier and more natural than how things were going with Beth.

In the days that followed, Peter slowly learned more and more about Amy, her Gift, and how her transition had started.

It was subtle at first.

Naturally upbeat, those closest to Amy often found themselves caught up in her energy. She was like a burst of sunshine on a stormy day. But more than just being invigorating to be around emotionally, Amy started to notice that people seemed to be physically more energetic around her.

Even more surprising—and disturbing—she began to notice that with the force of her will, she could *change* the way a person was behaving.

It had been easy to dismiss at first. Like the time she was at a track meet watching her boyfriend run. In the final moments of the race, Amy could tell that he was beginning to struggle and lose momentum. Completely caught up in the excitement of the crowd, she cheered that much harder and willed him to keep going. Suddenly he had a burst of frantic energy. He finished the race with his best time ever, but Amy was horrified when she later found him outside the locker room pacing and agitated.

He would walk ten feet up the hall, then ten feet back. Up and down. Back and forth. Over and over. Uncontrollably. When he tried to stop moving, his body would shake. Violently. His eyes were full of fear as he pleaded, "Help me! I have no control. I can't stop!"

He seemed emotionally distraught and on the verge of a panic attack. Not knowing what else to do, Amy called his parents and rushed him to the emergency room. The doctors were able to give him a sedative, and when his toxicology screen came back clean, he was told that it was just his body's over-reaction to the adrenaline of the race.

But in her heart, Amy worried it was something else. Something more.

Then she began to notice other things. Those around her were being affected, sometimes in extreme ways. When something funny would happen and Amy would feel amused, those around her would laugh disproportionately. When she was upset at school, other's in her class would become moody for no reason. Some would burst out into tears unprovoked. Others lashed out at each other. Sometimes aggressively.

A pattern was forming.

Terrified, Amy began to seriously suspect that it was her. Once she became convinced, she went to a very dark place emotionally. Being joyful and happy was her natural state, but knowing that she was harming those around her turned all that joy and happiness into fear and self-loathing. Both mentally and physically, she began to withdraw.

In the days that followed, food cramped in her stomach. Eating was painful. Through the raging storm of anxiety, sleep eluded her. When it did come, her dreams were ripped apart with nightmares; nightmares full of images of those she loved being harmed, either directly or indirectly by her, in whatever new and terrifyingly creative way her imagination came up with. Each night was torture and the thought of sleep filled her entire body with dread.

And then the headaches started.

Late that summer, before college, her hometown doctors did all kinds of tests and scans to see if they could diagnose the cause of her depression and migraines. They found nothing and sent her home with no answers.

A few weeks later she arrived at Grayson, unconsciously pulled there, almost against her will, as she had been content to just slide away into her misery.

That's when Peter found her.

Reflecting on these memories, Peter lay on his bed staring at the ceiling. What would it be like for Beth?

***

Peter hadn't realized that he had dozed off until he heard a rhythmic knocking on his door. Sitting up, he stretched out with a groan and ran his finger through his messy hair. "Come in."

Blake's massive frame entered the room. African American and six foot five, he practically had to bend over to walk through the entryway. A year older, Blake fondly treated Peter like a younger brother. Some people were intimidated by Blake's size and presence. But within an instant of being around him, it became obvious that Blake was more teddy bear than grizzly.

Blake's easy smile emerged as he plopped down on the bed— so hard Peter thought it might break. "Hey dude! So tell me about this new hotty that you found." Then, pretending to be worried, he added, "She is hot, isn't she?"

Peter joked back, "You mean being female isn't enough for you?"

"Oh, come on, man!" With that, Blake reached over and tousled Peter's hair. "Spill your guts."

"Okay, okay!" Peter dodged out of reach and shoved Blake away with a grin. "Not that it matters, but... She's pretty cute. You might want to take it easy with her though. She seems *very* shy. Even with my best efforts, she didn't seem too excited to come over tonight."

Blake laughed, "Ah, you're just getting rusty, my friend." Playfully flexing his biceps for emphasis, he added, "Just wait until she gets a load of me!" Then he stood up and offered Peter his hand. "Shall we get to your meeting?"

The two men headed downstairs together. Robert was still there, only instead of playing his video game, he sat on the couch taking apart some piece of electronic equipment, tinkering around with screwdrivers and a soldering iron. A metallic odor rent the air.

Skinny and unassuming, Robert's intelligence was off the charts. His brain functioned at such a high level that he often struggled to relate to everyday life and ordinary people—not that the Order qualified as ordinary people.

While Amy was the newest in the house. Robert the youngest.

His Gift was Life Boxes.

Put Robert in a room with electronics, or better yet, Life Boxes, and he could accomplish mind-boggling feats. However, put him in a room with a beautiful woman, and he was all knees, elbows, and mumbles. Often, his already broken speech would break down even further into an uncontrollable stutter.

Brushing his sloppy brown hair out of his large doe-like eyes, Robert looked up from his work. He grinned shyly at Peter and Blake's friendly chit-chat as they entered the room but said nothing.

Catching his eye, Blake flashed his large grin again, "And what's our boy genius up to today?

Robert flushed and sputtered, "Nah... nah... nothing. I was only just trying... trying to fix this broken signal line... see?" He helplessly gestured to the innards of some unrecognizable heap of wires and computer chips.

Just then, Amy bounced into the room and plopped down next to Robert on the sofa. "Don't worry Robby. Blake's just jealous of your gorgeous mind."

Taking no offense and with his hands raised in submission, Blake offered, "Hey, if I was a homework cheating kind of guy, Robert would be my man to cheat off of, no question." Perpetually grinning, Blake reclined against the far wall; his muscles relaxed. However, he fooled no one in the Order. Like a cat, Blake was more alert than he let on, and he could spring into action at a moment's notice, especially if someone he cared about was in danger.

Just then, Peter heard the front door open and close. Soon Donavon entered the room. He shrugged off his designer leather jacket and casually slung it over his forearm. Moving to stand behind the recliner that Peter was occupying, he leaned over to rest his arms on the back of the chair. From this position Peter could not see his face, but Donavon rarely wore anything but a serious expression.

Being the most powerful in their Order, Donavon had the highest sense of the good that surrounded each of them and the most natural ability with his Gifts. But instead of being the happiest of them all, he seemed the most sober.

Along with an elevated sense of the good, he also had a stronger sense of the Evil. No one else had struggled as quickly or as desperately as Donavon had when his talent first started to emerge. The more powerful someone's Gift, the quicker the Evil would swoop in. Where others could have months or even years to be found by a Locator—to be taught, trained, and saved—Donavon's life had practically changed in an instant.

In the end, Donavon had emerged as the strongest and most loyal member of the Order, but he had changed. He lost the innocence of his youth and no longer had a young man's belief that he was invincible. As far as everyone in this room was concerned, he had faced the ultimate challenge of them all, and he didn't dare forget what was at stake for others in his same situation—not even for a moment.

His hardships also gave him an incredible sense of empathy. He knew what it meant to suffer, and it seemed like that made it even harder for him to see others going through pain. It didn't even necessarily have to be something caused by the Evil for him to react. Donavon was sensitive to all kinds of suffering—emotional, physical, and spiritual—in everyone, Gifted or not.

And the one thing that could torture Donavon more than anything else was knowing that he himself had caused someone else's pain—especially if it was someone close to him. All of this had transformed him, making him very watchful and protective of those he loved—giving his all, especially in times of danger.

Peter realized what a burden this had become for Donavon. Normal life could be hard enough, but with the Evil involved, Donavon could become consumed, spending his days and nights trying to protect and save everyone around him from pain. It was exhausting, emotionally as well as physically.

To see those around him suffering, then to take that pain on as his own…Peter often worried that his friend was taking far too much on his shoulders.

Right now, everyone in the Order was safe. Protected. Trained, and prepared for their battles.

Beth, however… she was new and vulnerable. She could possibly turn into Donavon's current greatest weakness.

Turning his thoughts back to the present, Peter noticed they were all assembled and ready to start the meeting—all but one.

"Nancy!" Amy called into the next room.

Nancy had some personality traits in common with Donavon. Often stoic and serious, she had her demons that could surface and subdue a room. Within moments, she entered looking ruffled and annoyed. She had an apron on that was smudged with unidentifiable smudges of food. She had a slight crease in her forehead and a flush to her cheeks. Her long straight blonde hair seemed to be covered in flour.

Baking was her favorite hobby, although many would argue that she really wasn't very good at it.

Her cooking skills to one side, Nancy's natural grace ebbed from her tall and thin frame. There was a beauty about her face but it could be overshadowed by the severity of her expressions when she was upset—like now.

Over the top of Peter's chair Donavon calmly asked, "Problems?"

"No," was her curt replay. Taking a deep breath, she continued, "I thought it would be nice to have some treats for our meeting." Grumbling under her breath she mumbled, "But that clearly isn't happening."

Peter suddenly noticed a slightly burned smell coming from the kitchen.

Blake began to snicker.

Amy threw a decorative pillow from the couch. It bounced off Blake's muscular chest with little effect. Nancy glared and stuck out her tongue in mock annoyance, but then quickly had to turn her head away as a smile crept to her lips.

"Hey! Good shot Amy. You're getting b-better at that," Robert chimed in.

Amy smiled, "Blake gives me plenty of opportunities to practice."

And just like that, all eyes turned back to Peter. He took a moment to "taste" the atmosphere in the room. With an effort, he was able to bring down the subconscious walls that blocked out the hum of all the auras of his family members.

It was amazing.

The room hummed with energy and vibrancy. His entire body felt consumed with all the power. It was the best natural high in the world. Without even looking around the room, Peter could distinguish between everyone individually by feel. Donavon was the most powerful, so he was easy to find, in an overwhelming sort of way. Robert's aura felt more electric, like the snapping electricity of a Jacob's ladder. Amy's was softer, but tingled with anticipation. Nancy's was more somber, but he could feel the pull of her power like a magnet. Blake's just felt solid and dominant.

When Peter glanced around the room, the auras of his "brothers and sisters" were so tangible it was like they had visible colors emanating from around them—a shimmery haze of dancing light like a mirage. It all mingled beautifully together, just like a family should. It wouldn't have felt like home and the room wouldn't have been nearly as bright if even one of them had been gone.

Looking at their auras in this way, Peter thought of it as seeing things with his "Locator eyes" —a special ability that he alone possessed. Witnessing all that power in the room was the most amazing experience for Peter. But it was also extremely draining, and he could only sustain his special vision for a short time.

With a shift in his concentration, Peter had to put his walls back up to dull his senses.

They were waiting.

"I did make contact with someone new. Her name is Beth and she will be coming over tonight at eight." Amy and Nancy exchanged excited glances. "I was around her twice today, and both times she seemed to be in control. I didn't see any indication of headaches or anything else unusual. I feel pretty good that we may have found her before her Trial has started."

When the Evil starts to infiltrate someone's mind, that period of time was referred to as their Trial, and it was different for everyone. For those who are lucky enough to be found early and have slow growing powers, it could be relatively harmless. For others, like Donavon, it could be extremely dangerous.

Peter continued, "She seems almost painfully shy. I don't know how quickly she will open up to us."

While Amy was still new and learning, she offered, "If she is Gifted, she should be able to feel that we are on her side—to feel the good from us, right?"

Peter nodded, "True, but she might not be strong enough to detect things like that." Leaning over to rest his arms on his legs and clasping his hand together, he admitted, "I couldn't tell if her Gift has manifested or not." Pausing, he added, "Although, I'd guess that it hasn't too much as she was a bit tricky to find. And if her Gift is still buried, she likely won't be ready to accept what is going on."

Peter hoped his inability to instantly hone in on Beth was because her talent was in the earliest stages and still weak. How quickly a talent will blossom or how powerful it will become was always a mystery.

Nonetheless, Peter felt lucky that they found Beth while her Gift was so hard to sense. More than likely, that meant they had plenty of time to help her study, learn, and control her Gift. And, more importantly, more time to teach her how to resist the Evil.

"Well, I suppose then we should all just play it cool and see how she reacts to everyone." Nancy shrugged, "If she is as weak as you say, then we should have plenty of time to make friends before we need to reveal anything to her."

Blake chimed in, "So, what's the plan?"

As Locator, it was also part of Peter's skill to feel out what was the best way to handle someone—how many people should be around, who should do the talking, or who someone might respond the best to. Sometimes, Peter would have a very distinct impression about who might be able to interact most effectively with someone. Other times, it would be less concrete and anyone would do.

Searching over what Peter had felt when he was around Beth, the answer came clearly to him.

"I think she will respond the best to Donavon."

That got some hoots and whistles out of the crowd, but Donavon took it all in stride.

"Ah man!" Blake complained. "You dark and brooding types get all the luck."

Robert rolled his eyes, not the least bit interested.

Donavon would be the best choice. Beth seemed quiet and shy, and Donavon was not someone to move quickly or make a big deal over things. Slowly and carefully, he would handle the situation with the utmost caution.

Donavon's natural attraction for women also didn't hurt matters. Peter thought, "Beth will probably think she won the lottery."

All joking aside, once Donavon took Beth under his wing, she couldn't ask for a better mentor and protector.

Still… things had felt so awkward and off today. Could Peter trust his gut? What if Donavon wasn't the right fit? There was no way to know what events this single decision might set in motion.

CHAPTER 3: STUDYING

Now all the Order could do was wait. At the meeting's adjournment, everyone disappeared back to their corners of the house. Peter curled up on the couch, attempting to recapture his interrupted nap. Robert's tinkering in the corner was oddly soothing, and he sleepily mulled over possible scenarios for the upcoming night.

It was true that Peter did know a little bit about music, easily passing the class Beth was now enrolled in. He was confident that he could help her study and learn the material. During his years at Grayson, Peter had managed to take most of the entry-level classes for the different degrees so he could have an easy way of getting to know all the new students—primarily the Gifted ones.

But while studying for Music 1010 with Beth was not going to be a problem, it was mostly a front. He just needed a way for them to become friends and for her to trust him, and by extension, the entire Order.

Also, Beth would need to meet Donavon right away if he was going to be her mentor. Casually working him into the picture was going to take some finesse. Donavon was not a musician of any kind and therefore would have no excuse to come help Beth study. His only reason to even be in the house when she arrived was because he was Peter's roommate. But maybe that was enough.

If Peter's ability and intuition as Locator was working correctly, Donavon and Beth should naturally hit it off. If that happened, it would make life so much simpler, and was typically how these things worked themselves out. But after the rocky start today, Peter hesitated to put too much faith in his abilities.

For the second time that day, Peter hadn't notice that he had dozed off until he heard a loud crash from the kitchen and Nancy let out a small string of profanities. After their meeting, she had insisted on making another attempt at refreshments, this time intended for

Beth and Peter's study date. Stifling a chuckle, he opened his eyes to see her walking stone-faced up the staircase, apparently to go change her food-covered clothing. She delicately cradled a burned hand in her dirty apron. Amy followed, cheerily offering to take her to the store to buy something to serve instead.

Stretching and yawning, Peter got up from the couch to go to his room and retrieve his old music textbooks. He placed them on his desk and began to thumb through the first couple of chapters. After an hour or so, he felt fairly ready to tutor his new pupil.

The nap and studying had refreshed him. Peter always felt more aware after giving his brain a good workout. He thought it might be a good idea to hit the shower and freshen up before Beth arrived. Smelling extra good never hurt any social situation. Then it would be time for a quick bite to eat and maybe a little video game action.

Promptly at eight o'clock, Peter heard a knock at the front door. Gracefully, he unfolded himself from the floor, placed the video game controller on top of the television and switched the picture off. He jogged to the door and opened it to reveal a nervous-looking Beth.

Drawing immediately on his abilities as a Locator, Peter reached out with his skills and tried to make her feel more comfortable.

With his warmest smile, he said, "Beth! So glad you could make it. Come in." He stepped out of the way and indicated with a sweep of his arm that she was to enter.

Her eyes darting quickly around, Beth walked into the main hallway. A tentative smile played at the corners of her mouth, and her arms were protectively clutching her music books to her chest. Peter could feel the delicate hum of her Gift. It was very weak, but it reconfirmed to him that she was indeed Gifted. Peter offered to take her coat and backpack, but she hesitated.

"I was actually going to tell you that I only came because I think I don't need help after all." Her eyes were downcast and she jabbed her toe into the decorative Oriental rug on the floor.

"Okay?" Peter tried to turn up the charm a bit, "But you came all this way and even have your books." As his nerves jumped into high-gear, Peter struggled to keep his expression friendly and inviting.

If she left, he was sure his Gift would draw them together again, likely soon, but it would be so much more awkward than if he could help her have a good experience tonight. She needed to stay. He desperately needed more time with her. Surely, even with her Gift as weak as it was, she *had* to feel safe—at home.

Shyly glancing up to meet his questioning gaze, Beth slowly stopped fidgeting. Peter's efforts to make her feel more comfortable seemed to be working, bit by bit, although he had never encountered anyone so resistant before. If his motivations were deceitful in any way, his skills as a Locator would be useless. His abilities just didn't work that way. But, in this case, his motivations were honest and pure. He was simply trying to help Beth discover who she really was and wanted to keep her safe from the Evil.

Peter's mind wanted to scream, "Why is this so hard?" It was almost as if Beth's nervousness was rubbing off on him, making him doubt his purpose.

After a few agonizing moments that felt like an eternity, she relented, "I suppose we could study for just a minute."

Relief washed over Peter like a wave. He actually felt just a little weak in the knees. Not wanting the moment to magically slip away, he tried to not overly enthusiastically blurt out, "Excellent!"

Peter led Beth into the dining area that was attached to the kitchen. A large oak table held not only Peter's books, but a plate of store-bought cookies, courtesy of Amy.

"You baked?" Beth pulled one of the chairs out from the table to sit, and placed her books down.

"Oh, no. Those are from my housemates. They thought you might like some brain food while we go over things. They are hanging around here somewhere. Maybe you'll get to meet them before you leave." Peter was careful to sit down one chair away from Beth, giving her room to feel more comfortable.

Chuckling, he added, "You're lucky." Indicating the cookies, he continued, "We got these from the store. Nancy was trying to make you something homemade, but," he leaned across the table as if sharing a big secret and dropped his voice to a whisper, "fate intervened and you were spared."

Still nervous, but obviously trying to make an effort to play along, Beth raised her eyebrows conspiratorially and smiled. "Oh really?"

"I heard that!" Nancy called from the hallway moments before she strode into the kitchen. Laughing softly to themselves, Peter and Beth seemed to share a moment of genuine friendship. It almost seemed like too much to hope for.

Offering her good hand to Beth, Nancy said, "Hey there. I'm Nancy and I appear to be the butt of all the jokes around here."

Peter quickly intervened with a smile, "Not all the jokes, just the culinary ones."

Beth shyly took her hand and said, "I'm Beth." Glancing at the white bandages around Nancy's other hand, Beth inquired, "Are you okay?"

"It's nothing." Blushing slightly, Nancy grumbled, "Enjoy your cookies."

Peter stifled a snicker, and Nancy lightly punched him in the arm before she wandered over to rummage through the refrigerator. Earlier, Peter had asked her to find some excuse to hang around the dining area so Beth would feel more comfortable with another female around. Not even wanting to guess what Nancy was attempting to whip up in the kitchen this time, he turned his attention to the music lessons.

The time passed quickly and Beth was a willing student. She knew more than she gave herself credit for and was quick to pick up on the rest. As they worked together, Beth seemed to open up into an entirely different person. She smiled and stopped fidgeting with her papers. She took her coat off, nibbled on a cookie, and even laughed at Peter's attempts to make jokes. His confidence and bruised ego as a Locator were starting to heal, and he really felt like he was making some progress.

When they finally reached the end of the lesson, Peter groaned as he stood up and stretched the sore muscles in his back. Beth squeezed her eyes shut and covered a yawn with the back of her hand.

"Ah, come on! I'm not that boring of a teacher, am I?" Peter winked.

Sincerely smiling back at him, Beth replied, "You've been great Peter. I was pretty nervous to come over here today. I really like to keep to myself. But I must admit, you helped me out a lot. I might actually be able to pass this class."

Beth placed all her papers in her folder and bent over in her chair to put her books in her backpack. Just then, Peter heard the back door open and close softly. Glancing up, Beth saw Donavon enter the kitchen from the backyard.

Being a guy, Peter couldn't always tell what women saw in certain men, but Beth gave a little gasp at the sight of Donavon.

For a split second, Peter thought he could feel Beth's Gift intensify dramatically—like a power surge. However, as fast as it appeared, it also disappeared leaving her original mild hum in its place. Suddenly, all the awkwardness of earlier in the evening returned. Beth seemed to cave in on herself emotionally. She slumped in her chair, trying to make herself as invisible as possible.

The change was sudden and startling. Happening so fast, Peter could hardly take it in. What was going on? The fun, smart, delicate woman he was just starting to get to know was disappearing right in front of his eyes.

Donavon, however, was oblivious to it all. Instead, he saw Nancy right away and walked over to inspect her hand.

Unlike what Blake or Peter would do, Donavon didn't make any sarcastic comments about how she had gotten the burn. Instead he simply took her hand in his and unwrapped the bandages gently to see the damage. Then he placed his other hand over hers and closed his eyes. For just a split second, he seemed to concentrate very hard on something, his brow furrowing. Then he let his hands drop and gave Nancy a sympathetic look. The entire exchange had only taken moments.

Unexpectedly caught in the middle, Nancy looked worriedly between Peter and Beth at the table, and Donavon.

Peter and Nancy knew what had just happened. One of Donavon's talents was to manipulate a person's sense of touch. He couldn't actually heal Nancy's hand, but he could make the nerve endings less receptive so the pain would be minimal while she healed. It was the exact kind of thing that Donavon's compassionate nature would compel him to do for any member of the Order.

But in front of Beth! It went against all of their rules.

And of all people, Peter couldn't believe that Donavon would do something so careless—even if Beth probably had no clue as to what had just occurred.

Reeling, and a little afraid of what might happen next if he didn't intervene, Peter loudly cleared his throat to get everyone's attention. "Hey man! Want to come meet our guest?"

The whole exchange had only lasted a matter of seconds, yet Beth seemed to have picked up on the sudden uncomfortable air in the room.

At Peter's words, Donavon looked up, clearly startled upon seeing Beth at the table.

Peter's eyebrows shot up. Had Donavon really not noticed her there? That was entirely out of character for him.

Recovering instantly, Donavon strode over to the dining area and locked eyes with Beth. Reading the situation and sensing her discomfort, he angled himself closer to Peter to give her some space. A casual smile played at the corners of his mouth as he attempted to make her feel more comfortable "Hello. I'm Donavon... Donavon Grayson"

"Hi... umm... Beth." It was hardly more than a whisper, but her eyes were locked with his, and it appeared that she was more in awe than afraid of Donavon. She hardly took the time to blink as she gazed, almost afraid that he would disappear if her eyes closed for even a moment.

"Well, Beth. It's nice to meet you. Peter told me you were coming over to study tonight and I tried to stay out of the way. It appears he has been working you extra hard if you haven't gone home yet."

Flushed, her words suddenly spilled out in a rush, "Oh, I was just packing up to leave. I didn't mean to keep you out of your own home." Beth broke her stare away and suddenly changed tactics entirely. She began avoiding eye contact with Donavon at all costs. Recklessly grabbing papers, she attempted to stuff them into her folders faster, crinkling the pages and bending the corners. "I'll just be a minute."

Startled by her reaction, Donavon reached over and placed his hand on her shoulder, "There's no rush. Take your time."

For a moment, frozen, she stared at his hand on her shoulder almost as if she couldn't believe it was there. Shyly, she appeared to force herself to meet his gaze again but seemed completely unable to speak in return.

Donavon filled the silence instead, "It really was nice to meet you, Beth." He gave her a small, yet comforting smile, and then turned to face Peter. "I'm off to bed. See you in the morning."

"Good night, man." Peter casually slapped Donavon on the shoulder as he passed. Then he turned his attention back to Beth. Her bag was all packed now, and she sat looking miserable.

Peter wished he could understand women better. He stated, "He's right, ya know. I think I have worked you pretty hard tonight. We should probably give it a rest. When is your next class?"

Giving her head a little shake, almost like she was snapping out of a daze, Beth looked up at Peter. With a shaky voice, she said, "Wednesday… This is a Monday/Wednesday/Friday class."

"How about we get together again Wednesday night and see how things are going?"

Almost imperceptibly, her eyes flickered in the direction that Donavon had just left, "Sure... That sounds nice."

Peter couldn't help by think, "I bet it does."

Seeming to finally snap out of it, Beth took a deep breath and gave her head a firm shake. Focusing her attention fully back on him, some of the old Beth from earlier in the evening returned as she smiled and said, "Thanks again, Peter. You've been great. I'm not usually so lucky as to meet such a nice guy on the first day of school… or ever, for that matter."

And with that, she left.

***

As soon as Beth was gone, Peter helped Nancy clean up the kitchen. Over a sink of sudsy water and a stack of drying dishes, Nancy commented, "She sure seems jittery—like a rabbit caught in a cage."

"You noticed?" Peter smiled weakly. Beth was a hard case to figure out, and it wore him out. Not that people were supposed to be simple and boring. It just would have made life a little easier if he could predict her reactions even slightly. Peter was supposed to be good at this sort of thing.

"And what's with her reaction to Donavon? I didn't know if she was going to faint, run away screaming, or melt into a pool of desire." Nancy dried another bowl and returned it to the cupboard.

Peter shrugged his shoulders, "You're the girl. You expect me to understand?"

"Well, you're the Locator, and you said Donavon was supposed to be her teacher. They're supposed to have a connection, right?"

It was true.

However, if Beth's Gift had truly not manifested yet, then perhaps her connection to Donavon would not surface either. And even for a Locator, Peter was still pretty young and didn't even come close to having all the answers.

He wondered if he should ask his father for advice.

Nancy continued, "In any case, she sure seemed to open up to you. At least once you got into the swing of things. And, she's coming back over in two days, so that's good."

Peter finished washing all the dishes, and Nancy wiped up the water on the counter. He then headed up the stairs to try and find Donavon to get his take on the unusual encounter. Before he reached Donavon's room, he heard Nancy close the door to her own room downstairs.

Rapping softly on the door, Peter turned the knob and entered after he heard the familiar low "Come in."

Donavon's room was starkly different from Peter's. Peter had movie posters on the walls, a stereo on the shelf, his bed was hardly ever made, and his messy closet was always open for the world to see.

Donavon had his walls painted in somber colors—to help him sleep better, he once explained. His shelves were lined with books, and he had classical art hung up. His room was always clean and everything was exactly in its place.

Peter liked to live and let live, while Donavon needed order, keeping life's chaos under control.

There was a large recliner with a stand lamp in one corner, and Donavon was holding a novel open in his lap. He sat in the soft glow of the light with his dark framed reading glasses in his hand. It appeared he hadn't actually been reading, but rather was lost in his own thoughts.

Peter would have flopped down across the bed if he had been in his own room, but something about being in Donavon's room commanded the respect that Donavon himself obviously showed all his belongings. Instead, Peter pulled an elegantly carved chair out from the desk and sat down. He said, "I'm glad you're still awake."

Donavon set his glasses and novel on the end table by his chair. "I figured you would want to talk as soon as she was gone."

The whole day had Peter feeling dumbfounded. Not waiting, he launched right into the main issue that was bothering him, at least as far as Donavon was concerned. "Man… What was up with you using your Gift in front of her like that?"

Donavon's face became more serious, if that were possible. "I honestly didn't even know she was in the room. I swear I looked around when I came in because I knew she could still be there." As if to make sure Peter knew that he was to blame, Donavon added, "That was careless of me. I don't understand it."

Immediately, Peter regretted jumping on his friend like that. He knew he was probably just projecting his own mistakes and frustrations from the day on his friend, not wanting to fully accept his part of the blame for how things were turning out. Peter knew that Donavon would have a hard time forgiving himself if there was any chance his actions would harm the Order. Peter could see Donavon gearing up to torment himself, so he thought it was best to change the subject.

"Well, I don't think she noticed, so it's probably okay." Remembering Beth's reaction to Donavon's mere presence, Peter laughed softly as he added, "But you sure made her nervous."

Not ruffled, Donavon replied smoothly, "I got the impression that she is nervous by her very nature." Immediately, he steered the conversation back to the seriousness of the situation. "Did she seem okay while you were with her?"

That was the million-dollar question. As her teacher, Donavon would want to know if she was showing any signs that the Evil was setting in or if her Gift was starting to appear.

Peter ran a hand through his hair, rearranging the waves, "I did notice one odd thing. When you entered the room tonight, I felt a sudden spike in Beth's aura. It was almost like her Gift suddenly had a power surge. I've never felt anything like that before. It was so quick that I almost thought I imagined it." Rubbing his eyes tiredly, he admitted, "Maybe I did."

Standing up to place his book back on the shelf, Donavon mused, "Could it be my connection to Beth as mentor and student?"

Peter hadn't thought of that. "Maybe. I've been around other student-mentor pairs before though, and this was entirely new to me."

"Do *you* have any theories?" Donavon turned to stand in front of Peter's chair.

Peter folded his arms across his chest and thought for a moment. The Order kept some written histories—journals to help future generations navigate this strange life they led. Peter had gotten his hands on a few of them before, but none of them spoke of anything quite like this. He mused, "You *are* very powerful, Donavon. Maybe being around you, especially as her teacher, gave her a momentary jolt of your energy."

Donavon assumed the same pose as Peter, folding his arms across his chest. "Possibly. But if she took any energy from me, even unknowingly, I would think I would have felt something."

"Maybe."

"Perhaps your father knows what is going on."

Peter sighed, "I guess. I'll have to call him soon and see what he says."

Peter didn't like calling his dad every time something new happened. There was pride involved in figuring these things out on his own. And his dad was not the warmest and most inviting man. But he tried to balance that with not using his resources—wasting time trying to reinvent the wheel, as it were.

Something else was playing at the edges of Peter's memory, but he was just too tired to grasp it—something odd he had noticed about Beth. Donavon saw Peter's hesitation and raised a questioning eyebrow.

Then it clicked. "It might not have anything to do with you as a mentor *or* borrowing your power. I remember now when I first approached Beth that I felt her aura stronger when we were standing still. Then, as we walked away so I could show her how to get to class it faded a little. It wasn't like the sudden spike I felt tonight. This was more gradual. I've never felt someone's aura changing all the time like hers."

"Interesting. Although, I don't know what it means. You set up another appointment, correct?"

Peter nodded.

"Then let's give it time. We're in no hurry...yet." Donovan meaningfully stressed the last word.

Standing to leave, Peter walked to the door. Then turning, he added, "I'll let you know as soon as I know anything."

As he walked into his own room, Peter suddenly felt exhausted. Things were not quite as they seemed to be. The whole situation was unsettling. What did it all mean?

CHAPTER 4: FRIENDS

Peter and Donavon's history went back to boyhood. They were riding bikes, scraping knees, and swapping lunches long before either one discovered his Gift.

Peter was the adventurous one, always trying to get Donavon to explore the woods behind their homes. Once, they found a rusted-out abandoned car and transformed it into their secret base.

Peter thought the car was amazing.

The roof was ripped off, and the wheels were long gone. Moss and weeds grew all over the frame. The leather on the seats was slashed, and they could see the stuffing and springs in several places. The steering wheel was still attached, and both Peter and Donavon enjoyed playing with the dashboard switches and vents. The trunk didn't latch, but it closed enough to protect a collection of things that they stored there—magazines, snacks, and old blankets. On most afternoons Peter and Donavon would hike out to the car and sit inside, dreaming and planning their future.

Peter could remember one day sitting in the car when they were each ten. They decided that they were going to start up a band and tour Europe. It didn't matter that Donavon was completely unmusical. Peter had been taking piano lessons for years—two or three at least—and felt confident in his youth that he could teach Donavon anything he needed to know. Not worrying so much about what music they would play, or how they were going to pay for anything, they focused more on where they wanted to go. Donavon loved the idea of going to Italy and riding gondolas around the streets of water. Peter wanted to climb the Greek ruins.

By the end of the summer, they had stuffed the trunk of the car full of maps and itineraries for their trip, but never picked up an instrument to actually start a band. It was just more fun to sit in their old abandoned car and daydream than it was to practice.

Years later, they had a completely different experience out in the woods, one that would both strain their relationship, and then cement it.

In high school, Peter started to show signs that his talent was manifesting. Being from a family of Locators, Peter's father had been watching for this, and knew exactly what to expect. When Peter came home one day his senior year complaining of headaches and getting funny feelings around people, his father was prepared.

His relationship with his father had always been less than ideal. Sure, Peter loved him. But his father was gone a lot, and Peter often felt more abandoned than loved. Before his Trial, Peter knew nothing of Locators, Orders, or being Gifted. He had just been a normal kid, with typical dreams and fears. Peter thought that his father was never home because he had found something—or someone—more important than his son.

But later Peter understood. His father was not away on some corporate business trip, making money and forgetting about his family like Peter had once believed. He was out making a real difference in the world—a difference that people's lives depended on. Even though it was terribly hard for Peter to let go of the years of anger that he had built up, it was also hard to hold on to those feelings when he knew how important the work was.

As his father carefully explained to him when he began to manifest his talent, different clusters of the Gifted would each make their own Order. The wisest people from each Order would combine to form what was referred to as the Council. The Council was charged with placing all the known Locators in as many strategic places as possible.

They tried to make life as easy on the Locators as possible— keeping them near to their hometowns if possible. Or in Peter's case, sending the college-aged Locators to campuses so they could have some semblance of a normal life while getting their feet under them.

That was how Peter ended up at Grayson College.

Grayson was also special. No one was quite sure why, but Gifted for centuries had been naturally drawn there. Like Stonehenge or the pyramids in Egypt, this place held an energy vortex that drew in the Gifted. Like an earth chakra. It was no coincidence that a college had been established in this very spot for those college-aged Gifted that were just discovering their powers.

It was the perfect cover.

But Peter's dad was older and didn't have the luxury of focusing on a single location. It was his duty to go where and when the Council needed him—no questions asked. It didn't matter what was going on. If the call came, his father had to leave. Peter figured his father missed most of the important events in his life—Peter's birthdays, high school graduation, and even promised family vacations.

And with the supernatural pull of Locators to the Gifted, his father would have been compelled to leave, no matter how much he wanted to stay.

Being a family of Locators, no one understood what it was like to live with this Gift—or burden—like they did. Locators were a rare commodity. Even now, Peter could only think of a handful of other families that carried the Locator Gift in their bloodlines, and several of those lived in other countries.

Some of his feelings of patriarchal rejection melted away when Peter developed his own Gift. In fact, during his Trial, Peter didn't have to suffer for months in confusion while his talent started to emerge. He never even got so far as to hear the Evil talking to him. His father had a Life Box made for Peter months ahead, anticipating his Trial, and Peter was cleansed without having to undergo much of what the other Gifted did.

Maybe Peter should have felt more grateful, but he had not really understood what he had been spared until much later.

Sitting with Donavon in the car one late summer morning, he complained, "I know my dad works hard. But it would be nice if he could at least *act* sad that he is going to miss my birthday again!"

Donavon asked, "Where is he off to this time?" Donavon didn't know anything about the Order yet, so Peter had to be careful about what he said. The odds that Donavon would even be Gifted seemed so remote to Peter at the time that he never thought he would actually be able to tell his best friend the entire story.

"Who knows. Who cares." Peter had been picking apart a pinecone that had fallen into the car seat, which he now threw as hard as he could over the windshield to emphasize his anger.

"He doesn't need to be here for us to have a good time." Donavon got a mischievous look in his eye. "Well, you only turn eighteen once. What do you say we go celebrate becoming a man? Right now." He reached over and slapped Peter on the shoulder and then jumped out of the car.

Seeing that Peter was not following, he came around to the other side and started to haul his friend away by the arm. "Come on! Don't let him ruin the day."

They lived in a small town where everyone knew each other, so there was no way they would get away with trying to go to the local bar or anywhere else more exciting. Instead, they went to the ice cream shop and had celebratory milkshakes. Then they went to the matinee movie where just about everything blew up and the villains couldn't hit the broad side of a barn. Pure smash 'em up adrenaline, and Peter soaked it all in with his best friend.

They ended the day by hiking back out to the woods to sit in the car and stare at the stars. So far away from any light, the sky came alive. The Milky Way spread across the heavens, and everything was vibrant and beautiful. The whole day had been healing to Peter's soul. He had Donavon to thank for it.

Little did he know that soon after Peter's birthday, they both would be back at the car again, this time dealing with the horror of Donovan's Trial.

While Peter almost glided through his Trial, Donavon's was an entirely different story. Peter was relatively new to using his talent—only months old—when Donavon's Trial began.

Peter had been having the most success knowing that someone else was Gifted by his physical reactions to them—the tingling sensation that would creep over his skin. However, while his Gift was so new and weak, actually touching the person with his hands was the most effective way to know for sure. But that was not always possible.

Once he could physically feel someone's Gift, then he could focus his energy into using his eyes as a Locator to see their aura. It was a strain, and often he would only catch flickering glimpses of the multi-hued glow.

That day, Peter was supposed to meet Donavon out at the car. They were on fall break during their first semester at Grayson and their mothers were planning a big "Welcome Home" party. Both Peter and Donavon just wanted to escape the mayhem for a moment, so Peter had called Donavon up. He didn't care where they went, and wasn't surprised when Donavon suggested they visit their old hideout.

The hike didn't take very long, and Peter had enjoyed stretching his legs after the long drive home from campus. The evening was going to be hectic with the party going on, so he was glad to have these couple of hours of peace beforehand. When Peter approached the car—not seeing Donavon—he figured he was all alone. He climbed into the front seat and leaned his head back to look up through the branches that shaded the car. As he tried to relax, Peter began to feel his skin tingle in a way that was now becoming all too familiar.

Someone Gifted was nearby.

That was when he heard a moan from somewhere behind him.

"Donavon? Hey, man. Is that you?"

There was no answer.

Whether it was instinct or his Gift, he suddenly knew something was horribly wrong. He jumped out of the car to go investigate. Then, spontaneously and completely out of his control, Peter's Locator eyes jumped into sharp focus. He saw a mist swirling above the ground around the car. It only came up a couple of inches, but it wasn't white.

It was black.

Not wanting to touch the blackness, but seeing no other option, he cautiously walked to the back of the car to see what was going on. The edge of something was shining brilliantly on the ground just out of sight around the corner of the trunk. The glow intensified as more and more of the object came into view with each step. Shading his eyes with his hand against the intensity of the light, Peter finally saw what it was.

Donavon.

The black mist was swirling around his friend's body, trying to penetrate it. He was clutching his head, eyes closed, and there was a grimace of intense pain on his face.

Peter was instantly terrified of the inky blackness and did not want it to touch him any more than it already was. It moved and pulsed around his feet, alive and attacking. Yet his friend was in obvious need of help, so Peter rushed to Donavon's side and knelt in the blackness.

A couple of things became apparent to Peter at once.

First of all, his friend was not only Gifted—a fact that would have made Peter enormously happy in any other situation—but Donavon must have been incredibly powerful for someone as new and weak as Peter to feel his Gift so vividly. Peter didn't even have to *try* to use his Locator eyes. His special sight was reflexive and uncontrollable in Donavon's presence. Peter noted that his best friend's aura was beautiful and unmistakable.

Secondly, it was also clear as the Evil churned and attacked from all sides that Donavon's Trial had begun.

He couldn't help but think how he had just seen his friend a few days earlier at school and Peter hadn't detected anything different, even when they shook hands. It was unusual for someone to have their Gift manifest so suddenly, and for them to be in so much danger so quickly. Peter hadn't been told that such a thing could even happen.

Desperately, Peter shouted, "Donavon! Can you hear me? I need to get you out of here." As Peter touched Donavon's arm, it was like an electric current shot from his friend straight through Peter. The shock made him abruptly pull his hands away, suck in a sharp breath, and rub his tingling palms together. In response, Donavon was barely able to grunt and roll away, still grasping his head between his hands. He was trying to put distance between himself and Peter so as not to hurt his friend.

Peter grabbed his cell phone from his pocket and punched the only number he could think of— his father's.

Peter was just too new to this strange world to know how to help. And while he still couldn't shake the lingering bitterness he felt towards his father… if anyone could help, it would be him.

It only rang once.

"Dad! It's Peter. Donavon's in trouble." He quickly explained the situation. While they were both confused as to the suddenness and severity of what was going on, his father sprang into action and was immediately on his way into the woods. In one very small way, Donavon was lucky that day. Peter's father had been meeting with some other members of the local Order, and he did not come into the woods alone.

Peter heard their approach only moments before he felt the auras of those that were coming. With Locator eyes, Peter could see the shimmering forms of the three men that had come to his aid.

Being around Donavon's new found power was rapidly and mysteriously strengthening Peter's Gift. It was as if his own emerging talent had been hidden under a thick layer of dust. Instead of slowly and meticulously brushing that dust away with the gentle care of an archeologist's brush, the dust was being violently blown away by hurricane-force winds, leaving Peter feeling raw, exposed and overwhelmed. The light and dark flows of energy surrounding Donavon were so strong that he could see and feel things clearly—potently—things that he had struggled even to sense, let alone control, just seconds before.

"He's over he-." Peter's shout was instantly cut off by two things.

First was his father's warning, too late, "Peter, move!"

The second was the paralyzing pain that shot through Peter's entire body as Donavon took that moment to desperately reach up to his friend and take hold of his arm. It was like acid poured on his skin where Donavon's hand made contact, and that acid raced from his arm, through his veins, and coursed through his entire body. All the muscles in Peter's body locked in resistance to the assault. As much as he wanted to push himself away, the pain was holding him in place. It wasn't until Peter's father pried Donavon's hand off that he was finally able to catch his breath and fall away.

He rolled off into the leaves and sat himself up against the trunk of a tree. His breath was coming in ragged gasps. The sudden absence of pain made his entire body tremble and shake.

Peter couldn't see exactly what happened next, but within moments the three men had subdued Donavon, and two of them were carrying him out of the woods in the direction of Peter's home.

That was when Peter was finally conscious of the searing pain in his arm.

Rolling up his sleeve, he looked down and was astounded to see that Donavon's hand had left an angry red mark. He could see the exact shape and contour of Donavon's fingers blazing around his bicep. It stung when Peter tried to touch it, which made him hiss in response. He protectively cradled his damaged arm to his body, sweating and grimacing in pain.

A few moments later Peter's father came to kneel by his son. "Are you okay?" He panted and looked drained, showing what an exertion it had been for him to work with Donavon. He also looked worried, which again, might have made Peter feel a little better if it had been in any other situation. It was nice to know that his father cared.

"I think so. What's happening?" Peter looked in the direction the two men had carried away his best friend.

Carefully, Peter's father offered him a hand up. As they started to follow the others he said, "I'm not sure. But now that the attack is over, we need to get him to a hospital. Then we'll figure out what is going on."

"Can I help?"

His father, in an unusual moment of tenderness, placed his arm around Peter and said, "Just go home and wait." Squeezing Peter's shoulder, he added, "And be there for him. This will not be easy for either of you."

Calling his father had been the right thing to do. As much as Peter wanted to help his friend, he was acutely aware that he currently did not possess the knowledge or skill to do what was needed. It was a vital and humbling lesson, one that he would not forget as he learned to work with those who came into his own Order at Grayson College.

In the months to follow, as Peter would grow into his Gift, Donavon would tell him how much he was like his father. Peter couldn't see it. They might not always see eye to eye, but Peter knew his father was an excellent Locator, admired by those around him. Peter began to hope to become more like him—strong, confident, wise, and efficient.

That day in the woods had been the very beginning of Donavon's Trail. Peter hadn't been allowed to witness what happened after they took Donavon's limp body from the woods, which in some ways, he was grateful for. It wasn't until much later that he would learn the chilling details.

Details that would haunt any sane man.

CHAPTER 5: NEW IN TOWN

Weeks earlier... The first day of fall semester... Again...

Sitting on the grass, Rachel leaned up against the rough bark of a tree. Campus was buzzing with life, and she took a moment to watch all the people go by. It was fun to guess who they were, what they were studying, and if she would know any of them someday?

Grayson College was a busy place, and Rachel was excited to explore and see what it had to offer. She had arrived in town only the day before, was hardly unpacked, and knew absolutely no one. However, as the sun warmed her skin and she watched all the friendly, happy faces passing her, she just *knew* she was going to like it here.

This was her first year at Grayson, but she had attended community college back home in Florida for a couple of years so she was a littler older than some of the other students new to campus that day. Letting her imagination wander, her people-watching allowed her to fantasize about each person she saw, playfully wondering if her next best friend was just around the corner. Waiting for her.

Having just ended a semi-serious relationship a few months earlier, she couldn't help but also toy with the idea that her future boyfriend could be walking past at this very moment and neither one would even know it. It was an absolutely girly and ridiculous thing to think, but it made her smile and gave her hope and excitement for what might lay ahead for her future at Grayson.

A perfect example of the college dating scene suddenly began playing out right behind her. Rachel didn't really mean to eavesdrop, but it was hard not to. Sitting on the other side of the tree form her was a young girl who was suddenly being approached by a young man.

Rachel couldn't see their faces, but she heard the young man ask casually, ""I couldn't help but notice, do you need some help?"

He had a very inviting voice. Rachel had to resist the urge to turn and look at his face.

The girl replied, sounding surprised by the young man's approach, "Oh... I was just looking for my next class."

"Well, in that case, I bet I can help you. Why don't we start out with turning your map right-side up, eh?" Rachel stifled a giggle. "I'm Peter, by the way... Peter Bennett."

To be polite, Rachel did her best to ignore the rest of the conversation, which thankfully didn't last that long. As the couple walked away, Rachel stole a glance at the young man to see what kind of face went with the compelling voice.

He was tall, blonde, and well-built. While handsome, he also had one of the friendliest and most inviting faces she had ever seen. Rachel clicked her tongue in disgust.

Some girls had all the luck!

Not that Rachel had expected to meet the perfect man on the first day of class, but she certainly wouldn't have complained if someone so cute had offered to help her. The brunette he was walking with didn't even seem that interested in him. Too bad.

Sighing, Rachel leaned back against the tree again and closed her eyes, letting the breeze tickle across her face and the skin of her arms. Fall was her favorite time of year, and there would only be a few more days left of this perfect weather—perfect temperature, beautiful colors, and the excitement of a new school year with new people. What more could a girl ask for?

She thought, "Oh yeah, a cute boy to show you around." A small smile crept up on her face. There was plenty of time for that.

A short time later, deciding that she had lazed around long enough, Rachel got up off the grass and brushed the loose blades from her jeans. She also had to pick a couple pieces of bark from her long blonde hair which went all the way to her waist and often got mixed up in things. Gathering her books, she was about to step onto the sidewalk when the young man from earlier came strolling back around the bend.

She didn't really have any reason to, but the guilt of her earlier eavesdropping made her duck back behind the tree.

It was stupid. It was irrational. The guy probably didn't even know that she had heard a thing. But she couldn't help herself and stayed hidden.

When he was far enough away that she felt like she could make her escape, Rachel dived out from behind the tree and walked away a little faster than could be considered casual.

Inexplicably, she wanted to walk over to him. To hear his voice again. The strangeness of the urge was upsetting and out of place. Rachel shook it off and made her way to the student union building to find a nice quiet place to sit, study, and, later, get some lunch.

No more people watching!

As she made her way there, Rachel marveled at how much bigger Grayson was than her community college. The campus back home consisted of one large building with several wings. There were only hundreds of students, instead of thousands.

Here, booths lined the hallway of the student union, full of students trying to get people to sign up for clubs, sports, sororities, and fraternities. Rachel found a free study table across from one of the fraternities—Sigma Epsilon. They had a large poster inviting students to participate in rush week. Several guys sat at their table answering questions.

Sitting down, she placed her backpack next to her chair and rummaged through it to find the economics book she needed. Having good intentions, she flipped open to the introduction and began to read.

Shortly, her mind began to wander as the material got drier and drier. She unknowingly played with a lock of her hair—twisting and untwisting it around her finger. Then, started daydreaming… again.

Shaking herself, she tried to refocus on the material in front of her. But as the minutes ticked slowly by, Rachel began to feel her head throb. Headaches were a common problem for her when she read without her glasses, so sighing with defeat, she dug around in her bag until she found them.

However, despite her halfhearted efforts, Rachel's head began to pound harder. Annoyed she ripped the glasses form her face and stuffed all her belongings back into her bag. A migraine was building and she no longer felt hungry for lunch. She began making her way to the bus stop, absently rubbing her temples and longing for the dark and quiet of her bedroom.

She was so preoccupied with her pounding head, that she was startled when someone tapped her on the shoulder.

"Sorry! I didn't mean to scare you." It was one of the men from the fraternity table. He was a tall, skinny red-head with tan skin and light brown freckles spattered across his face.

Hesitantly he reached his hand out and offered her something. Her skull was throbbing so hard that she frowned in concentration, trying to focus on what he was holding out to her.

It was her reading glasses.

The smile on his face dissolved as he became obviously uncertain by the grimace plastered across hers. He tentatively said, "Um… you left these at your table. I thought you might want them back."

Rachel felt like she was being rude and tried to force a smile. Waving her hands around her head she said, "I'd forget my head if it weren't attached. Thank you." Her humor was an attempt to try and defuse the tension.

Just then, another lightning bolt of pain shot through her brain, and she grabbed her head with a groan.

Reaching a hand out to steady her, the young man asked, "Are you okay? You look awfully pale."

"Yeah, I don't feel so good right now."

"Maybe you should sit down." He started to guide her towards a nearby bench in the bus depot.

"Wow, that's embarrassing." Rachel sat down and smiled meekly at the young man next to her. "Thanks for coming to my rescue."

Reclining next to her on the bench with his arm over the back rest, the young man grinned and did a John Wayne impersonation, "That's alright, little lady. I'm always on the lookout for a damsel in distress." Offering his hand, he added, "I'm Stewart, but people call me Stu."

She shook his hand, "I'm Rachel." Rubbing her temples, she added, "Sorry for all the drama."

Raising an enquiring eyebrow, Stu asked, "Migraine?"

Nodding as minimally as possible, she replied, "I guess so. I've been getting more of them lately. This one hit me pretty fast."

"Yeah, my sister gets migraines too. They really wipe her out. Always looks like she has been hit by a truck when they are over." In a teasing tone he added, "But I'm too nice of a brother to tell her so."

Even with her pounding head, Rachel managed a weak smile. "Well, you've proven that you are a gentleman today. I appreciate your help." Teasing back, she added, "I'd even tell your sister that if you needed me to."

Chuckling, Stu smiled. Then his expression became more serious as he inquired, "Are you sure you are going to be okay? I could call someone to come pick you up if you need. I got my cell."

Waving the suggestion away, Rachel said, "That's okay. I'm just going to take the bus." To lessen the blow of her refusal, she tried to think of things to keep the small talk moving. Remembering his fraternity, she offered, "I actually don't live that far from Sigma

Epsilon. I saw the sign for your building just up the street from my apartment" What she was actually thinking was that she lived alone, so there was no one Stu could call to help her.

Delighted, he exclaimed, "Small world! In that case, I could give you a ride if you wanted. I just finished my shift at the table and was on my way home anyway."

Oh dear. That had not been her intent.

Rachel got the impression that Stu was a pretty nice guy, but it still seemed unwise to accept a ride from a complete stranger. Maybe that's how relationships in college got started, but she wasn't ready to risk being whisked off to who knows where.

"Thanks anyway. I think I will just sit here and get a little air while I wait for the bus. I don't like to mooch off people."

Just then, another stabbing pain ripped between her eyes. Stu gave another worried look at her quick intake of breath.

"On second thought," she admitted through gritted teeth, "maybe I'll take that ride after all." She felt like a moron, but the realization that she could be waiting as long as another twenty minutes for the bus in the sun made her suddenly nauseous. The day had gotten hotter, as summer was refusing to give up its grasp on the afternoon heat. She needed to get home and the sooner the better.

Smiling weakly, she started to rise from the bench.

Stu was quick to get to his feet as well. Scooping up her backpack, he offered his arm and pointed off to the left, "Sure thing! I'm parked in the parking garage over there."

Rachel tried to block out most of the movement of walking to Stu's vehicle. She did however notice that his arm felt remarkably strong and steady as he helped her along.

He pulled out his keyless entry and pushed a button. Off in the distance, Rachel saw the lights on a black truck flash. It was large, and she had a little bit of a hard time getting up into the cab while he held the door open.

Stu ran around the vehicle and hopped inside, obviously used to the height of the truck. Loud booming music blared out of the speakers as he twisted the key in the ignition. Automatically reaching over to turn the volume down, he gave her an apologetic look. She tried to smile back at him, but instead ended up rubbing her temples more furiously and closing her eyes.

Perhaps, thanks to the experience of his sister having migraines, Stu kept remarkably quiet on the ride. He only asked the minimum number of questions to find her apartment.

Switching off the engine upon their arrival, he acted like he was going to open the door and get out when Rachel stopped him. "That's okay. You don't have to get out. I really appreciate the ride though." She opened the door and slide unceremoniously to the ground.

He offered her one last smile and replied, "Don't give it a second thought. If you feel like doing something nice for me, you know where I live, obviously." He nodded in the direction of Sigma Epsilon. "I know how you hate to be a mooch." He gave her a playful wink as Rachel shut the door behind her.

She hardly paid any attention as she rushed up the stairs of her building. Unwisely, but blessedly, she had left the door unlocked and did not have to mess with keys to get inside. Feeling more cautious now that a stranger had given her a ride home, she locked the door behind herself, dropped her bag just inside the entryway and made her way to the couch. She was lying down and nearly unconscious almost before her head touched the cushions.

**

She awoke to discover that it was dark outside.

What time could it possibly be?

Thinking back to her afternoon on campus, she was sure she had left no later than two o'clock. She grabbed the digital clock on the end table and twisted it around to read the face. It was eight-thirty at night.

Amazingly, her headache was completely gone. She stretched lazily on the couch before pushing herself up and stretching her back. It had been a hot afternoon, and her living room retained some of the residual heat. She could feel moisture on her chest under her shirt from sweating in her sleep.

Feeling sticky and groggy, she trudged to the bathroom and proceeded to take a nice long shower. She even scrubbed her hair twice with shampoo, just to enjoy it that much longer.

With a towel wrapped around her, Rachel made her way into the bedroom to put on some fresh pajamas. It was only nine, and it was too early to go back to bed. Besides, she was not the least bit tired after her too-long power nap.

Rachel began to reflect on her day and her thoughts kept coming back to how nice Stewart had been, to not only track her down and give her glasses back, but to give her a ride home when she was in obvious distress. Plus, earlier that day she had been so optimistic about her new life at Grayson and making friends. Maybe now was as good a time as any to get out there and make a connection.

He had said, "If you feel like doing something nice for me, you know where I live." Feeling determined, she was going to take him up on that offer.

Afterall… she did hate to be a mooch.

Rachel went into the kitchen and opened up her pantry. There were a couple of bags of store-bought cookies, but she thought something slightly fresher would be better. She grabbed a box mix for brownies and set to work mixing the powder, water, oil and eggs together. Scraping the batter out of the bowl and into her baking dish, she put the entire thing in the oven and went into the living room to watch some television while it baked.

Twenty minutes later the smell of brownies filled her apartment. When they were cooled and ready to go, she got out a paper plate and some plastic wrap. Filling the plate, she carefully covered it with the wrap and went back into the bedroom to throw on some sweats to deliver her treat up the street.

It was only ten. She thought, "Frat boys never go to bed before midnight, so he should still be awake."

The night air had cooled considerably from the heat of the afternoon, and Rachel felt particularly refreshed as the breeze ran through her wet hair. This was one of the moments when she wasn't jealous of the ease of short hair. She preferred that her longer hair took a while to dry so she could feel this refreshing cooling sensation.

Within minutes, she was standing outside the door to Sigma Epsilon. The lights were on inside, and she could hear thumping music coming from behind the door. She knocked loud enough that she figured she would be heard.

Suddenly, she began to be self-conscious about the fact that she was a lone single girl knocking on the door to a house full of twenty-something single men. Her heart began to pound and her palms got sweaty. She was about to bolt back down the sidewalk when the door opened.

Replacing her panicked look with a friendly yet awkward smile, she tried to cover her feelings with a boisterous, "Hi! Is Stewart here?"

The generic-looking college guy who answered the door yelled over his shoulder, "Stu! Girl's here." He stepped away and motioned that she could come inside.

Rachel felt a blush start to creep up her neck as she wondered what kind of situation she might be walking into. The house was surprisingly clean for a house full of men, but the stench of cheap alcohol was in the air, presumably perfumed from all the plastic cups scatter around here and there half full.

Stu came bounding down the stairs, and a smile lit his face when he saw who was waiting for him in the entry way.

"Hey you! You look like you're feeling better."

Feeling a little awkward, Rachel held out her offering and said, "I brought these for you—to thank you for the ride. I'm feeling much better now."

"That was sure some attack you had." Stu reached out for the plate.

"I hope you like brownies."

In mid-reach, he paused as a strange expression crossed his face, and he suddenly asked, "Did I upset you today by giving you a ride?"

Perplexed, Rachel wrinkled her brow and said, "No... Why? Do you hate brownies?"

Chuckling slightly, as if embarrassed, he tried to offhandedly reply, "Oh, okay then." He took the offered plate of goodies. "It's just that last year a bunch of the boys got sick from a plate of brownies that some girls brought over that were laced with laxatives. I didn't think you would do something like that over getting a ride home, but I just wanted to check."

As a show of good faith, Rachel reached over and grabbed a brownie from under the plastic wrap. Making a dramatic show of it, she took one large bite, and with her mouth stuffed full said, "Yum!" and swallowed. Raising an eyebrow, she added, "Okay, now your turn."

Stu mockingly rolled his eyes, "Oh, all right. If you twist my arm." He took one from the plate for himself and stuffed the entire thing in his mouth in one big bite. "These are amazing," he gushed, and promptly took another brownie. This time he took several bites to finish it off. In between chewing she was able to make out, "You didn't have to do this."

Laughing, Rachel smiled and wondered if she really had found a good friend, and on the very first day. It was getting late, and she had early classes in the morning, so she didn't stay very long before she said her goodbyes and made her way back home.

Before she left, Stu gave her his cell phone number—just in case she needed another ride. He hesitated a minute after the number was given, possibly trying to think of an excuse to ask for her number in return. Coming up empty handed, he was about to let it drop when Rachel decided to take pity on him and gave her number over as well. She thought, "How many white knights is a girl likely to find anyway?"

Once home, she quickly got back into her comfy pajamas and settled down on the couch. She was still too well rested from her earlier nap to go to bed quite yet.

The clock read ten thirty, and Rachel decided to give her homework one last go around. Not to tempt fate twice in the same day, this time she put her glasses on immediately.

In record time, she made it the rest of the way through her assignment and was just starting to feel drowsy again when the pain returned.

Instead of gradual headache like earlier, this time the pain hit with a vengeance. When Rachel could open her eyes and look around again, she discovered her homework had scattered across the floor and she too was on the floor curled up in the fetal position. The pain was so intense that once over, she had a hard time remembering exactly how bad it had been—almost like her body was trying to protect itself by forgetting.

Her breathing was ragged. With a shaky hand, she pulled herself up off the floor and made her way to the bedroom. Crawling into bed, she closed her eyes and tried to steady her breathing. Her entire body was trembling from the shock of it all.

Slowly she began to drift off to sleep.

Before she was pulled completely under, she could have sworn she heard a voice speaking to her.

A voice with golden tones that whispered three little words:

Enough… for now.

CHAPTER 6: CONFRONTATION

Peter lounged in the recliner contemplating his evening study date with Beth. Things had progressed nicely over the last two weeks, and he felt like tonight he should confront her with the truth. But did Beth even realize that she was special?

She had yet to display any signs of a Gift, and—thankfully—any signs of the Evil. In asking offhandedly how she felt, Peter never got more than a "Fine."

There were two things that could draw a Locator's attention to someone Gifted. One was the feeling of the person's Gift itself—a warm and good sensation. The other was the dark and uncomfortable feeling of the Evil.

So far, Peter had only been having fleeting impressions of Beth's aura, and even that would come and go. Usually, her power felt like a weak and unsteady hum. But sometimes, without warning, he would feel a sudden spike in her aura that would practically knock him off his feet.

It was like nothing he had experienced before.

Following Donavon's advice, Peter called his father to see if this was something that had happened to others. His father referenced another case, but was unsure on the details.

"I'll call you once I check a few sources." he had said. That had been almost a week and half ago. Peter impatiently wondered what could be taking him so long.

Beth was due to arrive any minute now. Peter rubbed his hands together in excited anticipation of finally revealing this secret world to her. Even though he was not totally sure that her Gift had manifested yet, he knew that time was likely running short, especially if she was truly unstable. He also didn't want her causing unintentional damage with her powers because she didn't know how to control them.

Also, most people could sense the Order was where they belonged. It was part of being Gifted. Peter hoped that this would be the case today, and that Beth wouldn't be too scared by what he intended to reveal.

Beth seemed to genuinely like Peter and enjoy his company. As they continued to study together, she would open up more and more, and Peter discovered a hidden gem underneath all of the shyness. Bright and sensitive, Beth had a great sense of humor and was one of the kindest people he had ever known. Peter began to feel a bit protective of her. Like he wanted to shield her from all the things that would scare her back into her shell.

But Peter also knew there was a more compelling reason why Beth would come to visit. As much fun as they had together studying, Beth had her eye on a different prize.

Donavon.

Peter had never felt that surge of power in Beth's aura like he had that first night. Not even when Beth and Donavon were in the same room together. But it made little difference. That surge of power was still there, transformed into a smoldering heat behind her eyes as she looked at Donavon.

For being such a shy person, Peter often thought he would blush if he could read Beth's mind in those moments. Many times, that was because he would catch Beth in the act and cause a blush to cover her face as well.

Donavon seemed oblivious. He treated her as he treated everyone—calm, cool, and polite. In his own way, he would try to make Beth feel at home in his presence, but Donavon was more focused on his role as a mentor—trying to glean any useful information from his student about her Gift without being obvious about it.

But both Peter and Donavon were becoming impatient. Precious time was slipping by. Peter needed to rely on his friendship with Beth—and her pull to Donavon—to be enough to anchor her through this evening.

He had to trust his instincts as Locator. It was all he had, really.

***

Beth arrived precisely at the usual time: eight o'clock. Only tonight—instead of sitting at the kitchen table while other members of the house would randomly walk by—everyone in the house was assembled in the living room, waiting to confront Beth.

Peter opened the door when the bell rang and reached out to take Beth's coat. She winced slightly as she pulled the coat off her arms, and Peter noticed that her skin was unusually bright pink. As he stood closer, he could feel heat radiating off her body.

"You okay?"

Beth self-consciously bit her lower lip and looked away as she answered, "I got sunburned today."

If her skin already hadn't been so red, Peter was sure she would be blushing underneath. "Ouch! Too much fun in the sun, eh?"

Beth nodded slightly and smiled a tiny smile, handing Peter her coat.

After hanging her coat in the closet, Peter led Beth into the living room. She immediately hesitated when she saw the entire household had assembled there. There was a definite feeling of excitement in the air.

Her eyes scanned the room, momentarily lingering on Donavon.

Over the course of two weeks, Beth had managed to meet every member of the household. She seemed the most at ease with Amy's bubbly personality and Robert's awkwardness. In contrast, Peter was pretty sure the first time Beth had met Blake she had been completely overwhelmed by his effervescent personality.

Of course, that never stopped Blake. Despite her bashfulness, he would invade her personal space—sometimes with a hand on the shoulder, and sometimes scooping her up into a bear hug. Beth didn't seem to know what to make of the over-friendly man, but every day she seemed less and less surprised by his flamboyant overtures.

"Hi Beth! I saved you a spot." Amy's high voice flitted across the room as she slid over to make room for Beth on the couch. Peter thought it was be more comfortable for Beth if she sat between Amy and himself.

"Umm… thanks." Looking around nervously, Beth slowly approached the couch and sat. "Did I interrupt something? Peter and I were supposed to study tonight, but if that's a problem I can come back some other time."

"Actually," Peter began, "I thought we could all talk for a minute." Peter thought he could feel Beth's pulse pounding louder as he sat down beside her. Her nerves were kicking into high gear. He couldn't help but wonder what she thought was going to happen.

"There is no easy way to start a conversation like this, so I guess I'll just jump right in." Searching her face for any sign as to what she was feeling, he asked, "Do you believe in the supernatural or paranormal?"

There was a long pause and dead silence.

Unexpectedly, Beth's frame began to tremble and then shake as a fit of giggles took over.

Dumbfounded, Peter thought, "She's laughing?" He had been so worried that she would be scared or upset. But laughing? This was the last reaction he expected.

She seemed unable to answer for several moments while spasms of amusement rocked her body. Peter glanced around the room to gauge everyone else's response. Nancy looked back, confusion in her eyes. Donavon just regarded the scene in the same calm and detached manner he always did.

After a few more seconds, Beth appeared to regain some of her composure and she breathlessly said, "Oh Peter! You're such a kidder. And here I thought, by the looks on all your faces that this was some kind of intervention. That you were going to ask me something serious."

Beth's smile slowly started to fade as she regarded the still serious expressions of those around her, smothering the last of her mirth.

"Oh," she gasped, "you're serious."

Blinking in confusion, she locked eyes with Peter and wide-eyed said, "I'm not sure what you mean." Peter felt a slight surge in her aura as she began to take the situation more seriously.

Without a word, Donavon stood up from the recliner to cross the room. He kneeled in front of Beth and Peter thought he felt her heart start to pound even more violently. It was as if Donavon's extremely close proximity was causing huge waves of nervousness and emotions to roll off Beth, like waves crashing on the shore.

Donavon gently took both her hands in his and closed his eyes—just like he had done with Nancy that night in the kitchen. His breathing was slow, deep and even as he began to use his Gift on her.

Peter took this brief moment, knowing it wouldn't last, to drop his barriers and sense the auras around him in the room—to see them with his Locator eyes.

Beth's aura was clearly visible, pulsing and blending with the others in the room. As he watched Donavon work, he could see power flowing from his hands. It sparkled and shimmered around Beth's entire form, basking her in an angelic glow. Her power ebbed and flowed as it mixed together with Donavon's.

It was beautiful.

It only lasted a moment, and the effort exhausted Peter. But being able to see—really *see*—in the fullest sense with his Gift was one of Peter's favorite things about being a Locator.

Reluctantly, he put his walls back up. The room seemed lifeless when seen with his normal eyes.

He tried to concentrate on Beth's reaction.

A small gasp escaped her parted lips, and she stared with wide eyes at Donavon, who opened his eyes to study her. "It doesn't hurt anymore." Disbelievingly, she traced her finger tips up and down her arm—over her sunburn.

A slight smile played at the corners of Donavon's mouth. Softly, he replied, "I'm glad." He stood and returned to his chair.

Beth turned her wide, innocent eyes on Peter. Then she took in the entire room. "How did he do that?"

Her expression changed as another piece of the puzzle seemed to suddenly slide into place. *"All of you can do that?!"*

Peter explained, "No, not that... exactly." In an unspoken signal, he inclined his head towards Robert.

Suddenly the lights in the room brightened. Everyone expected this, but Beth was caught off guard and had to shield her eyes with her hand. Just as suddenly the lights dimmed, leaving a glowing impression from the contrast of bright and dark floating before everyone's eyes—as if a giant flashbulb had gone off in the room.

Finally, the lights returned to normal. The entire time, Robert kept a small blue arc of electricity hissing and popping between his two hands.

Chuckling, Blake rubbed his eyes and gave Robert an accusing look, "Show off."

Robert blushed, the arc suddenly snuffing out.

Peter then made eye contact with Nancy, and suddenly the room was filled with the sound of birds chirping. Other nature sounds joined in, and it was like being transported to the middle of a rainforest.

Then, just as suddenly, all the sound ceased. An unnatural silence permeated the room. It was uncomfortable, the way the sound of everyone's breathing stopped. Amy shifted her legs, but the rubbing of the material was silent in the void. Unnervingly absent were all the little sounds of life that are typically filtered out by the subconscious.

Like the steady turning of a volume dial, things returned to normal and the sounds returned.

Locking eyes with Amy, Beth asked, "What about you?"

"I'm sort of a natural sedative or caffeine jolt. Whichever is handiest at the time. Neat, huh?" Amy's expression was like that of an eager child, almost as if she were sharing the coolest news she'd heard all day. Playfully, she waggled her fingers in front of Beth's face, "You're getting sleepy… very sleepy." Then she giggled, dropping her hand, obviously teasing. "I can also be a kind of emotional mirror, where what I am feeling can be passed on to others."

Beth's expression was hard to read. She mechanically turned her head to look at Blake. "And you?"

Blake's big grin widened as he replied, "I'm pretty good with air." With a wink, he added, "I can take your breath away, baby."

Finally, her gaze rested on Peter again. "And what about you?"

Peter felt very unsure of himself under her penetrating stare. For someone who was usually so timid and shy, suddenly Beth's eyes made Peter feel like he was under a microscope. Feeling the sudden need to clear his throat, Peter coughed, then said, "Well, I'm not exactly like the rest."

Nancy scoffed and rolled her eyes. "Yeah. You're mister normal, alright."

"That's not what I meant. I just mean that it's different for me. I can't influence the physical environment around me like everyone else can. My skills only really work well with people like us." Peter's eyes took in everyone in the room, finally settling on Beth. Cautiously he added, "People like you."

He felt another flux in the aura around Beth at his inclusion of her—a palpable surge of strength. She didn't seem to notice it herself, which made Peter worry that she was going to be in complete denial of the situation. With some frustration, he thought, "How can she not feel it when her energy spikes like that?!"

Amy abruptly became concerned, "Are you feeling okay? You look a little green."

Beth's eyes were glassy, and she was still stroking her own skin disbelievingly—waiting for the sting of the sunburn to return. She whispered, "Like me?" Lucidity slowly began to return to her face as she added, "What do you mean?"

This was the window that Peter had been waiting for.

"I realize that you may not even know it yourself, yet, and that this can all be a little overwhelming. But we want you to know that something special and wonderful is coming, and that you are not alone." He continued, "We are all here to help you in any way that we can." Beth suddenly glanced up at Donavon expectantly and Peter couldn't help the small stab of jealousy that pierced him.

No, jealousy wasn't the right word.

It just would have been nice if, for once, someone was excited to have his help and not getting weak in the knees over Donavon. He wasn't jealous, he was just envious. Defensively, his mind added, "Two completely different things."

Shaking her head, Beth stood up and started to pace. "I don't know if I believe all of this… or that I have anything to do with it."

Robert, usually so quiet, said, "Do you deny what we j-just showed you. Do you deny the proof of your own skin?"

Beth came up short. A spark of anger flashed in her eyes. "I don't know what I saw! And that doesn't mean I'm involved."

She turned to face Peter again. The anger was gone as suddenly as it had appeared. Instead she looked on the verge of tears. Her emotions were all over the place, which was to be expected.

With trepidation she asked, "So what can I do?"

Peter stood to place his hands on her bare arms. The tingling sensation returned where his skin touched hers. "We don't exactly know. Sometimes it takes a little time to figure it out." Adding some reassurance to his voice he pushed ahead, "But you are not alone. Often there are people who came before you with the same Gift that you will have. We can learn from their experiences. We've got extensive records that date back a long time."

Changing the direction of his thoughts, he asked, "Have you noticed anything yourself? Do you have a gut feeling about what it could possibly be?"

Beth looked completely lost. Very quietly she answered, "No."

Donavon briefly closed his eyes and exhaled loud enough that she noticed. He was clearly disappointed that Beth was not providing any answers. As her mentor, this made his job more difficult.

Beth reacted to his sigh, looking almost like a small child that was upset at disappointing their parent.

Always the optimist, Amy popped off the couch and wrapped an arm around Beth, "It could be something exciting and wonderful. Maybe you will be able to move things with your mind. How awesome would that be?" Squeezing Beth around the waist, she added, "And like Pete said, you won't be alone."

Cocking an eyebrow and pointing his finger, Blake smiled and contributed, "I got your back, kid."

Peter could see the questions swirling around in Beth's mind. "But how do you know that I am like you at all?"

Peter sighed. Confession time.

"Well, that's sort of my job—my Gift. I'm a Locator."

"A Locator?"

Amy gushed, "Yeah, like a detective, sort of. Only he can only find people like us."

"So don't go to him if you lose your keys." Blake claimed a seat on the couch, since everyone seemed to be standing now. "I tried once. It cost me a bit to get those keys replaced."

Shaking his head at Blake's attempt at levity, Peter shrugged his shoulders, "I can sense the Gifted. Everyone with a talent has energy around them that I can feel. It's not usually even that hard because we seem to be drawn to the same places—like Grayson. I just have to be close enough to feel their energy and then I just… know. I can't explain it exactly, but sometimes I just know where to be or where to go. The Gifted and Locators are continually drawn to one another."

Robert chimed in, "Like magnets."

A slight hint of betrayal entered Beth's voice, "So that day on campus…" She trailed off as they looked at one another. Nothing else needed to be said. But Peter got the distinct impression that Beth now viewed their meeting as possibly tainted in some way. It hadn't just been a nice boy seeing a nice girl who need directions. Peter had known things—kept things from her—from the very beginning. Guilt blossomed in Peter's gut like a rot, hidden deep inside. His intentions that day has been pure, but Peter was afraid Beth might not see it that way.

Her whole world was being turned upside down. Things that she had been taught were only real in comic books or movies suddenly were blatantly staring her in the face. Not only were these things real—not only did they exist—but she was supposedly a part of it all. Her life was becoming something from a bedtime story.

"How come I've never heard of people like you before?"

Donavon decided to answer this question. "We are very careful. You can probably see why discretion would be important to us."

Blake added, "Salem witch trials ring any bells?"

Looking even more shocked, Beth asked, "So, you are witches?"

Amy burst out laughing. "No, silly! There's no such thing. No potions or hexes or bibbidi-bobbidi-boo. We work with energy—nature—that sort of thing."

"Nature?"

Amy continued, "Yeah. When you look at it like that, I guess we are more like hippies."

Blake smiled, "Hippies with freakin' cool powers."

Even Beth smiled at that.

Seeming to settle down just slightly, Beth asked, "So, what do I do now?"

Peter walked away to lean against the wall. He wanted to give her some space to breathe—to think. "That's entirely up to you."

Almost disbelievingly, she asked, "You mean I'm free to go?"

Donavon frowned ever so slightly. "Not exactly."

Peter was quick to try to minimize the discomfort. "What he means is, of course you are free to go. But it's more complicated than that." He stopped to take a deep breath.

So far, they had all avoided talking about the darker side of their lives. The Evil. With Beth's delicate nature, Peter had been dreading this part, but thought, "Ready or not. Here we go."

"These... Gifts... they come with some danger too. When your talent starts to emerge, you will notice that you have a stronger sense of the good things in life. But along with that, you will have a stronger pull from the bad."

"Bad things?" Beth's tone was skeptical.

Nancy decided it was her turn to help out. "Call it the devil. Call it Satan. Call it bad karma. Call it the dark side. Call it whatever the heck you want, but Evil is real. It's out there, and it will be just waiting for you to become strong enough to feel it before it tries to corrupt you."

Robert interjected, "We call it your Trial."

Beth was rapidly turning pale again. "So I am in danger? Does this happen quickly?"

Trying to soothe her with his Gift as Locator, Peter locked eyes with Beth again. "It varies from person to person. You don't need to worry about it too much right now. From what I can tell—and it's my job to know—your power is still very weak. I found you in plenty of time. It's like I said. The Gifted and Locators are continually drawn to one another, especially during the critical time of their Trial."

Beth reclaimed her seat on the couch. She slumped into a posture that Peter was becoming familiar with—retreating into herself. "So, now what?"

Nancy responded first, "We've found it to be helpful to stick together. That's why we all live together. We're offering to let you move in with us. It's really the safest way. Then we can be here to support you whenever you need."

Peter continued, "So our study sessions are pretty much over." Knowing this could be the carrot that made all the difference, he plowed ahead, gesturing to this best friend, "Donavon is going to be your mentor now."

Beth's aura surged again. The feeling was so potent to Peter, he just wished he could reach out and bottle it to show her.

A small gasp escaped from her lips, and for a moment Beth looked like she just wished she could disappear into the couch. But as she looked from Order member to Order member, their welcoming smiles calmed her. Finally, her eyes rested on Donavon. With some of the first confidence she displayed all night, she replied, "Okay, I'm in."

CHAPTER 7: TAILSMANS

"I have so many questions," Beth said the next day as Peter helped her carry boxes up to her new room on the second floor.

"That's why we're here," Peter said, "To help you figure it all out. Donavon is your mentor, but don't be afraid to ask any one of us anything." They walked into her just-cleaned room, courtesy of Nancy and Amy. She was one door down from Donavon, which Peter hoped would be comforting.

Since it was the beginning of the school year, Beth sold her old apartment contract to a late-coming student in a matter of hours. She was also surprised when Amy told her that she wasn't going to need to pay rent in her new home.

"I can't possibly stay here for free!"

Amy smiled, "Sure you can. We all do. Donavon's family owns this house and they don't want any money. The Graysons are really understanding that way."

Her brain clicked, "Grayson? As in Grayson College, Grayson?" Beth looked a little embarrassed that she hadn't made the connection sooner.

"The one and the same."

Being Gifted didn't necessarily run in a person's family. Locators were kind of the exception to that rule. So, while it was true that Donavon's parents weren't Gifted, his grandmother was. And she had enthusiastically supported her grandson when he revealed he was Gifted, both emotionally and with her vast reserves of wealth.

But even though the Order was not obligated to pay rent, it didn't mean that the occupants got off without making some kind of contribution. Everyone was responsible for some kind of upkeep.

Beth was eager to pull her weight. She decided to take advantage of the beautiful autumn day outside and help Nancy and Amy clean out the last of the vegetable garden. Peter and Blake were going to trim back some bushes so they would be pruned and ready to go in the spring. Donavon was mowing the lawn for the last time this year.

Robert was the only one who was absent from today's chores.

Peter could overhear the girls chatting while he snipped the branches on a nearby bush. Snip. Snip. Snip.

"I feel like I am never going to get my Gift figured out. How did you find out what you could do?" Beth asked Nancy while she made a pile of debris from the overgrown lettuce.

Wiping a gloved hand across her damp forehead, Nancy sighed as she sat back on her heels. "At first, I had no idea what was going on. I actually thought that maybe I was going crazy. I can remember one time sitting in school and I overheard some girls gossiping about someone."

Nancy bent over to keep pulling up the carrots with the help of her trowel before continuing, "I don't remember what they said exactly, or who they were talking about, but I remember being really annoyed. They were like seething vipers, and it just went on and on. I got so mad that I couldn't hardly stand it anymore. And then suddenly," she dramatically jerked a carrot free, "Bam! Complete silence."

She smiled a bit at the memory. "I was so relieved that they had stopped talking that it took me a moment to notice that *everything* had become deathly silent. I looked around the room, but no one else seemed to notice. My teacher was up at the front, still prattling on about our homework assignment but I couldn't hear a thing. His lips were moving, but I wasn't able to pick up so much as a peep."

Beth's eye got big with worry, but Nancy chuckled softly, "I actually started to freak out, and I practically ran from the room. I went straight to the bathroom and hid in a stall. I found out later that everyone assumed I had suddenly gotten sick and ran off to puke."

Still laughing at the memory, she continued, "I didn't need to run away though. Once I had gotten away from those gossiping girls, all the sounds returned."

"That must have been a crazy experience." Beth took a sip from her water bottle and waited for Nancy to continue.

"Yeah. But there were other strange things that happened too." Nancy stood up to dump her pile of carrots into a waiting bowl. "My parents fought. A lot. And it was really hard to watch as a kid. My dad wasn't the most loyal guy. This one time he came home smelling like perfume and my mother jumped all over him, accusing him of having an affair." Nancy seemed a little embarrassed to add, "Again." She plowed on with her story. "The screaming and yelling got pretty bad. I was up in my room with the door shut lying on my bed. When I heard them come pounding up the stairs, I tried to pull my pillow over my face to block out most of the sound. It wasn't working.

"All of a sudden, I started to hear a ringing in my ears. It was *way* better than hearing my folks fight, so I started to really concentrate on the ringing. It grew louder and louder, until I couldn't hear anything else. It only lasted a short while, but when it faded away, my parents had stopped fighting. Instead, I heard my mother sounding all frantic in the next room.

"I got scared that something bad had happened to her while I was blocking out all the fighting, so I ran from the room to see what was going on." Nancy's face got darker, as she paused to take a breath. "I found her kneeling next to my dad. He was lying on the ground, holding his head and sort of moaning. When he moved his hands away, I saw there was a little blood coming from his ears. Some of it had pooled on the carpet." With a distant look in her eye, she added, "That stain never did come out."

Beth, looking a little pale herself, tried to make Nancy feel better. "You didn't know what you were doing. It really wasn't your fault."

Nancy's face turned into a grim smile. "The funny thing was, I didn't really feel that bad afterwards. I maybe should have, but I thought he got what he deserved. Actually, less than he deserved. We took him to the hospital, and found out that his ear drums had ruptured, or some such nonsense. He healed pretty quickly, but his ears are pretty sensitive now." Looking Beth in the eye, she added, "A little pain hardly seems like fair compensation for a life time of cheating on your spouse."

Beth seemed a little taken aback and Nancy noticed the look on her face. "Well, it's not like, now that I know how to control it, that I would do that again. It was an accident. But I can see some sick justice in it too."

Beth, looked away, feeling uncomfortable. "I see…"

Peter hadn't noticed that he had stopped trimming until Blake punched him in the shoulder. "Gonna make me do all the work?"

"Sorry man." Peter started clipping again. Snip. Snip. Snip.

Trying to change the subject, Beth asked Amy, "So, where is Robert, anyway?"

Amy—looking all too happy to move on to a different topic of conversation—energetically replied, "Oh, he's probably off working on your Life Box."

Beth stood up and went to work on another patch in the garden. "I'm not too clear on the whole Life Box thing. How does that work?"

"Well, you'll have to ask Robert to get all the details. It's very confusing. But basically, Robert has to make a unique box for every member of the Order. Robert showed you how he is good with energy and electricity. Things like static cling. Well, he's also good with metals."

Looking thoughtful, Beth interjected, "Metal... Electricity... I can see how that might be related."

Amy went on, "It takes some time to make a box from scratch, and so he's probably busy making yours. It needs to be ready before we can try to protect you from the Evil. Once it's inside you, the Evil has to come out and go somewhere. Your Life Box will become the perfect container. It will go along with this." Amy gestured to the intricately-designed choker around her neck. Beth had noticed that Amy never took it off.

Really looking closely now, Beth caught her breath at its brilliance. The white gold was delicately braided into a thin chain embedded with diamonds. Hanging from the center was a pendant of delicate flowers. Each blossom was incrusted with amethysts and more diamonds. The sun sparkled and winked as it bounced off the faceted jewels and onto Beth's face.

"That's amazing!"

Amy giggled. "Well, *I* like it. Robert is such an artist. I can't believe the things he comes up with. Show her yours, Nancy." Amy was practically bouncing with excitement.

Nancy took off her left-hand glove to reveal another stunning work of art. This time it was a bracelet, delicately made of yellow gold. Oval rubies were separated by silky white pearls, forming a ring of satin and sparkle that fit snuggly against her skin.

Amy gushed, "The men have them too, only they all wear rings."

Pausing in his work, Peter absently rubbed the fingers of his right hand together to consciously feel the ring there. It was so much a part of who he was now that he never really thought much about it. His ring had five small square sapphires entrenched in silver, with a few small diamonds on either side of the row of sapphires. The gems made a slight s-curve around his finger.

"So, what are they for?"

Amy's eyes sparkled, "Well, besides being absolutely gorgeous… these are our link to our Life Boxes. Anytime Evil tries to touch us, it is channeled through here," she lightly placed her hand on her throat—over her choker, "into the heart of our box."

Not understanding fully, Beth asked, "Does your box ever get... full?"

"Oh no! It would take more than one lifetime to attract enough Evil to fill a Life Box." Amy jumped up to go toss her pile of weeds into the waiting wheelbarrow.

Beth continued, "Aren't you afraid that you will lose it or it will get stolen?"

Amy giggled again, "Not really. Robert is good at his Gift. He binds the jewelry to us. If you look closely, you will see that there is no clasp." Beth leaned in for a closer inspection. The choker was one solid piece of jewelry with no obvious way of removing it. Amy added, "I don't think it's possible to take it off without Robert's help. Besides, why would I want to take it off? It's my protection. I feel so much safer with this around my neck than I ever did walking around vulnerable to the Evil."

Nancy looked up, "They are our talismans. When Robert has your box and talisman done, then we will hold a special... event." Amy rolled her eyes at Nancy's choice of words, so, looking at Amy she added, "Well, *ritual* sounds too much like a cult, I think." Amy rolled her eyes again and shook her head like she thought Nancy was being silly.

Nancy took a deep breath and blurted out, "Fine! We'll hold a special *ritual*," she greatly emphasized the word, "where we will Cleanse you of any Evil that might already be trying to hurt you. The Evil will get channeled from you, to your talisman, and then finally to your Life Box. There it will be trapped so it can't hurt you or anyone else ever again. Your talisman will also act as a sort of shield that will protect you from any future contact with the Evil."

Amy got a look of excited anticipation and said, "But you haven't told her the best part!"

Beth looked at Nancy expectantly.

She explained, "While it's true that by the time a Life Box is ready, most people have a pretty good idea of what their Gift is going to be." Looking sympathetically at Beth, she continued, "I know you haven't been having too much success at accessing your Gift yet, but during your Cleansing—that's what we call it—any Gifts that you currently possess will become apparent to everyone in the ritual."

As a side note, she added, "Although, that doesn't mean that you might not start to develop more Gifts later. It is rare but not unheard of. However, by then you should be a lot more experienced at recognizing the energy around you, so it shouldn't be as difficult for you to figure out what is going on."

Excitement sparkled in Beth's eye for the first time as she eagerly asked, "What do you mean by my Gift will *become apparent?*"

"Well, it's hard to explain exactly." Nancy's forehead crinkled, "During the ritual, everyone's consciousness will become linked with yours. This is necessary because, if we are going to be able to dispel the Evil from your mind, we need to be able to feel it. Then, we can find it and lock it away.

"While we are all connected, we will also be able to tell what your current Gifts are." Nancy paused, frowning. "I'm not explaining this very well. It's such a unique experience. I'm sure Donavon or Peter could probably do a better job telling you about it. You'll have to ask them sometime."

Amy added, "You know, it's almost like having a vision. We should be able to see all the things that you currently can't see about your Gift because we have more experience recognizing the pull of the energy around us. Having that brief experience of being inside your head, and feeling the world around you exactly like you feel it, we should be able to sense what kind of power you are drawn to. Not only that, but because our minds will be linked, *you* should be able to see it through our eyes too."

Peter smiled to himself. The girls were really trying to help Beth feel better and to have hope that she would figure out her Gift one way or another. But the Cleansing was hard to describe, which is why they typically left it up to him or Donavon. They had more experience explaining these kinds of things.

As the discussion turned to more trivial things—like Amy trying to imagine what kind of jewelry Robert would create for Beth—Peter recalled his own Cleansing. It had been astonishing. Standing in the middle of the circle, surrounded by those who were Gifted—there was such power there. And love.

Well, that was not totally true. Like Nancy said, they had to find and dispel the Evil. That was horribly unpleasant. It almost made Peter shiver to remember the feeling of the Gifted sending their energy into him, concentrating the Evil that had infused in his mind and pulling it out. For the rest of his human existence, he was sure he would never experience anything like it again.

But, on the other side of the spectrum, there had been the absolutely incredible experience of feeling his mind linked with all the Gifted in the circle. Peter's father had been with them during his Cleansing, and as a Locator himself, had especially been able to show him the Gift and power that Peter held.

In that moment, Peter had learned more about his Gift—seeing it through his father's eyes—than anyone ever could have explained with words. It was like a window had been opened between their minds. Everything had felt so clear. Coming out of the Cleansing, he had felt so confident about his place and purpose in the world.

But then Peter had started to use his Gift in the real world. Not every situation he came across was ideal, but Peter was required to do what was necessary regardless of his personal feelings. It didn't matter if he felt a twinge of guilt while manipulating a person's senses. It didn't matter if the newly found Gifted One seemed like a immoral person worthy of saving. Those were not Peter's calls to make. He simply had to get the job done, and help everyone he could.

But Peter feared the day would come when he would be faced with a situation where he was not emotionally ready to handle it. He could only pray that he would be strong enough—and trained well enough— to do the right thing.

CHAPTER 8: UNEXPECTED

Peter felt antsy—like he was missing something.

In the past two weeks, Beth's progress had been slow, almost frustrating, but he still figured there was plenty of time to help her. Donavon also seemed totally devoted to her welfare now that she was moved in and he could work with her. He would carefully walk her through exercises designed to help her focus her mind and concentrate on what she might be able to manipulate. But when she had no idea what to concentrate on yet, it seemed an impossible task. Always patient, Donavon would coax her through the frustrating moments and encourage her to keep trying. Smiling slightly, he would remind her that it was only a matter of time—that these things couldn't be forced and her Cleansing was coming.

A Gift typically surfaced in one of two ways. Either it would emerge during a moment of extreme emotional turmoil, or it could be coaxed out with a calm focus. It was obviously safer if they could help Beth figure things out when she was calm, rather than upset, so Donavon taught her various tricks to meditate and center herself.

When Peter observed them, Beth acted self-conscious and shy, just as she had been that first day with Peter. Donavon worked patiently but unrelentingly. Right now, Amy and Donavon sat on the coffee table while Beth sat on the couch, ready to learn. Peter leaned against the doorway, observing.

"You have to focus on the moments when you think your sixth sense might be telling you something," Donavon explained. "In those moments, when you feel the most aware, you might be able to stretch out enough with your feelings to begin to recognize what your subconscious is trying to tell you. The unconscious part of your mind probably already knows exactly what is going on, but the conscious part of your mind doesn't want to believe it."

He turned to Amy, "Okay."

Amy looked at Donavon and concentrated for a moment. Peter watched as a Locator, and could see the flows of energy that Amy directed toward Donavon. Peter assumed she was trying to give Donavon an energy boost, which was safer than trying to make him tired—especially while he was trying to teach. But Amy also had to be careful not to overdo things, or Donavon wouldn't sleep much tonight.

"Do you feel what she is doing?"

Beth sighed, her eyes closed, "I'm not sure."

"A little more, please, Amy."

Peter saw the flows intensify slightly. A flicker of recognition crossed Beth's face. "I think I am getting something."

"Good!" Donavon smiled at Beth, and she in turn seemed to blossom under his gaze with a warm blush. Amy clapped and cheered enthusiastically.

Donavon took Beth's hands in his. "Now see if you can feel this." The flows changed as Amy shut down and Donavon took over.

For once, Beth didn't seem to react to Donavon's touch in a self-conscious way. Instead, caught up in the moment of her victory, she closed her eyes again and concentrated on feeling Donavon's energy.

As the seconds ticked by, Peter could sense Beth's frustration increasing. Her breathing got deeper and more irritated. Donavon was slowly, methodically increasing the flow of his energy around their touching hands. He wasn't exactly trying to send his energy into Beth, because she would feel that right away. But rather, he was just surrounding Beth in his energy, hoping that she could feel the flows of power around her. "Don't push too hard. That will only be a distraction. Take all the time you need… It will come."

Glancing to look Donavon in the eyes, Beth took a deep breath, straightened her shoulders and closed her eyes again to concentrate. She shook her head to toss her hair over her shoulders, and unknowingly leaned a little closer to Donavon.

The aura around them continued to increase in strength little by little, until finally Beth gave a small start and suddenly jerked her hands free from Donavon's.

Immediately alert, Donavon asked, "Is everything okay? Are you all right?" His eyes flickered to Peter. As their glances locked for a split second, Peter knew that Donavon was thinking about that time years ago in the woods, when Donavon had unknowingly burned Peter's arm with his touch. To this day, there remained a scar around Peter's bicep in the exact shape of Donavon's hand. Despite being covered by the sleeve of his shirt, Peter instinctively reached up and protectively covered the mark with his hand.

Donavon hadn't meant to hurt Peter that day. He had simply been reaching out to his friend for help. Not understanding what was going on, or the nature of his Gift, he had poured so much energy into Peter that it physically hurt him. Over time, as Donavon learned to control his Gift, he had told Peter that he wasn't even sure if he was capable of releasing that kind of power again. Only under the extreme torment of the Evil was he able to do what he did that day. With his Life Box and ring in place, he felt he should be safe enough now to never hurt anyone like that again.

Or was he?

Peter glanced at Donavon's right hand and saw the protective ring that Robert had created. Both Peter and Donavon had initially been given rings made by someone in a completely different Order. Now, living with Robert, they had... upgraded, in a way. With Robert's help, Donavon's ring was now a work of art.

It was dual tone. A slim yellow gold band connected to a wider white gold band with a trench of alternating diamonds and emeralds in between. It was classy, and like nothing Peter had ever seen before.

Peter knew that Donavon was worried that he might have hurt Beth just now. His concern for her was written all over his face as he watched Beth rubbing her hands together.

She glanced up, and reading his expression, tenderness covered her face as she smiled, "Oh, I'm fine. It just tickled, is all." Holding her hands out, palms up, she explained, "See. I was just surprised by the suddenness of it."

Donavon genuinely smiled back and laughed a little to himself. In his sometimes overly formal way, he said, "Well, I was going for something like that, but I was hoping to be more subtle until you could just barely sense it. I apologize for startling you."

Beth laughed back, "Oh no! It was great. I could really *feel* something. Out there. Surrounding us."

Donavon reached over and lightly placed his hand over hers again. "That's wonderful. It should really help you start to sense your energy." Beth deeply blushed, but her eyes beamed with pride and joy.

Peter, also smiling, chimed in, "I'd say that's pretty good work for one day."

Peter knew that one of these days Beth's Gift would spring into existence, but he couldn't help the uneasy feeling he was getting—especially when Beth would leave the house to go to class or shopping. It didn't matter where she was going. Just as soon as she was gone, Peter would start to pace around the house like a caged animal. He anxiously felt like something was wrong and he didn't know what it was.

Later that evening, Peter was coming down the staircase when he spied Donavon and Beth working in the living room again. Beth was sitting on the couch, arms folded in her lap, eyes closed, and brow furrowed in concentration. There was a storm forming outside, and the sheer curtains were billowing in the breeze.

Donavon sat next to her, speaking in soothing tones. "Don't try to force it. Just relax and try to clear your mind. Reach out with your senses and try to feel, *really feel* the room around you. Feel the air, the material of the couch, the carpet under your toes. Think of something pleasant—something that makes you happy. Let those good feelings flow through your entire body."

As he spoke, Donavon moved to kneel in front of Beth. "A Gift is full of pleasant feelings. It heightens your senses. It should be enjoyable, satisfying, and warm. You should be able to feel the presence of the goodness around you." Donavon reached out and placed his hands over the top of hers.

Peter dropped his guard and let himself see the unseen flows of power swirling around Donavon and Beth. His own power was invisible to himself. He had no idea what he looked like when he was absorbed in his Gift as Locator. But he *could* see what was going on with Donavon and Beth.

Donavon, in an attempt to help Beth find her sense of the good, was pouring his energy over and around her. It flowed and shimmered, settling in a soft cloud. He continued, "Stretch out with your senses. Try to feel my aura around you—my hands on yours. Feel the breeze from the open window. Feel the oppression in the air from the energy of the storm." He moved closer to Beth, dropping his voice. His energy continued to emanate around her in a swirl of light.

Just as she had earlier, eyes closed, Beth leaned closer to Donavon's voice. He reached a hand up towards her face and allowed his power to flow stronger as he rested his palm against the side of her face.

Without warning, lightning struck outside. The brightness burned into Peter's eyes, and he instantly shielded himself, both physically and mentally—his Locator eyes momentarily overwhelmed. When he could focus again, he could no longer see the auras in the room below.

What he did see surprised him.

Beth had her arms around Donavon's neck. She was clinging to him while her lips were feverishly pressed against his mouth. Guessing how she felt about Donavon, Peter couldn't be too surprised by what he saw. He was, however, surprised by the suddenness of it.

What shocked him more than anything—and made him feel suddenly very self-conscious—was that Donavon had his arms wrapped around her waist and was kissing her back with equal intensity. They pulled each other closer as the wind continued to blow the curtains out and round them, completely lost to the rest of the world. Beth had a hand tangled in Donavon's hair, crushing her face to his and Donavon was arching up to meet her from his kneeling position on the floor.

Stunned, all Peter could think was, "Didn't see that coming."

Before he could wonder if he had been wrong to underestimate Donavon's feelings for Beth, and before he could lift a foot to move discretely away, Donavon was pushing Beth into the back of the couch and attempting to untangle his arms from around her. His expression was dazed and confused. His voice sounded husky but also surprisingly uncomfortable as he said, "I'm sorry…" Attempting to rise from the floor, he seemed to be regaining some composure and became overly formal again. "That was not my intent. I don't know what came over me." His voice remained hoarse and rough, yet there was an underlying irritation to it. "I certainly didn't mean to take advantage of you while you were concentrating so hard."

Beth looked at him, dumbfounded. "I'm sorry," she mumbled. "Did I do something wrong?" The pain of the rejection clearly showed on her face, and her cheeks burned with a fierce glow.

"Oh, no!" Donavon was quick to sit down next to her on the couch. He placed his arm around her shoulders. It looked brotherly and awkward, especially compared to the intimate embrace they had just shared. "I just..." he seemed at a loss for words. "I... I just don't know what came over me" he finished lamely.

Beth's lip started to tremble and her eyes were shiny with tears. Her face was becoming more flushed with each passing moment.

Peter could see the conflict in Donavon's eyes. It was as if he wanted to reach out and comfort her, but was unsure if that was the right thing to do. Peter always thought of Donavon as a man with high ethical standards. He didn't know what to make of the behavior he just saw and the immediate reversal of course that had taken place.

At the most inopportune moment, Blake decided to come around the bend from the kitchen. Oblivious to what was going on in the living room, he spotted Peter frozen on the stairs. He chortled and said, "Hey dude. Playing freeze tag?"

Peter mentally rolled his eyes and chanted in his mind, "I'm not here. I'm not here. I'm not here. Please, ignore the completely mortified blonde guy on the stairs."

Locking eyes with both Donavon and Beth, Peter swallowed loudly and finally completed his journey down the stairs.

In a blind flood of tears, Beth raced from the couch to the closet. Snatching her coat, and with her hand covering her mouth, she avoided eye contact with Peter and rushed out into the storm.

For a split second, Peter and Donavon locked eyes with one another, matching stunned expressions on their faces. Peter didn't have a chance to wonder if he should run after her—or tell Donavon to run after her—because at that exact moment an overwhelming sensation knocked the air completely out of Peter's lungs. He doubled in half, clutching his mid-section, while Blake and Donavon ran over to help.

Blake got an arm around Peter and tried to help him straighten up.

"What's wrong?" Donavon eyes were focused and serious now—the embarrassment of the moment forgotten.

Peter gasped. "Something is wrong. I have to go. I have to go *now!*"

Without even bothering to grab a coat, Peter dashed out the door. The storm was really picking up. The rain pelted down, soaking him to the skin almost instantly. The wind whipped and howled. Peter could see the trees bending at sharp angles, leaves and debris flying across the ground. Water flowed in the street gutters like white rapids.

Something was pulling Peter down the street, an invisible force he couldn't ignore. He was only vaguely aware that both Blake and Donavon had followed him out into the torrential downpour. They had both grabbed jackets to help keep the rain off.

"Peter. What is it?" Blake was jogging alongside, keeping up with Peter's stumbling yet brisk pace.

His Locator instincts were in high gear. He was driven to move and move now!

"I don't know. Something is wrong. I have to be somewhere… somewhere right now. It's important." With each passing step, Peter could feel the pull growing stronger. Still clutching his side because of an overwhelming pain, he started to jog, each step splashing up water—the rain soaking his clothes.

"Is it Beth?" Donavon's eyes were full of suspicion and remorse.

Peter thought, "He must be afraid she's out here, upset and in danger… and worried it's all his fault." He could feel sympathy for his friend. He seemed in such obvious distress. Maybe there was more going on with him and Beth than Peter had realized.

Grunting through clenched teeth, Peter growled, "I don't know what it is for sure. I just know there isn't much time." The pull was changing. It was becoming tainted—dark and oily. Peter's skin felt unclean and he could feel the pulsing darkness of the Evil. His instincts as Locator were screaming at him to hurry. Something terrible was happening.

Peter heard Blake's sharp intake of breath. They exchanged a look and Blake responded, "I feel it too, man." Donavon nodded in agreement.

The invisible pull brought Peter to a street where most of the fraternities were located. He wasn't overly familiar with where they were, as the fraternities were not his favorite place to hang out. Toga parties and all night keggers were the exact opposite of a Locator's lifestyle. Peter had to be focused—and sober—to be a good at his job.

Not knowing exactly where they were, Peter ran up to what looked like an apartment complex. He could feel the Evil surrounding them. It was everywhere. Anyone else who was not Gifted probably wouldn't notice anything amiss, aside from the storm. However, to Peter, the air smelled of sulfur and the taste of bile was in his throat.

He dropped his defenses and looked at his surroundings with the eyes of a Locator. In the middle of the darkness, Donavon and Blake stood out—their auras making them glow like angels. Their talismans sparkled beautifully with a fierce light, indicating the strength of the Evil around them. The only other time Peter had seen his ring glow with such force was the day he found Donavon during his Trial.

Swirling around the apartment complex was a thick cloud of black energy. It was dense and stifling—in sharp contrast to the brilliance of their auras and talismans. The wind was howling through the trees, but Peter could also hear another kind of wailing coming from deep within the churning cloud—the wailing of voices in pain and torment.

"In here." Peter indicated the second stairwell for the building. The men ran up the stairs, taking them two at a time. Peter halted on the top floor, scanning and being guided by an unseen force. Then, he started pounding on the second door he came to.

Blake and Donavon exchanged a worried glance. Thunder rumbled outside and lightning illuminated the hallway in an eerie way. Peter tried the doorknob only to discover that it wouldn't open. "It's locked." Peter roared, "We have to get this damn door open NOW!"

"I got it." Blake maneuvered in front of Peter. With his defenses down, Peter could see Blake drawing the surrounding energy to him. He was a big guy, and maybe he could have broken the door down by himself, but Blake wasn't taking any chances. They all had a bad feeling about this.

Blake rushed at the door and smashed it off its hinges with a solid wall of air. It sounded like a battering ram. Being the first to step into the room, Blake was immediately knocked down to his knees by the overwhelming presence of the Evil in the room.

Donavon seemed less affected by it as he strode in, scanning the room with a dangerous gleam in his eyes.

Wiping the rain from his face, Peter entered the room as well, and immediately his eyes fell upon the two people present. A distressed redheaded man—although he currently appeared more like a boy than a man—was crouching over a blonde female. She might have been beautiful, but Peter couldn't tell. Her face was contorted in pain and her hands were forming claws and scratching at her face. She hadn't drawn blood... yet... but dark red lines ran down her cheeks. She was thrashing around on the floor, groaning in obvious pain.

The ring on Peter's hand started to glow as it absorbed some of the attacking energy of the Evil. The sapphires flashed a dazzling blue, glowing in a way that only Locators could see. The Evil screamed and hissed in response as it was attacked by the talismans of the Gifted men.

Then something else extraordinary happened. At first Peter thought it was another bolt of lightning. However, unlike lightning, it was sustaining, illuminating the room. An enormous field of energy was developing around the blonde female and Donavon. As Donavon continued to approach the girl, it grew stronger, brighter and more intense. When Donavon reached out to touch her, the green emeralds of his ring radiant, the energy exploded into blinding colors that made Peter cringe and hide his face.

Unable to see the same things, Blake was touching Peter's shoulder and shaking him. "You okay? Hang on, man. We're getting her out."

Donavon scooped up the girl and started for the door. The redhead jumped to his feet to protest, obviously recovering from the shock of a huge black man busting down the door. "Hey! Who are you guys? You can't just take her."

Donavon's face was a mask of complete fury and protectiveness. He shot the redhead one withering look which offered no room for argument. The redhead hesitated and instead stood clenching and unclenching his fists in frustration, too afraid to cross the possessed stranger.

They all rushed out into the hall, Donavon carrying the woman who weakly moaned, "No, no, no…"

CHAPTER 9: NIGHTMARES

Early that same morning, Rachel sleepily hit her alarm. Glancing at it through tired eyes she suddenly awoke with a start.

She'd overslept, again!

Frantically she rushed to grab her stuff before the shuttle bus came. In her hurry to stuff her homework into her bag, one of the paper sheets neatly sliced the end of her finger.

Cursing, she shoved her finger into her mouth, grimacing at the salty taste. The cut simply added to her irritation. Pausing, she glanced at the hallway mirror.

The sight made her sigh.

She hadn't been sleeping well over the last two weeks. Dark circles rimmed her eyes in deep shades of purple and blue. Her hair was in a messy knot at the nape of her neck. Her glasses sat askew on her face, and she wasn't about to mess with make-up.

The problems had started the night of her horrible migraine attack. Since then, every time she tried to close her eyes she couldn't relax. For some reason, she felt insecure, alone, and afraid. When she would finally nod off, exhausted, she would be restless and her dreams were full of disturbing images.

And a Voice.

Enough, for now.

That's what the Voice had told her.

The morning after it had all started, she tried to convince herself that she must be delusional. During the daylight hours, it was easy to dismiss something that strange as a trick of the migraine.

Nighttime was a different story, though. The Voice would come to her in fitful dreams. It would tell her to do things—evil things. It would whisper to her, asking her to drop her defenses. Other times, there was simply a flow of words coming from the Voice— words she wished she could scrub from her memory.

In those moments, it was impossible to deny that the Voice was real. It was Evil. She would sit up in the middle of the night, covered in sweat, to discover that she had violently ripped her bed apart in her frantic attempts to wake herself up. Shaky, she would rise to go to the bathroom and splash water on her face, washing the sweat away.

No matter how vivid the dream had been, within moments it would start to fade, and she would be unable to recall the exact details.

The headaches had also continued, but never as severely as that first day of school. She constantly wore her glasses now, in the hope that it would help prevent future attacks.

Turning away from the mirror, Rachel walked into the bathroom to rummage around and find a bandage. As she carefully wrapped her paper-cut finger, she heard the unmistakable sound of the brakes of the bus squealing and protesting at the stop outside her apartment.

"Ah, crap!"

Rachel dashed to the window and peeked outside. Sure enough, she was just in time to see the red tail lights go out as the bus pulled away. She felt a prickling sensation in her eyes and fought to hold back tears of frustration. She mentally kicked herself because she realized it was a stupid thing to cry over.

She thought, "If I just had more sleep, this wouldn't bother me at all. I'm such an emotional wreck."

She crossed the room and snatched up her backpack. In the side pocket, she found her cell phone. Gritting her teeth, she punched in Stu's number and waited for him to pick up.

A groggy voice answered on the other end, "Hello?"

She sighed. "Hey, Stu. It's Rachel."

She heard Stewart clear his throat on the other end. He still sounded groggy, but was trying very hard to wake up quickly. "Hey, Sunshine! What can I do for you, this fine day?"

Rachel couldn't help but smile at Stu's optimism. "You sound like you just woke up. How do you even know it's a good day?"

He chuckled, "Any day that starts out with a call from you is a good day."

Rachel was so glad to have met Stu. They were becoming fast friends. He was really easy to be around.

Rachel bit her lip, and then took a deep breath, "Can I ask you for a favor?"

She could hear the smile in Stu's voice, "Of course you can. And I won't even call you a mooch."

Rachel rolled her eyes, but plowed ahead anyway. "I sorta need a ride to school." She grimaced and waited for Stu's reply. She had already asked him for a ride twice this week, and she was sure he was going to tease her about sleeping in again.

Instead the concern in his voice took her off guard. "Still not sleeping well?"

"Yeah, last night was rough." Rachel had ended up confiding in Stu about her sleeping problems after the last time she had to beg for a ride—minus the part about the Voice. It wasn't like she was excited to talk to *anyone* about that. At the time, he could obviously see that she was exhausted and he refused to start up his truck and take her to class until she told him what was going on. Trying this time to avoid another barrage of questions about why she wasn't sleeping, she offered, "I'll make you dinner."

Like most college guys, Stu was quick to accept the offer of food. "Deal! See ya in a few."

With that, they hung up and Rachel decided that maybe she had time after all to put on some makeup. It might help to make her look more refreshed than she felt. She really didn't want Stu to worry more than he needed to.

A few minutes later, Rachel peered into the mirror to check out the quick beauty job she had done and was pleased with the result. She still looked tired, but not as zombielike as before. She walked into the kitchen to see what she had on hand to feed Stewart for dinner.

Munching on a breakfast bar while she foraged, she took some chicken breasts out of the freezer to thaw while she was away. She also spied a new bag of salad mix in the crisper drawer. That, along with some instant potatoes and some ice cream in the freezer, she had the meal makings to feed a hungry college guy.

Rachel heard the now-familiar sound of Stu's truck honking in the parking lot. Tossing her bag hastily over her shoulder, she opened her apartment door and stepped into the hallway. While she was busy locking the door with her key—she was more careful about those kinds of things lately—she heard the door right next to hers open.

Tiffany, her neighbor, was just leaving her apartment as well. However, by the looks of her neighbor, she wasn't going far. She was dressed in a pair of tattered pajamas, and her hair was a miserable mass of snarls. Her heavy black eyeliner and mascara were smeared under her eyes, and she smelled of something worse than cigarettes— although Rachel couldn't positively identify the smell since she had never used drugs in her life.

Tiffany was known to be sort of a wild child. In her apartment, the bedroom shared a wall with Rachel's bedroom. It was not uncommon for Rachel to hear all sorts of things going on next door at all hours of the night—things Rachel would really rather not hear. Tiffany's endless stream of boyfriends convinced Rachel to make a mental note never to rent an apartment that shared a bedroom wall with a stranger again.

Be that as it may, there was no changing it now, at least not until Rachel's contract was up. So, she tried to make the best of an unpleasant situation by being as friendly as she could. She smiled as Tiffany trudged by in a daze. Her efforts received a grunt and a glare in return.

Grateful that at least Tiffany hadn't given her the bird, Rachel rushed down the stairs. She reflected on how she came from a good family and a small town. She frankly didn't know how to relate to someone like Tiffany. Sex, drugs, and rock-n-roll were not something that she was interested in.

It was more than that though. The idea of that kind of lifestyle was just scary to her—danger, death, and addiction. Being so high or so drunk on something that you didn't have control over who you were frightened Rachel.

As she got closer to the front door, Rachel could hear the low thumping of the bass from Stu's truck. Sex and drugs, not so much, but Stu was all over the rock-n-roll scene.

As he spotted Rachel approaching, a big grin split his face and he waved energetically. He had the enthusiasm of a child. His upbeat personality could be infectious, which was exactly what Rachel needed right now.

"Hey there Sunshine! Your chariot is ready and waiting. Where to?"

Rachel had to stop and think. "Chemistry building. It is Wednesday, right?" At Stu's nod of acquiescence, she continued, "All the days are blurring together. It's hard to keep it straight."

"So, another rough night, huh?"

Rachel nodded. A worried expression overshadowed Stu's smile, so she quickly backpedaled with, "But it's not that bad." She added with a self-depreciating laugh, "I'm just a wimp."

Stu didn't seem to be fooled by her blasé attitude, but he also didn't seem to be willing to push things this morning. They drove for a short while in silence.

It was the middle of the morning, and Rachel was enjoying the bright sunlight and fresh colors of a new fall day. Everything was beautiful and easy to look at. It was so much more pleasant than the way things could look in the harsh afternoon sun. She felt like her moods could be easily swayed by the atmosphere around her. If it was a nice bright day, then she was in a good mood. If it got dark and stormy, her mood typically became dark and stormy as well.

And if the weather turned extreme... she shuddered, unwilling to think about that night in Florida long ago. Those memories still haunted her.

As they pulled into the parking lot by the chemistry building, Stu was chatting incessantly about his fraternity brother's new video game system. She didn't hear half of what he said because it was mostly technical mumbo jumbo that went over her head. Oblivious, Stu kept gushing, "The graphics are just awesome. So life-like. I must have been up half the night playing. I bet I got less sleep than you did."

Rachel grumbled, "I doubt it."

"So, I'll see you tonight for dinner? Better make lots because I can eat like a horse."

As she climbed out of the truck cab, Rachel tossed over her shoulder, "Pig!"

"Mooch!" was the equally playful reply from the cab. Rachel rolled her eyes and gave a quick friendly wave.

Most of the students were already in the middle of their classes, so campus was pretty empty as Rachel made her way down the sidewalk. That may have been a good thing, because hardly anyone noticed when Rachel stopped dead in her tracks, the color draining from her face.

I'll hurt him, Rachel. You won't listen, so I'll hurt him. I won't kill him, because I love you. I'll just make him suffer a little to prove my devotion to you. Acknowledge me. Let me in, Sunshine.

Rachel felt her stomach heave at the Evil's use of Stu's nickname for her. She had to clutch her sides to keep from losing her breakfast on the sidewalk.

Her mind was screaming at her, "It's daytime! This doesn't happen during the daylight! No, no, no!"

A few passersby gave Rachel cautious glances, but no one stopped to offer her any help. They seemed to move by her in slow-motion, and it felt like the ground was suddenly sloping away from her, trying to knock her off balance. She was sure that if she didn't sit down soon, she would end up on the ground one way or another.

Rachel stumbled over to a bench shaded by some large trees. She sat, panting, with her head between her knees. The sun went behind a cloud and she shivered—maybe from the cold, maybe from the shock.

Her mind was reeling.

Was she really going crazy? Was her mind coming unhinged and attacking her? She had never thought she had a dark side to herself. But if this Voice was coming from her subconscious, then it had to be from a twisted part of her brain that she never knew existed.

"Like my nightmare..." The thought suddenly sprang into her mind. With a gasp, she had a sudden, perfect recollection of the previous night's terrors.

She remembered standing in a room, but in a way that only happens in dreams, the room was actually two different rooms fused together. One half of the room was an ordinary looking hotel room, complete with boring wallpaper and generic abstract paintings on the wall. The other half of the room was the front foyer to her parent's home in Florida. Rachel stood in the center, right over the blurry line that divided them.

In the foyer, her mother was struggling to keep the front door closed. A hurricane was raging outside and the front door was trying to come off its hinges, to be sucked into the storm. Rachel could see the dark clouds through the open doorway, and the trees in the front yard were whipping in the wind. Her mother was desperately calling to her to come help with the door before it was too late. The hurricane's familiar freight train-like sound was deafening.

Rachel hesitated to go to her mother's side.

In the hotel room, the scene outside the windows was very different. It was a beautiful sunny day. The light streamed into the room in an almost blinding heavenly way. The sound of the raging storm was replaced with birds singing and a lawn mower in the distance. Her father was on the floor, clutching his chest. He reached a shaky hand in her direction, pleading with Rachel to help him.

She didn't know where to go—who to help.

You can't save them both, Rachel. You must choose.

Her father's face contorted in a spasm of pain. His face turned a frightening shade of red, and the veins in his forehead were bulging from the pressure. Through gritted teeth, he called, "Rachel! I need you! Help me!"

I can give you the power to save him. Come to me. Or I can make his heart explode… and the blood flow!

Her eyes locked with her father's as a wail of agony escaped his lips. The sound was abruptly cut off as he began to gurgle and blood was bubbling out of his mouth.

"No!" The force behind the word should have ripped it from her throat, but as is also common in dreams, Rachel was hardly able to make it more than a whisper.

Blood dripping. Hot and sticky. Thick and soothing. Drip, drip, drip…

Rachel tried to go to her father, but her feet felt heavy and useless. It was like they had been cemented in place.

Drip, drip, drip… Can you hear his heart, my love? Thump, thump, thump…

The scream that Rachel was trying so desperately to voice suddenly came from a different direction. Unwillingly, Rachel's gaze shifted from her father's tortured expression to her mother.

"Rachel!"

Her mother was no longer trying to pull the door closed, but was suddenly hanging on to the doorknob, being sucked outside into the storm. Her feet had been blown out from under her, and her body flapped in the wind like clothes on a clothesline.

"Rachel! I can't hang on! Help me!"

Her mother's screams were hard to make out over the roar of the hurricane. Rachel could see the muscles in her mother's arms straining to hang on, her knuckles white as she desperately gripped the door.

I can save her, too. I can save everyone. I love you. I would save them for you, Sunshine.

Rachel grabbed the sides of her head. The beginnings of a migraine were setting in. The throbbing in her skull made her eyes blur.

Or, can make her bones snap! Marrow, bones. Snapping, cracking.

Impossibly, over the sound of the hurricane, Rachel heard the distinct sound of something snapping, and then saw her mother's mouth open to howl in pain.

"No, no, no… it's not real. It's just a dream. Wake-up, Rachel. WAKE-UP!"

The gurgling sound of her father increased, and his eyes began to roll up inside his head. Smothering, choking sounds escaped his mouth as blood spilled down the side of his face. He began to convulse.

Drip, drip, drip… thump, thump, thump…

Rachel moaned. She willed her body to move, but nothing happened. She didn't know which direction to turn anyway.

Snap, crackle, pop! What a lovely sound.

Her mother's screams were cut off, as the fingers in her hands splintered. The wind had won. The arms of the storm claimed her mother and pulled her out into the deathly black sky.

Thump, thump…thump…

Thump…

Silence.

Too late, my love. But you will learn. Kiss.

Her father's dead and unseeing eyes stared back at her accusingly. The sound of the freight train ceased, and Rachel could again hear the birds singing and the lawn mower rumbling. The normal sounds of a beautiful summer day clashed sickeningly with the scene before her eyes.

And then she had woken up.

Now sitting on the bench, the vivid memory of the nightmare was too much for Rachel. Her stomach heaved and retched as she lost her breakfast. Rachel felt a quick twinge of regret for whomever was going to try to sit on this bench later.

Panting, she wiped her mouth on the sleeve of her shirt. Sweat was beading on her forehead. Her hands trembled as she tried to catch her breath. She shook herself.

It was not real.

While her father had died of a massive heart attack alone in a hotel room in Wyoming the same night as the hurricane when she was young, there had been absolutely nothing she could do about it. And her mother was fine, safe at home. She again shuddered, trying to shake off the unrealities of the nightmare. The horrible falling sensation in the pit of her stomach slowly faded.

Rachel focused on her surroundings. She wiped the tears from her eyes and took a deep cleansing breath.

Feeling again like she could breathe, she stood, just as the sun began to reemerge from its cloudy hiding place. She basked in its warmth and, for a moment, felt safe.

CHAPTER 10: BLOODY SHARDS

Rachel couldn't face class. Instead she went into the bathroom in the campus library to rinse the bile out of her mouth.

As she looked at herself in the mirror, the words of the Voice kept playing over and over in her mind. Should she warn Stu of the imminent threat? Or would he think that she was being silly?

Rachel didn't consider herself to be an overly superstitious person, but her gut was telling her that it would be very unwise to dismiss what the Voice had told her, even if it turned out to be nothing. What if something did happen to Stu? Her guilt would be overwhelming.

Therefore, she needed to warn him without sounding crazy.

She had his cell number. It would be easy enough to call. But what did someone say in a situation like this? "Hey. Something bad is going to happen. The voice in my head told me so."

Umm… no.

Maybe she should call him every so often, just checking in to make sure he was still kicking around somewhere—to hear his voice and make sure he was still alive.

She could go hang out at the fraternity and wait for Stu to get back from classes for the day. But if he only had one class this morning, and if Rachel beat him home, he would know that she had ditched after begging for a ride. That might make him worry more about her.

A friend could only take so much strange behavior.

And if she suddenly was trying to spend an entire day with Stu, he could also get the wrong idea about their friendship. He might start to think that she was developing a crush.

Maybe the simplest thing to do was send him a text. She could make it short and sweet. Of course, he would probably wonder what was going on, and what had prompted such an odd message. Rachel figured she would just deal with that when the time came. It was better than living with the guilt.

Having decided on a course of action to follow made her feel much better. She wound her way through the stacks until she found a private and secluded corner of the library. The air smelled stale.

Rachel tapped her phone, making the screen light up. She opened a new texting thread. This was the hard part. What to say that didn't sound insane?

After several agonizing minutes of writing, rewriting, and then writing again, Rachel sent this message:

Stu—Had a funny feeling today and just wanted to ask you to be careful. It's probably nothing. See you tonight! I'm getting that horse ready for you to eat.—Rachel

She hit send. It was good. Short, sweet, and it didn't sound ultra-crazy.

Now, she needed to figure out how to waste an entire day. Her homework load was pretty light at the moment, so there was no hope of distraction there. She needed an escape from real life for a while—something to keep her from thinking too hard about all the nightmarish images. Maybe she would go home and watch a movie to pass the time.

Rachel made her way out of the library and headed for the nearest bus stop. The ride to her apartment was on the campus loop, and in minutes she was back at her place, trudging up the stairs.

Once inside, she walked over to her bookshelf to pick a movie to distract herself. She had a fairly small collection consisting of her absolute favorites. She wrinkled her nose in disgust at the horror flicks—she so didn't need that right now—and instead selected a nice romantic comedy.

She whipped up a light lunch and settled on the couch to waste the day. Far too quickly the credits were scrolling up the screen. Rachel stood up and stretched.

She had a few more hours before Stu would arrive for dinner, so she tried to tidy up the apartment. Rachel lived by herself, and she wasn't a very messy person by nature, so it only took her a matter of minutes to straighten up every room. Not sure what else to do, Rachel grabbed a book and settled back into the couch again.

Her sleepless nights were really taking their toll on her, and before she knew it, she dozed off. It was a shock when she opened her eyes again, glanced at the clock, and realized that she only had another thirty minutes before Stu would be there. She also realized, with a smile, that she had finally slept dream-free, and felt more rested than she had in days.

With a renewed burst of energy, Rachel began to grill the chicken, set the table, and get everything prepared for dinner. She felt so much lighter that she even softly sang to herself while she worked. In no time, dinner was ready, and Rachel started to wash a few of the dirty dishes.

As the pace of the evening started to slow, her good mood was also starting to fade, and the earlier feeling of apprehension started to grow in the pit of her stomach.

What if Stu didn't come?

How would she know what was going on? What if something had happened? What if he never got her text? Some things get lost in cyberspace. It was possible that he had never gotten her warning and done something foolish.

As worries swirled in her head, Rachel distractedly reached for a glass on the counter. As she pulled it over to the sink, her soapy hands lost their grip and the glass tumbled into the sink with a crash. With a curse under her breath, she reached into the water. She found that the glass had not broken after all. Taking a dish rag and shoving it inside, Rachel discovered that it had cracked in the fall and it gave way under her pressure. It broke into several pieces underneath the soapy water.

Oh crap.

Hastily, Rachel pulled her hands out of the sink. She would have to be careful and drain the water before she tried to clean up the glass shards. It was too hard to see where they were with the soapy bubbles.

Perfect. Just perfect.

Just then, there was a knock at the door, and Stu's voice filtered in from the hall, "Knock, knock!"

Rachel let out a breath that she didn't realize she had been holding as relief rushed through her at the sound of his voice. The sink was forgotten as she dashed around the corner to see with her own eyes that Stu was safe and sound.

He had just closed the door behind him and was entering the room. She smiled warmly and Stu chuckled, "Happy to see you too, Rach. So, where's that horse you promised me?"

"So, you got my message?"

Stu threw his coat over the back of the chair. Rachel quickly scanned him from head to toe and didn't see anything amiss. Her relief was so great, she could have kissed him. Of course, she didn't, and instead stood there with a silly grin plastered to her face.

She thought, "He's going to think I've lost it."

Stu smiled back, "Yeah, I got it. As you can see, I am perfectly safe and sound. I think your psychic skills are a little rusty."

She giggled nervously, "I don't know what's wrong with me." Turning to face the dining room table, Rachel gestured for Stu to sit. "Shall we eat? I need to pay up."

"That's right, mooch." Stu playfully punched her in the shoulder as he sat at the table.

The meal went off without a hitch. Rachel was a pretty good cook and even knew how to add sour cream and cheese to the instant potatoes to make them less instant-tasting. Stu ate two platefuls, and would have gone for a third except that Rachel promised dessert.

She felt so much lighter, now that she could see that Stu was safe. She felt like she had so much pent up energy that she was going to burst, and she was in the mood to splurge.

"There's a pastry shop just down the road and I'll pay."

With a mischievous twinkle to his eyes, Stu asked, "Can I get anything I want?"

Rachel laughed, "Sure—anything you want."

"Deal!" Stu jumped up from his chair, grabbed a few dishes and headed for the sink. "You know, I hear they have this killer cheesecake there—all kinds of flavors."

Rachel was so distracted by her sudden good mood that she had completely forgotten about the broken glass in the sink. Before she could warn Stu to be careful, he plunged his hands into the soapy water.

"Ahhhh!" Stu's face contorted in a grimace of pain as he hastily pulled his arms back out of the water.

Rachel felt a cold sweat break out over her body, and the room started to swim as she saw the large shard of glass sticking out of Stu's palm.

With a shaky hand, he pulled the glass out and dropped it on the countertop. Rachel felt nauseous and all the muscles of her body locked in place.

Drip, drip, drip… what a lovely shade of red. If only he'd cut deeper, so you could see the pretty deep colors underneath. I'll make lots of pretty colors for you, my love.

Stu clutched his hand to his chest scowling and groaning with the pain. The blood was flowing down his wrist and making a mess of his shirt. Trying to stop the flow, he was attempting to wrap his shirt around his wound and apply pressure.

"Ah, man… uuuhhh." His words of pain helped to propel Rachel forward. She stumbled into the kitchen and grabbed a towel, wanting to help.

"Here, let's wrap your hand in this. I am so sorry Stu. I broke a glass in the water earlier but forgot all about it when you showed up."

Stu held his hand out to her, and she had to swallow to keep from gagging as she saw a fresh gush of blood escape the cut. She wrapped the towel around his palm as tight as she could, and started to apply pressure to stop the flow.

Stu's face was quite pale, but he still tried to make a joke through gritted teeth, "And here I'd been so careful all day, and your kitchen was the booby trap after all."

"You are probably going to need stitches." The towel seemed to be getting soaked through, so Rachel tried to press harder. Stu winced a little at the added pressure.

Squeeze, my love. Squeeze harder! See the pretty colors. I made them for you. Look at the pain on his face. SQUEEZE!

Rachel immediately dropped Stu's hand, sickened by the thought that she might be purposely trying to hurt him more. She couldn't believe these thoughts were coming from her—*her* mind. Her hands were shaking, and her legs felt weak. "You better keep applying pressure," she whispered, quickly turning her face away. "Can I drive you to the emergency room?" Rachel's voice was thick and her throat kept trying to cut off her words.

Stu began to press on his hand as he nodded his acceptance. "My keys are in my pocket in my jacket."

Rachel wasn't sure she could make her wobbly legs take her to the living room to get his keys, let alone drive Stu anywhere, but she had to try.

Staggering away, she retrieved his keys and held the door open while Stu followed her out into the hall.

Tiffany's door was open, and Rachel could see her sitting on the couch in her messy apartment. Unpleasant odors drifted into the hall, and Tiffany seemed to be leaning over something on the coffee table. With glassy eyes, Tiffany looked up. Seeing Stu's pained face, and the bloody towel wrapped around his hand, Tiffany snorted and turned her face away.

Rachel didn't have time to be annoyed with her strange neighbor. Instead, she rushed Stu down the stairs and out to his truck. Moving protectively and awkwardly, she tried to do everything she could to help. She even tried to help Stu climb into the cab, but her "help" was making things harder. Stu finally threw his good hand up in protest and chuckled, "I got it Rach. I'm not dying here."

"Not funny."

Rachel climbed into that cab and gunned the engine to life.

"Hey! Careful with my baby! She likes to be stroked, not punched." Stu caressed the dashboard with his good hand, teasing Rachel.

Rachel's mind hissed, "How can he be in such a good mood when I practically just cut his hand off?" She was fuming.

Only she was mostly mad at herself. All day long, she had been worried about Stu hurting himself. She couldn't wait until she got to see him again and make sure he was okay. And there he was, safe and unhurt on her doorstep.

Only in reality, he would have been safer if he had stayed as far away from her as he could!

Maybe she should just tell him what was going on—confess that he was friends with an insane person who hears voices in her head. Not only that, but the voices are horrible voices that can reach out of her head and hurt those that are closest to her.

As much as Rachel wanted to be friends with Stewart, she was becoming convinced that he wasn't safe with her.

Her thoughts churned, "Something horrible is going on. Maybe I truly am going crazy."

Rachel wasn't sure how many red lights and stop signs she ran, but she got Stu to the hospital in record time. He insisted on getting out of the truck under his own power and smiled at her exasperated expression.

Moments later, they were in a sterile exam room. Stu sat on the hard exam table, the paper sheet under him crinkling loudly. A friendly plump nurse was taking notes on what happened.

"And how exactly did you cut your palm?"

"There was broken glass in the sink that I didn't know was there until it cut me." He shot a glance at Rachel, and chuckled to himself at her green complexion.

"And you were at your girlfriend's place when this happened?"

Rachel felt color flooding her cheeks, and she spoke up, "Oh, I'm just a friend."

Over the top of Rachel, Stu said, "Yup."

Stu and the nurse exchanged a loaded glance, and they both grinned as she replied, "Ah-huh."

Rachel bit her lip, annoyed.

The florescent lighting was irritating to Rachel's eyes, and she could feel the beginnings of another migraine coming on. Rubbing the sides of her head, she leaned forward to keep from glaring at Stu and the nurse.

The doctor entered the room next. He had distinguished salt and pepper hair, a crisp white coat and a stethoscope. "So, who's dying today?" he said with a note of humor in his voice. Rachel's frown deepened.

So not funny.

"That would be me." Stu held up his hand wrapped in the bloody towel.

"Well, let's take a look at that, shall we?"

The doctor expertly started to remove the towel. He examined the damage, numbed, washed and stitched the area. At one point, he glanced at Rachel, who was still holding her head and staring intently at the floor. The doctor spoke up, trying to be helpful, "If your girlfriend is uncomfortable watching this, she can wait in the waiting room."

"I'm not his gir…" Rachel gave up, and instead smiled as best she could, "I'm fine. Really."

It must not have been a very convincing smile because both Stu and the doctor looked away and Rachel could have sworn she saw the corners of their mouths turn up in smiles.

Rachel thought, "Just wait until you know everything is okay and you can punch him later."

After an hour and ten stitches, they were allowed to leave the hospital. Rachel promised Stu that she would pay his medical bills. He waved her off, saying that he had insurance and it was his fault for being so hasty. Rachel didn't like it, but they could fight about this later. She wasn't in a fighting frame of mind at the moment.

The wind had started to blow and the sky was becoming grey and overcast. The pounding in her head was getting worse, but Stu asked if they were still going to stop for dessert. Rachel was hardly in the mood to eat anything, but she *had* promised, and she owed Stu his reward for the night. So, they stopped and picked up something to take back to Rachel's apartment.

"Aren't you afraid to come back to my place?" Rachel asked.

"Heck no! This little cut is hardly enough to slow me down." Stu thumped his chest dramatically with his good hand, "Me, man, tough!"

Glancing at Stu's new crisp white bandages, Rachel couldn't shake her bad feelings about the night, so she locked the door behind them after they entered her apartment.

Rachel's head pounded so hard that she had a hard time stomaching the first few bites of her cheesecake. Her stomach was rolling with the waves of pain in her skull. Giving up, she walked into the kitchen to put her leftovers in the fridge.

A bloody shard of glass was sitting on the countertop where Stu had left it—a grizzly reminder.

The wind was really starting to howl outside now, and Rachel could hear the rain hitting the glass on the living room windows. It was perfect weather for her mood.

Frowning and grumbling, Rachel plopped back down on the couch next to Stu and started to rub her temples again. He had long since wolfed down his cheesecake, and was reclining against the cushions, cradling his bad hand against his content stomach.

"You don't look so good, Rach. Does the sight of blood bother you? You keep turning green." There was a twinkle in his eye that was annoying Rachel.

She thought he really should be more upset about the evening. *She* certainly was.

Rachel didn't feel like talking. Her ears were ringing and her entire skull felt like it was going to burst. She just nodded weakly, and then whimpered when the movement made her head pound worse. Strange lights were dancing before her eyes, and it was hard concentrate on anything but the pain.

Stu slid over and placed his good hand on her shoulder. He gently asked, "Is it another migraine? Can I get you something? The doctors gave me some pretty good painkillers."

Just then, Rachel's heart started to pound. A sickening heat began to develop in her feet, and slowly spread to her entire body. Sweat beads popped out on her forehead as she began to rock herself back and forth. Her stomach began to cramp painfully. The ringing in her ears intensified and was suddenly accompanied by a rushing sound. She reached out to Stu, her hand shaking and sweaty.

Stu's expression got very serious and worried. Almost panicky, he asked, "Hey, hey! Is everything all right? What can I do for you?"

His words didn't make any sense. She couldn't respond, even if she wanted to. All she could do was hang on to her head, trying to keep all the pieces together. If she let go, she felt like she would splinter apart.

She could still hear the rain pounding on the glass outside, and the wind was blowing so hard that the window frame was shuddering.

Rachel started to see spots swirling before her eyes, and the Voice came back.

I ask so little of you, Rachel. Don't make me hurt you anymore. Your pain is my pain. I can make it all go away. Just prove that you love me. Hurt him. He won't even know it's coming. Look at the worry on his face. He trusts you. Gouge his eyes out with your fingers! Feel them pop under your nails. The sweet ooze.

Rachel's stomach did another back flip. The pain was maddening. Stu had his arms around her and he was rocking back and forth with her as she moaned.

The Voice was right. He did trust her. His hands were rubbing her arms in comforting strokes.

Only, it wasn't comforting. It was annoying. With every pass of his hands her irritation grew. She wanted to violently shove him away to make it stop. Her skin felt too sensitive under his touch, but she couldn't let go of her head to push him away. His hands continued their path—up, down, up, down. He was softly cooing something in her ear, but she couldn't make it out.

I can make it all go away. Just DO IT!

Up, down, up, down.

Rachel moaned and tried to struggle against Stu's grasp. She let go of her head with one hand and weakly pushed against his shoulder. She whimpered, "I don't want to hurt you."

The sweet ooze. Can't you taste it on your tongue? Do it. Do it. Do it.

Stu laughed, "I don't think you're in any shape to hurt anyone, Rach." His mirth was grating. Her head was so full of pain and anger. She would do almost anything to make it stop.

Up, down, up, down.

DO IT!

Stu kept rocking her back and forth. The intimacy of his embrace was infuriating. The heat from the way his body was pressed up against hers only added to the sweat on her face. It was uncomfortable. He had no right to hold her this way. Rachel wanted to scream, "I am not your girlfriend!" Instead, she groaned again, and Stu held her closer, and rhythm of his hand increasing in tempo.

Up, down, up, down.

You don't belong to him. You belong to me. Make him let you go. Scratch him. Make him bleed. Just a few pretty colors and then it will all go away, my love.

"No, no, no…" Rachel started to grab the hair on the sides of her head. The slight pain from her fingers pulling at the roots was nothing compared to the throbbing in her skull. It was almost a pleasant distraction, so Rachel pulled harder.

She could feel Stu's hands abruptly stop rubbing her arms as he frantically tried to pry her hands out of her hair. She almost sighed with relief at the absence of his touch, but her teeth were locked together in a grimace. If it kept his hands busy and away from her, she would pull her hair out all day.

Rachel fought against him. She struggled to keep her hands tangled in her hair. Her frenzy was giving her unnatural strength, but in the end Stu was still far stronger—and more well-rested.

He forced her hands down into her lap.

A howl of rage erupted from Rachel's throat. She hardly even recognized her own voice. His scorching touch on her wrists was aggravating. She felt so hot and irritable. She was desperate to find a way to escape and put some distance between his body and hers.

As she thrashed about, she was able to pull herself to the floor in front of him. Her eyes were wide open and frantic, but she wasn't seeing anything around her. She only saw waves of red in varying shades—the color of blood. Her screams continued as she struggled against his grip.

Beautiful music. Scream, scream louder! Hurt him. Make him scream with you. Make beautiful music together.

"No, no, no!" Rachel could hardly recognize the words that were coming from her mouth. She only felt the slight relief that came from the exertion of her protests. Her breath was ragged as she pulled huge gulps of air into her mouth to continue her screams. Her hands had formed into claws, and she was raking them across her cheeks. The stinging was another delicious distraction.

Deeper, harder. I want to see your pretty colors too, love.

She could feel her nails biting into the flesh of her face.

Up, down, up, down.

And then it was too much. Darkness started to descend around her, and she could feel herself being pulled under. Unconsciousness was waiting to claim her, and she was happy to rush towards it. She was vaguely aware of her screams getting softer and softer, but she unwillingly continued to chant, "No, no, no…"

Before she completely succumbed to the pull of oblivion, Rachel thought she heard a loud crash. Then, a warm light flooded her senses. Even though her eyes were closed, she could see brilliant colors behind her eyelids. She had the slightest impression of weightlessness, and the cool air was rushing past her face. It felt wonderful against her hot skin—refreshing, clean, and untainted.

However, it was also trying to bring her back from the depths of blackness.

She frantically thought, "No, I don't want to come back! I don't want to ever wake up!" Rachel just wanted to slide away and be free—even just for a moment.

Even he can't save you. I control you now. There is no escape unless I will it. You will learn. I will make you learn.

Faintly, she cried, "No, no, no…" Rachel tried to weakly snuggle closer to the glow that was surrounding her. She thought she felt the arms of the light respond and pull her closer. Her body trembled, and the air continued to rush past her skin. She begged for unconsciousness to claim her, and finally, mercifully, it did.

CHAPTER 11: UNKNOWN

Peter's breath caught in his lungs as he stepped out into the bitter wind. Donavon, carrying the limp form of the blonde woman in his arms and sheltering her body as much as he could, raced down the street towards their house.

Blake stood arguing with the redheaded guy about what was going on.

"It's okay, dude. We know how to help her." Blake raised both of his hands up in front of him, palms facing outward, in a gesture meant to say, "I mean you no harm." He was backing away slowly, trying to appear as non-threatening as possible. Blake knew the power of his intimidating physical presence.

The redhead wasn't buying it. His green eyes blazed in anger and suspicion. "Who are you guys? What's going on? Where are you taking her?" Peter could see the panic on the young man's face, and he knew that he would not be able to follow Donavon until he used his Gift to calm this unfortunate bystander.

Annoyed, Peter thought, "Witnesses are always so inconvenient."

As Peter gave him a knowing glance, Blake turned and took off after Donavon, splashing water with every stride.

Peter was annoyed that he couldn't follow his friends and help, but this was part of his duty—to stay behind and tie up loose ends.

His talent was not nearly as strong with the non-Gifted. In order for his ability as Locator to have the greatest impact, it required someone already sensitive to the forces of good and evil around them—someone Gifted. But in intense situations, when people were already emotionally excited, it was possible for Peter to use his Gift to reach the non-Gifted as well.

He focused his energy on the redhead, and in a soothing voice drawled, "It's okay. Everything is going to be all right. We're friends, and we know how to help. We know what's going on." The man turned his attention away from the retreating forms of Blake and Donavon to focus on Peter. Trying to sound casual, Peter added, "What's your name?"

"Stu." The man replied and then instantly looked as if he regretted it.

Peter could be irresistible.

Stu continued, "Rachel never mentioned having any friends like you guys." Stu's eyebrows were pulled together, and his face screamed suspicion.

Peter's mind instantly took note, "Ah! Rachel. Thank you."

Peter took a hesitant step in Stu's direction. "Rachel has been having headaches, right? Not sleeping well?" Peter had noticed the dark circles under her eyes and felt safe in guessing. He continued to send feelings of trust and peace towards the young man.

Stu nodded his head in agreement.

"She's very sick right now, and we need to help her as fast as we can. I'm sorry that there was no time to explain things to you. I know that must be upsetting. If every second weren't so crucial, we could have taken the time to introduce ourselves properly. I'm Peter, by the way." He couldn't help but feel a little ridiculous, making introductions in the middle of drenching rain.

Peter extended his hand, and Stu accepted the gesture and shook. The redhead immediately pulled his hand back, and glanced at it like he couldn't believe what he just did. Peter smiled reassuringly, but Stu folded his arms across his chest, locking his hands to the sides of his body, as if to restrain them from moving of their own accord.

That was fine, Peter could see that he was having an impact on him, and it didn't matter if it took a few minutes.

Peter asked, "How do you know Rachel?"

"We met the first day of school. We're friends." Almost defiantly, he added, "How do *you* know Rachel?"

Peter had to be very careful about what he said. If he lied to Stu, his abilities as a Locator would stop working and the feelings of trust he was fostering would disappear. It was impossible to create something from nothing. Stu obviously wanted to believe Peter and trust that Rachel was in good hands. Peter was just enhancing those impulses.

He would have to phrase all of his answers very delicately so he did not turn those feelings back into suspicion.

Peter thought for a moment and then replied, "We're like family."

Stu seemed a little stunned by this answer. "Oh! I didn't know. Rachel never mentioned having family close by." He didn't seem to notice that Peter had prefaced "family" with "like," and instead took the statement literally.

But Peter couldn't help how his words were interpreted. It only mattered that he told the truth and that his intentions were pure.

Peter kept the good feelings flowing. "Well, school hasn't been going that long. I was bound to drop by on her eventually." To himself, he added, "I am a Locator after all."

Stu seemed to immediately reevaluate the situation now that he thought Rachel's family was involved. Some of his urgency to follow the others seemed to evaporate and he relaxed slightly. His budding trust seemed to waiver for a moment though as he thought of another question. "How did you know she was in trouble?"

Peter took a deep breath, "I just had a bad feeling—like I needed to check on her." He smiled reassuringly, "You know what that's like." Then he quickly continued before Stu could question him too much about it. "When I knocked on the door and no one answered, I knew something had to be wrong."

Knocked? Pounded the hell out of it is more like it.

Peter was hoping that Stu had been too worried about Rachel to notice how little time they had given for someone to answer the door before Blake busted in. "I don't usually make such a dramatic entrance. Speaking of which," Peter indicated the apartment building they had just left, "Perhaps we should go fix that door before we leave. I don't think Rachel would like all of her stuff to get stolen while she is gone. It should only take a minute."

The more time Peter could spend with Stu, the greater influence he would have over him. That could turn out to be very helpful in the near future, seeing as how Peter was not sure what was going to be waiting for them when they arrived at the house. Once all the emotion of the moment was over, Peter would have a harder time controlling Stu.

The young man's eyes nervously flickered to where Donavon and Blake had disappeared. Peter reached out again, and this time let his hand lightly rest on Stu's arm—sometimes physical contact could strengthen his influence—and he tried to soothe him by saying, "She's going to be okay. She's in good hands." Following Stu's gaze with his own, he added, "I trust them like brothers."

Stu grumbled something under his breath that sounded like, "Easy for you to say," but he let Peter lead him back up the stairs to Rachel's apartment. It was a bit of a relief to be out of the raging storm and battering winds. Peter wiped the rain from his face and shook out his dripping hair. He imagined his wavy locks were poking out all over his head.

Standing in front of Rachel's apartment, they surveyed the damage. It actually wasn't too bad, all things considered. The door frame had cracked in a couple of places and the hinge was bent where the bolts had been ripped out of the wall. The door itself was intact. They might need to replace part of the frame and get a new hinge, but they could at least temporarily set the door upright and latch it into place to keep strangers out. They just had to hope that no one came and put any pressure on it, or the door would pop open very easily.

They worked together to jimmy it into place as best as they could. Peter looked at Stu as they worked. Not being Gifted, Stu would not have been aware of much of what had taken place earlier with Rachel. He probably didn't feel the Evil surrounding the apartment.

He only knew his friend was in severe pain.

On the other hand, Peter could still feel the taint of the Evil that had been in the room only minutes earlier. The faint sulfur smell lingered in his nostrils, and he had an almost uncontrollable urge to scrub his skin raw. But whatever had been attacking Rachel was gone. Only lingering impressions made Peter's skin crawl. He glanced out the window to see that the storm was finally abating outside, he could almost make out a sunset.

He thought, "It might be a beautiful night, after all."

Peter wasn't sure there was any way to keep Stu from following him home to check on Rachel, so he hoped that his housemates had come up with a game plan by the time they arrived. The best he could do was to continue to make Stu feel as comfortable as possible, so he would feel good enough to believe whatever story they came up with and leave them alone.

Once the apartment door was safely latched back into the frame, Peter turned to Stu and smiled, "Shall we go check on our girl?"

Stu's tense face relaxed. "Yeah, I feel bad leaving her for this long, but like you said, I am sure she will appreciate not having all her stuff gone when she gets back."

The two men headed for the parking lot. As Peter began to walk toward the street, Stu stopped him. "I got a truck. You want a ride?"

Happy that Stu was making such a friendly offer, he accepted. They drove in silence, apart from the occasional direction to the house. Peter tried to keep the calm and peaceful vibes flowing around them in the enclosed space of the truck, but it was difficult because Peter was still on edge himself.

How come he had been so slow to find Rachel? Locators were supposed to find the Gifted!

He angrily berated himself mentally, "How could I be so blind?"

Peter's Gift as a Locator had been growing and developing steadily over several years now. His twenty-third birthday rapidly approached, which meant he had been honing his skills for just over four years. While that was still relatively young in the world of Locators, Peter felt like his senses were growing stronger all the time.

He was so pleased with himself that he had found Beth while she was still so new and weak. There were still moments when her aura was so weak that Peter could almost miss it. So, how could he find Beth, but not have any idea that Rachel was living just a few blocks from his house? Not only that, but she was obviously either incredibly powerful or incredibly far into her Trial to warrant such a massive attack from the Evil.

Neither option appealed to Peter.

The first option meant that she might be facing a situation similar to what Donavon had gone through. The vivid memories and horror of Donavon's Trial would be forever emblazoned in Peter's memory. Even now, he shied away from thinking about it.

To be so powerful so quickly, it didn't give them much time— or hope—to be able to give Rachel the skills she would need to survive. Donavon had been lucky, and Peter was sure fate would not allow him to witness something that miraculous again in his lifetime.

But, if Rachel was so powerful, then why didn't Peter find her sooner? Long before tonight her aura should have blazed like wildfire on the horizon—visible for miles around. He should have been able to locate her apartment in his sleep, or unconsciously follow her around campus on a daily basis. Why hadn't he bumped into her at the grocery store, or sat next to her at a football game? All of these scenarios were the kind of thing that "just sort of happens" to Locators all the time.

The second option was equally depressing. If Rachel was already a fair amount into her Trial, then they had already lost so much time. Who knew how much longer her mind could hang on to fight back the Evil's seduction? If they were too late, they may have unknowingly carried a monster back to their home. The idea of his brothers and sister sitting around at home, unsuspecting how dangerous Rachel could possibly be at this very moment... Peter suddenly got very anxious to complete the drive back.

Peter wanted to hit the dashboard with his fist in anger, but instead continued infusing flows of peace and calm into the atmosphere. It only took a minute or two to drive from Rachel's apartment back to the house, but in Peter's mind the journey felt ten times that long.

His father would be so disappointed in him.

Peter had been entrusted to be the only Locator at Grayson. It was an honor for someone so young to be on his own in any location. Peter's friendship with Donavon had also been a key factor in this decision. Peter seemed to draw a great deal of strength from Donavon, allowing his Gift to manifest itself quicker and stronger than most. With the two of them living together, it was felt that he should be able to handle the job of being the sole Locator at college.

Peter could see it now.

First, his father would be upset that he had not been able to find Rachel sooner. Second, he would probably reprimand him for being so indiscreet in his behavior tonight. His father would never be so careless as to leave behind any evidence, like a broken door. He also certainly wouldn't have had any witnesses to deal with if it could have been avoided.

Peter could feel his calm exterior slipping as he thought of what a mess he had made in such a short amount of time. He was immensely grateful when they finally pulled up in front of the house, and he was able to slip out of the truck cab. Walking as quickly as he could in front of Stu, Peter took the front steps two at a time and barged into the house.

His eyes swept the room and tried to instantly take in all of the information that he could. Blake was leaning against the fireplace and Nancy was at his side. Blake had his arm around her, and they both had a look of worry on their faces. Peter was a little surprised by the intimacy of their proximity to each other, but didn't have time to speculate further.

His eyes continued to sweep the room. Amy and Robert both sat on the loveseat in the corner. Robert was leaning forward, hands clasped and arms resting on the tops of his legs. His eyes were on the floor. Amy was apparently hugging herself—concern also evident on her face. At Peter's entrance, she instantly launched herself in his direction with an exclamation.

"Oh, Peter! I'm so glad you're back."

She wrapped her arms around him and buried her face in his shoulder. She didn't seem to mind that he was completely rain-soaked.

Then he noticed that Beth was back. Her face was pale and her eyes were red-rimmed.

Confused by Amy's exuberance at his return, and not knowing if Beth's tears were leftover from earlier in the evening or some new trauma, Peter's heart began to beat faster. The panic and concern on Beth's face was haunting and contagious. Peter felt a cold sweat break out on his skin under the dampness of his clothes.

With horror, he thought, "Were we too late?"

That was when he was finally able to finish his sweep of the room, and his eyes settled on Donavon and Rachel. Rachel's body had been gently placed on the couch. Donavon's jacket was covering her, and Peter could see it slowly rise and fall with her every breath.

He was startled by the amount of relief he felt just seeing that she was still alive.

Peter could only see Donavon's back. He was kneeling by Rachel's side, holding her hand. He was blocking her face from Peter's view. It was comforting to see that she was no longer moaning and writhing in pain. She appeared to be at peace—resting.

Peter left Amy and crossed the room to stand by Donavon. Stu silently shadowed him, throwing uncertain glances at the other occupants of the room.

Peter sucked in a sharp breath as he beheld the woman before him. Her cheeks were slightly marred by the red trails left behind from where she had been dragging her nails across her face, but Peter could hardly see them as he looked at her features. She was stunning. Her hair was a shimmery gold color, and it cascaded down her body to her waist. She was slender, and lying on the couch, looked fragile and extremely breakable—like a beautiful doll.

He felt like he needed to memorize every detail.

Her lips were the color of pale rose petals. Her dark lashes were thick and full, lying feathery soft on her cheeks. Although he did not know the color, he imagined that her eyes would sparkle like precious gems. And although he didn't know the timbre of it, he imagined her voice to be sweet like honey. The terror he had seen on her face in the apartment was completely gone now, replaced with an angelic serenity. Peter almost had to cover his mouth to keep from saying the word out loud—angel. It seemed as if her name was being whispered to him over and over again, from every direction.

Rachel, Rachel, Rachel…

He had an overwhelming desire to protect her—protect her from the Evil that he had felt smothering her in the apartment.

He knew he could be strong enough.

He would be able to be everything that she needed.

It wouldn't be too late for her. Peter wouldn't let it be.

Suddenly, it was irritating that Donavon was hovering over her, holding her hand and being so possessive. What gave him the right? He didn't know her from Eve. Peter frowned as he watched Donavon's fingers stroking patterns over the delicate skin of her hand. He could feel the anger starting to well up inside him.

Angrily, he thought, "You don't know her."

Just then, Donavon looked up at his friend, and the look on his face made Peter feel like he had just been dropped in a bucket of cold water. There was so much trust and brotherly love on Donavon's face. He looked relieved to see Peter there, and it was disarming.

Peter took a deep breath and shook his head. Something was wrong with him.

The thought occurred to Peter that he didn't really know Rachel from Eve, either. He didn't understand where these strong feelings were coming from.

The thought came again, only this time directed at himself, "You don't know her."

It didn't matter. He didn't care. All he knew was from the first moment he set eyes on Rachel, his life was never going to be the same again.

He might even go so far as to say that it was love at first sight.

Things were spinning out of control. He needed to get some air—fast!

He turned to Stu, "I'll leave it up to my family here to introduce themselves. I need to go check on something."

His abrupt departure might have appeared rude, but with his uncontrollable emotions, it seemed like the smartest thing to do. Peter cut through the kitchen and went out the back door to the porch. The cool night air felt good in his lungs, as he took several deep steadying breaths. He walked over to lean against the railing.

Night was starting to set in, and it was the last moments of the day when the sky pulsed with rich and vivid shades of red, orange, and purple. In a few more moments, the darkness would begin to take over. Everything would lose its brilliance of color, retreating first to shades of grey, and then finally black, until tomorrow, when the first rays of morning would touch them again.

Out here, Peter felt better—more like himself. The evening had been such a flood of sensations and emotions. First the incident with Donavon and Beth on the couch, immediately followed by the pull of Rachel and the danger surrounding her.

Everything seemed to culminate in this moment and the first glimpse of her face.

The pull of his emotions seemed weaker out here, and he wondered if perhaps these strong feelings for Rachel were some sort of strange leftover reaction to the tremendous amount of Evil he had just been exposed to. Looking at his ring with Locator Eyes, he could still detect a faint glow, and knew that the strength of the Evil had been staggering. Maybe it was dangerous and foolish to trust anything that he might be feeling until things returned to normal. His nerves felt raw and exposed. Peter drew his protective walls back up around him, trying to settle his mind and block out the barrage of forces that seemed to be weighing on him.

The colors in the sky had faded completely now, and it felt like the world had entered a new season.

He heard the door behind him open and close softly. He turned slightly as Beth made her way over to the railing to join him. Her eyes looked a little less red in this light, but there was still an urgency about her features.

"How are you holding up?" Peter gave her his most sympathetic smile.

Beth smiled back weakly, "I'm better, I guess. What a night, huh?" She turned her face away to admire the view. "I'm sorry you had to witness my moment of mortification earlier."

Peter felt himself blush a little, and he coughed to cover up the tension in his voice, "Ah, that's okay. I didn't mean to intrude on such a private moment." Clearing his throat, he tried again, "You know, Donavon's a good guy. I'm sure there is a reason why he did what he did. He would never intentionally do anything to hurt you. You can trust him, you know."

"I know." She sighed. "It was my fault. At first, I was unsure about what happened. But after I left and," she glanced at Peter, blushing, "cooled down a bit, I realized that it had probably been all me. I shouldn't have kissed him like that."

Beth looked down, a small tear escaping her eye.

Peter couldn't stand to see her beating herself up like this. Hoping to make her feel better, he added, "You know, it takes more than one pair of lips to make a kiss."

Beth looked Peter in the eye, a fierce determination suddenly coming to her face, like she had just made up her mind about something. "You think he wanted to kiss me back?"

Warning bells went off in Peter's head, "Careful. Don't get in the middle."

He looked away, "Well, I can't speak for him." The last thing he wanted to do was give Beth any false hopes. He certainly didn't want to speak for his friend without having a better idea himself as to what was going on. Peter was a little overwhelmed at the moment with his own emotional trauma.

He suddenly felt frustrated to be having this conversation with Beth. "I just meant... oh, I don't know what I meant." He turned around to lean against the rail with his back, and Beth continued to stare out over the grass. Using both his hands, he pushed himself away to go back inside. Maybe things would be different now. Maybe the strange emotions he had felt for Rachel would be gone as suddenly as they had appeared. Besides, he wanted to be there when she woke up.

To see her eyes... To hear her voice...

Peter violently shook his head again and thought, "Seriously! What is wrong with me? I don't even know her!"

Beth decided to go back inside with Peter and she actually entered the living room ahead of him.

The questions and confusion that had been on her face intensified as she looked in Donavon's direction. Seeing that he was in the same place, holding Rachel's hand, her expression turned fierce and resolute.

Peter got the serious impression that Beth was not going to let Donavon get off easily after tonight's events.

She gave Peter one final look. As their eyes locked, Peter could see the undeniable determination in her face.

He pulled his gaze away, eagerly looking at the couch. Rachel's eyes were just starting to flutter open. He took a sharp intake of breath. Rachel's eyes were a luminous shade of blue, more beautiful than he had imagined. The perfection of her face took his breath away. Even the marks from her nails had faded completely.

Donavon was the first person Rachel could see, and she smiled as she looked at him.

Sharp jealousy stabbed at Peter's heart. It was indescribable how much he wished his had been the first face she had seen. The anger from earlier bubbled to the surface and he struggled to fight it down again.

Peter's heart trembled as her gaze slipped past Donavon and rested on him. Surprise crossed her face, and her lips parted slightly as she looked at him. She used her arms to push herself up slightly from the couch.

Instantly, Donavon was reaching out to help her. His movement irritated Peter.

Then… one glorious word escaped her lips.

"Peter."

He didn't even have time to wonder how she knew his name. Hearing it spoken by her was like hearing his name for the first time. In that moment, the world stopped spinning. The sound of her voice was like soothing salve on his frayed nerves. His heart beat frantically. He could feel himself plunging deeper and deeper, away from reality. It was almost against his will, except he wasn't struggling. He wasn't fighting. He was melting—changing. He would never be the same again.

There was no coming back from this.

She was everything he wanted and everything he needed. His confidence in that was unquestionable.

This was love—the kind of love that was powerful and all consuming—a dangerous kind of love. But a lingering doubt filled his heart.

You don't know her.

CHAPTER 12: A NEW LIFE

Love. Peace. Safety.

Rachel's mind floated serenely. Her body felt weightless, effortless, almost like she had no body. She was everywhere, yet she was nowhere.

A shape in the distance formed—a man. He was walking towards her with slow, even strides. She felt like she should go to him. He was her protector—her warmth and strength.

An urge to laugh tickled her brain, yet she wasn't sure where her mouth was, or how to make the sound. Instead, she was simply happy to be—to drift with the ebb and flow. Time had no meaning, and the meaninglessness was comforting.

And then a cold breeze stirred, its icy fingers trying to penetrate her peace. It was irritating. Nothing cold should exist in this place. She stirred restlessly, trying to move away from the chill. She would have frowned, but she wasn't sure how to make her face work, or if she even had a face. The breeze swirled around the form of the walking man, gently rustling his hair and clothes.

She wanted to dive back into the warmth, towards the man, but the breeze was persistent, and it was pulling her back up, out of the warm embrace and back into the harshness that was waiting for her. Her body slowly resurfaced and with every passing moment she discovered a part of herself anew—her fingertips, her lungs, her legs. With the discovery of her face, she wanted to pull her eyebrows together in annoyance.

This wasn't the direction she wanted to go.

As the sense of her body returned, so did the weight of it. She could feel how heavy her arms were. The air was pressing down on her, pinning her to the soft cushion she was lying on. Her hair lay damp, cold, and uncomfortable against her skin.

Everything was cold.

Except her hand.

She tried to concentrate on that—the warmth of her hand—willing the warmth to consume her again. She wasn't ready to wake up yet.

Her body started to ache, as physical discomforts began to resurface. Her face felt raw and sensitive.

She was afraid that the man in her dream was going to disappear as she drifted farther away. The thought sent a stab of fear through her heart. She knew, without him, she would be in danger—vulnerable. She would be without her protector.

But the pull was irresistible. Against her will, she could feel herself resurfacing.

Even with her eyes still closed, she began to be aware that she was in a room, lying on a soft surface—presumably a couch. The air tasted different, and she knew she had never been to this place before. A warm, earthy smell filled her nose—leather.

She shifted her weight, and a quiet moan escaped her lips. She realized that the warmth of her hand was because someone was holding it, and her moan had caused that person to grasp it tighter. Having her eyes closed, it was as if some other sense that she didn't know she possessed was being enhanced. She could feel an energy in the room—alive and inviting.

In fact, as her senses continued to awake, she became aware of people softly talking to each other. It was only a mumble, and she couldn't make out the words, but she was definitely not alone.

She was tempted to continue to keep her eyes closed—just breathing and enjoying the last remnants of her blissful slumber. But something was tugging at her subconscious, and just like the weary sleeper who gives up and reluctantly gets out of bed in the morning, she knew there was going to be no more rest for her. Something was coming—someone.

Rachel could hear their footfalls down the hallway, but she could also feel the energy in the room change. Without seeing anything, it was as if it got brighter, and she knew that someone new had come into the room. The energy quickened and her skin began to tingle. There was also an edge to the power. Something darker, something that was trying to bring back a memory that she was unwilling to recognize. A memory of…

The Voice.

Panic shot through her as the memories of the evening came crashing down on her. Her heartbeat sped up, and her breathing got ragged. Suddenly it was frightening to not see, to be blind to the danger around her. Where was she? Who were these people?

Or…

Was it better not to know? Would the reality be worse? She wasn't sure she would ever again have the courage to open her eyes and face the world.

In response to her fear, she felt someone lean in closer—the person holding her hand. She felt the warmth of their close proximity, and felt their fingers gently stroking her skin. Where their skin touched, she felt more of the energy. She felt soothed. She *had* to see, to open her eyes and know what was going on. There really was no other choice.

Her eyes opened, and when they focused, there he was—the man from her dream. Even though she hadn't been able to see his face clearly, she knew without a doubt that he was the one. Her protector.

Her thoughts tumbled together, "But, how can he be real? As flesh and blood, right beside me? Maybe I'm still dreaming."

She had been so afraid to wake up, to return to a place where the Voice could reach her again, but to find *him* here watching her she felt that there was still hope.

Before she had blacked out, she was so sure that the Voice would win. She thought that surely she had gone insane, and that there was no escape.

But then why would the man from her vision suddenly find her? Why, for the first time in what felt like forever, did she finally feel safe again? If there was no chance for salvation, why didn't the Voice just take her?

Maybe she could fight back. Maybe she wasn't insane.

But then there was the unbelievable reality that this man could be right here, right now... Maybe she *was* going crazy. But this was a different kind of insanity—a pleasant kind. If losing your mind meant that you could finally feel safe, feel at home, then it was the kind that she would gladly accept. This man was here for a purpose, and Rachel knew that they were connected in some way.

Or was it a cruel trick?

The man looked at her worriedly, and she wanted to reassure him of the hope that she had just discovered. She smiled, and it was as if her smile were the key to melting away the pain and tension in his face. He smiled back and the skin of her hand where he held her tingled and felt even warmer.

This is no trick.

But his was not the movement that drew her eye. Another man had entered the room—the man whose footsteps she had heard in the hallway. Rachel's mind reeled as she recognized the blonde man from that first day of school. She had been sitting under a tree, and this man had come and shown another student the way to class. She might not have recognized him, except that she remembered how guilty she had felt for eavesdropping on his conversation that day, and when she tried to make her escape, he had come back around the corner and forced her to hide like the coward she was.

Not believing her eyes, she tried to prop herself up better with her elbow. The other man, her protector, moved to help her sit up.

She remembered the blonde man's name from the conversation that day, and it left her lips before she could stop herself.

"Peter."

The way she said his name, it was a statement of fact—he *was* Peter—but it also sounded like a question of shock.

Rachel's mind raced from this feeling of unreality, "How did I end up here?" She began to question her sanity... again.

She saw surprise cross Peter's face, but her attention was quickly pulled away as Stu rushed to her side. "Rachel! I'm so glad you are awake." He looked between Peter and her. "So, you guys do know each other."

Maybe it was a good thing that Stu had distracted her, because she might have been frightened by the sudden burning passion in Peter's eyes when she spoke his name. Instead, she was simply confused by Stu's assumption.

Again, her mind questioned, "We know each other?"

Of course, Stu would think that. Hadn't she just spoken Peter's name aloud? But how was she supposed to explain that? It was an embarrassing story, and her head was still spinning from the events of the day.

Stu didn't really wait for her to answer anyway. Instead, the man holding her hand gently moved aside and allowed Stu to sweep her up in a hug. She felt weak, and the support of Stu's body felt nice. She was still seated on the couch, but she felt like she might fall over if he let her go too suddenly.

Her hand unexpectedly felt much cooler, and she thought of the man who had just been holding it and wished he hadn't let go. The feeling of warmth and security that she had been clinging to faded a little as he moved away. He didn't go far, but it was still too much. Looking at his face, she could see that he also seemed reluctant to leave her side.

But these were such strange feelings to be having. By all accounts, she should feel more comfortable in Stu's arms. More comfortable with someone familiar, instead of longing for a man who was more dream than reality.

She hugged Stu back, and when he released her, she pulled the jacket back up over her shoulders. Rachel couldn't help but shiver from the sudden chill that she felt from the dampness from the rain.

The jacket was leather, and Rachel enjoyed the scent. It was mixed with something else—*his* scent.

Stu was trying to ask her how she felt, but instead of concentrating on him, Rachel glanced around the room and saw all the other unfamiliar faces there. Across from her on a loveseat sat a young woman with curly brown hair. There was a kindness to her face—a face which was currently beaming with a huge welcoming smile. Rachel immediately could sense that this girl was going to be one of the happiest, friendliest people she would ever meet. She couldn't help but smile back at her.

Also, on the loveseat sat a skinny young man. He seemed to be younger than her. He also had brown hair, which flopped into his eyes. He seemed awkward and shy, but he too was smiling slightly at Rachel. When she met his gaze, he immediately dropped his eyes to smile at the carpet instead. Apparently, carpet was much less intimidating than she was.

Leaning against the fireplace was probably one of the biggest men she had ever seen. Lean and muscular, his skin was a beautiful shade of deep chocolate brown. He too smiled almost as welcomingly as the girl in the loveseat. She felt immediately at ease around him, despite his intimidating size.

The black man's arm was lightly tossed around the shoulders of a skinny blonde woman. Her face was beautiful in a sharp way, and even though she smiled like the rest of them, her smile just didn't seem as warm and welcoming. Instead it seemed both genuine, but reserved.

Rachel just about didn't notice the last person in the room. It was almost as if this girl didn't want to be seen. She stood off in a corner, with her arms folded across her stomach and her shoulders hunched. Rachel practically looked right past her, until it dawned on her that this was the girl that Peter had escorted to class that first day of school—Beth. She tried to catch the girl's eye, but she was stubbornly staring at the floor, avoiding eye contact. Rachel tried not to extract any meaning from the girl's antisocial behavior. It couldn't really have anything to do with her. The girl didn't even know Rachel.

But it was hard not to wonder when everyone else in the room seemed so sincerely happy that Rachel had woken up. In fact, the relief in the room was almost palpable.

Except for Beth.

Then, Beth did raise her head to look up. But instead of looking at Rachel, she looked directly at the man that had been holding her hand, and Rachel understood. The jealousy was plainly written across her face. This girl did not want that man anywhere near Rachel. She couldn't help but feel a little guilty.

Guilty, because it was arrogant to assume that she could just magically wake up and this beautiful man would be unattached. She was a fool. People had lives. Not only that, but people had lives *with* other people. Beth probably felt the same warmth and security when she was around him as Rachel did. What girl wouldn't be attracted to that? And it seemed safe to assume that Beth probably already knew him—his *name* at the very least.

Rachel finally focused back on Stu. Shaking her head to clear her thoughts, she asked, "I'm sorry. What did you ask me?"

Stu just laughed softly and smiled, "That's okay. You've been through a lot. I was just asking how you were feeling."

Stu was too nice to her. She didn't deserve it. Rachel hated to make him worry any more than he already was. "I am much better now." She sat up, placing her feet on the floor. She noticed his bandaged hand and a fresh wave of guilt hit her. "What a mess I've made of our evening together! First your hand, and then this," she gestured to her head. "I'm really sorry."

Peter came over to the couch and sat in the open space she had just made. He had a warm and friendly face, just as she remembered. He said, "I know it must be disconcerting to suddenly wake up here. We were all very worried about you." It was incredible—the good vibes that were coming from this guy. Rachel felt far more comfortable than she had any right to be. "Can we get you anything to drink?"

For some reason, it seemed horribly rude to refuse the offer. "Um... sure. That would be nice."

Peter looked at the woman on the loveseat, "Amy?"

Amy bounded up from her seat. "Sure thing Pete. Stu, you want to help me?"

"Of course."

Stu seemed oddly comfortable here as well. He left with Amy to get the drinks. Rachel couldn't help but wonder what it was about this place that was so comforting.

Rachel crinkled her forehead in puzzlement.

As Amy and Stu left the room, she could feel the energy around her diminish, ever so slightly. Even more strange, she was sure it was something to do with Amy alone, and not Stu.

With Stu gone, it seemed like Peter suddenly felt the need to get introductions out of the way. In a manner that felt slightly rushed, he quickly introduced Rachel to everyone. It was almost as if he wanted to get it taken care of before the drinks came back. Rachel couldn't help but find it a little odd.

Why the hurry?

It was nice to have names for all the faces that were looking at her—Nancy, Blake, Robert—but especially Donavon's. It was an unusual name. Rachel wasn't sure she had ever met a Donavon before. But that seemed fitting, as Rachel was pretty sure she had never previously met anyone quite like him.

Peter was watching the hallway anxiously as he continued to speak. "Rachel, we know what is happening to you—the headaches, the sleepless nights and the Voice. We want to help you, but it's a very delicate situation. You are perfectly safe here with us. We understand if it will take some time for you to feel comfortable, but you must understand that there could be precious little time left for us to make a difference."

Despite the ominous sound of his words, Rachel felt strangely calm and accepting of the situation. She had an overwhelming desire to trust Peter, and the others in the room. If they could help her, then she needed to trust them.

He continued, "We can explain everything to you, and you can ask as many questions as you want. However, Stu is a completely different matter. It's better…" Peter gave her a knowing glance, "No. It's *safer* if he knows as little as possible about what is going on."

Thinking about Stu's hand, and the threat the Evil Voice had made against him, Rachel knew exactly what Peter was talking about. Without even thinking about it, she was nodding her head in agreement.

Rachel thought, "Yes, Stu needs to be kept safe. I mean, look what I did to him tonight. He never would have ended up in the emergency room if he had stayed away from me."

Peter looked at her with such honesty and desperation in his face that Rachel couldn't help but feel herself respond to it. His voice was pleading as he continued, "I'm going to have to ask something very difficult of you now. I am going to have to ask you to trust us," his hand swept around the room, indicating everyone present, but

Rachel's eyes landed on Donavon before she turned back to Peter, "and help us get Stu to go home. We need to have him leave before we can tell you what is going on. Can you do that?"

Peter's eyes bore into hers with such intensity and determination. Rachel could feel that he only had her best interest at heart, and she felt so at home in this place, with these people. It was not a difficult choice to make.

She just hoped that she wouldn't have to lie to Stu—at least not very much.

Again, her mind chided her, "He deserves better. So much better…"

Rachel could feel Amy's presence get stronger and stronger as she came closer to the living room. She and Stu were chatting happily as they brought the drinks back. Amy carried a tray, and Stu had napkins in his good hand.

Laughing as she entered the room, Amy joked, "Stu thought it would be safest if I carried the glasses." Stu flashed a big grin at Rachel, and she smiled back weakly—embarrassed because she knew exactly what they were referring to without Stu's bandages as evidence.

It was okay. She deserved a little teasing.

Stu quipped, "Ah! Don't look like that Rachel. I mean, what's a few stitches between friends."

Blake piped up in his booming voice, "Here, here man. Well put."

Nancy elbowed Blake playfully in the ribs, but he didn't seem to hardly notice. Being as big as Blake was, it would take more than Nancy's elbow to get his attention.

Robert quietly got up to leave. Rachel got the impression that he was extremely shy, but he also appeared to have some task to do. He stopped to whisper to Donavon briefly before leaving the room, and the only part Rachel was able to make out was, "I'll let you know as soon as I am done."

Donavon's expression was serious and grave as he nodded to Robert, who then quickly left the room.

The drinks were passed out, and Rachel took a sip. The cold of the soda startled her for a moment, but then refreshed her parched throat. She was thirstier than she thought and gulped the remainder down. Stu came to sit at Rachel's feet by the couch. He looked up at her and commented, "I don't know what they did to help you, but you look so much better right now." He turned a questioning stare to Peter.

Giving off an air of absolute certainty and confidence, Peter replied, "I think she's going to need some extra rest, and we'll be careful to help her avoid anything that can trigger a migraine—like caffeine, chocolate, alcohol, bright lights…" All of that was true and could cause a migraine, but Rachel was sure they had nothing to do with her special kind of headaches. The Evil Voice didn't care if she ate chocolate.

In a way that would appear comfortable and familiar to Stu's watchful eyes, Peter put his arm around Rachel and joked, "No strong drinks for you tonight, sweetie."

Trying to play along, Rachel smiled and leaned into Peter's embrace. "Thanks Peter. I know you're watching out for me."

When she tried to smile back at Peter, his eyes were suddenly very serious and sober. He whispered very softly, "I am." His voice had a husky edge to it and he squeezed her shoulder tightly.

He immediately snapped out of it, and smiled casually at Stu, who had missed the brief exchange between sips of his drink.

Donavon was watching them as well. He seemed to be struggling to stay the few feet away that separated them. Almost unconsciously, he would move his hand, as if he was going to reach out for her, and then he would instead place his hand in his pocket, or shift positions. It was subtle, but Rachel felt uneasy with him away from her too, and she could read the signs in his movements.

Thinking that she should do her part to help get Stu safely away, Rachel covered her mouth as she yawned. She was so exhausted from lack of sleep that it was not a hard thing to do. Trying her best to look sleepy—also, not hard to do—she looked at Stu and said, "I am really tired. I think I'll just sleep here tonight, so my friends can watch me." Rachel saw Amy beam a huge smile at the word "friends." Then Rachel added, "I really don't want to be alone after getting so sick."

Stu couldn't possibly offer for Rachel to sleep at the fraternity, and Nancy chimed in helpfully, "The guest bedroom is all clean and ready to go." Rachel smiled at her gratefully.

Stu still seemed hesitant to leave and let her get some rest. He gave the room one last suspicious look before Peter commented, "Don't worry, Stu. We'll take good care of her." The waves of honest to goodness trust and sincerity that were coming off Peter were staggering. She desperately wanted to ask Peter how he was doing it. Rachel wondered if Stu could feel the same thing she was feeling.

To answer her question, Stu suddenly seemed to relax. He stood up then leaned down to give Rachel one last parting hug. He whispered in her ear, "Get feeling better, Sunshine." As a protective afterthought, before he let go, he added, "I'm just a phone call away."

Rachel could almost feel tears coming on. Stu was such a good, caring friend. "I know. I'll call you in the morning." Before he reached the door to leave, Rachel called after him, "Thanks for everything tonight Stu. I really needed a friend."

Stu smiled, nodded his head at her, and left.

Straightening up and away from Peter's shoulder, Rachel turned to look at everyone. She had the distinct impression that things were about to seriously change for her. It was as if she were standing on the edge of a cliff. Instinctively, her muscles tensed as if bracing for impact.

The energy in the room pulsed powerfully. She had never felt anything so potent and intoxicating.

But she also had the distinct impression that she was finally *home*—exactly where she belonged, with these people that surrounded her. She looked straight at Donavon.

With him.

CHAPTER 13: THE ORDER

Rachel looked around the room expectantly.

Blake and Nancy sat together on the loveseat, while Amy plopped down in the middle of the floor to sit Indian style. Donavon stood off to the side, watching, and Beth was still in the corner, hugging her sides in a defensive posture.

So far, Peter seemed to be the spokesman for the group, so Rachel turned to him for some answers. After a short uncomfortable silence, when it appeared that no one was going to say anything, Rachel decided to take the lead.

"Can you please tell me what is going on? What is happening to me?"

Peter exhaled slowly. He was still sitting next to Rachel, but he slid over just slightly so he could turn his body to face her better. "It would be helpful if you could tell us, first, everything that you know. Then we can better fill in the gaps for you. For example, how long have you been having your headaches?"

Rachel thought for a moment. "Well, I've had headaches my entire life. But they haven't been really bad until a few weeks ago."

Peter nodded and looked relieved.

Donavon spoke up next, "And how long have you been hearing the Voice?"

It was the first time Rachel heard Donavon speak. His voice was a deep, rich baritone that brought tingles to her skin. For a moment, she forgot he had asked her a question. Looking deep into his eyes, she realized she should answer: "Since the first day of class."

The stormy look that crossed Donavon's face made Rachel feel afraid again. She saw him clench his fist at his side, and he almost took an involuntary step in her direction. He seemed to want to come to her—her protector.

Amy was no longer smiling, and Peter also looked concerned. As if he were doing the math in his head and trying to force the numbers to be different, he whispered to himself, "You have been having migraines for a few weeks, and have been hearing the Voice for at least two?"

The atmosphere in the room grew colder. Rachel couldn't help but lose some of the hope that she had been trying to hang on to.

With dismay, she thought, "Maybe it's worse than I realized."

Rachel wanted to leave the couch and go to Donavon's side. She couldn't explain this strange desire to be near him when she was scared. She tried to swallow down her anxiety. This strange pull to the man from her dream seemed fantastic and surreal. She needed to keep her emotions under control before she lost herself to this raging tide that was threatening to sweep her away.

Suddenly, she felt exhausted all over again. So much had happened in such a short period of time. She wasn't sure how much more of this she could take in one day.

Scared to know the answer, but unable to resist asking, Rachel inquired of Peter, "Does that timeframe mean something?"

He replied, "It means we are going to have to work very fast."

Peter seemed so compassionate and genuine. Rachel wanted to trust him, even though she somehow *knew* that he could manipulate her feelings. As if in response to her thoughts, Peter looked at her, focusing. She felt a sudden change of the energy around her, like some invisible weight was pressing down on her body, forcing her muscles to release their grip on her—to relax. Rachel couldn't help herself this time. She had to ask, "How are you *doing* that?"

Peter tilted his head to the side as he looked at her, confused, "Doing what?" He seemed to take a moment to look at himself and make sure he wasn't unknowingly touching her in some way or doing something else upsetting.

At the tension in her voice, it felt like Peter began to try even harder to make her relax. The air around her got heavier and it made Rachel feel even more tired—something she didn't need at the moment.

"*That!*" Rachel waved her hands around in the air surrounding her head. "I'm already tired enough and you are making me feel like I am going to collapse any second." She stifled a yawn just then, emphasizing her point.

Donavon chuckled and folded his arms across his chest, assuming an amused stance. Peter's jaw dropped as the realization of what she was saying sunk in.

Wide-eyed, he gasped, "You mean you can feel what I am doing?"

Not sure what the big deal was, Rachel replied, "Of course. It feels like you are trying so hard to influence me that I am surprised you haven't broken out in a sweat yet."

Instantly the pressure in the air disappeared, and she felt relieved. It was much easier to concentrate now that he had stopped. She looked at Peter and added, "Thank you."

Again, Donavon dropped his head, avoiding eye contact with those around him as he smiled. It looked like his shoulders were shaking slightly from laughter.

As Rachel looked around the room, everyone seemed surprised—Beth especially. She got the feeling that maybe she should be more concerned about this. Except Donavon didn't seemed bothered in the slightest. A little more timid this time, she continued, "You mean that's not normal?"

Rachel thought she heard Beth snort softly and say under her breath, "Not really."

Amy shot Beth a sympathetic look.

Peter shook his head, recovering from his astonishment. "Most people can't do that so quickly."

Oh…

He apologized, "I'm sorry. I didn't mean to upset you. You just felt so anxious."

Rachel wanted to roll her eyes. "Well, wouldn't you be a little anxious in my place?"

She looked up at Donavon then, and when they exchanged glances, Rachel was sure he was entertained by the situation. Possibly feeling the need to explain why his reaction was so different from everyone else's, he commented, "It seems we need to be careful not to underestimate you."

Peter's expression changed. "Obviously, you can tell that something out of the ordinary is happening to you." Without waiting for her to confirm this, he continued, "And obviously you can tell that you are surrounded by people who are familiar with things being a little out of the ordinary. So perhaps we should just lay it all out in the open for you. Do you feel ready for that?"

"Yes." Rachel hoped there was as much confidence in her eyes as she tried to put in her voice.

***

An hour later, Rachel's head spun with all the explanations of Orders, Locators, Cleansings, Life Boxes, the Evil and the Gifted. It all sounded rather fantastic, and a few months ago she probably wouldn't have believed a word of it.

But now...She felt she really did not have a choice.

Peter told her how the Gifted had a greater sensitivity to the good around them. She could feel the good vibes around her right now and could intuitively tell that they were telling her the truth.

She thought to herself, "All of this was real, and it is happening to me."

Peter looked at her and asked hesitantly, "You seem to be taking this all rather well. How do you feel?"

Rachel thought a moment, and then smiled at everyone in the room. "Relieved, actually." She could almost feel the collective sigh that everyone in the room let out. Apparently, they were preparing themselves for all kinds of different reactions from her. "I was starting to think that I was going crazy, and so it's nice to finally have some answers."

Amy seemed particularly pleased by this response. "That's how it was for me! It's almost like, just to have answers, even if they are hard to believe, was still comforting."

Rachel nodded.

Beth cautiously took a couple steps toward her. With a fierceness that surprised Rachel she quietly inquired, "Do you have any idea what your Gift might be?"

Rachel shrugged again. She hadn't really noticed anything unusual happening around her—apart from the Voice—or that she responded to things any differently than anyone else. "How would I know?"

Suggestions came from around the room.

"Maybe you feel a tingling or energy around you."

"During high stress situations, something strange may have happened."

"Just recently you may have started having sensations that are completely new to you."

Rachel just shrugged. "No, besides the Voice and the headaches, I really didn't notice anything. I mean, I felt what Peter was doing to me, but I've never noticed that I can do anything like that."

"That's okay." Peter said quickly. "That's what we are here for—to help you figure these things out."

It was getting late. And Rachel was glad she had agreed to stay the night. The idea of going back to her apartment, alone, was just too scary.

After wishing everyone a goodnight, with Donavon specifically admonishing her to wake him at the first twinge of any problem, Amy took Rachel upstairs to show her the guestroom. It was at the very end of the hall, across from the bathroom. Inside stood a queen-sized bed, a small desk, and a bay window that looked out over the backyard.

Amy pleasantly chatted about the details that went along with staying the night—like where the extra blankets were and where her room was if Rachel needed anything in the night. Nancy was about the same size as Rachel, so they were letting her borrow a pair of pajamas to sleep in. When it looked like she was about to leave and let Rachel get ready for bed, Amy finished by asking, "So, do you think you need anything else?"

"No, this should be great. I was hoping to ask you something, though."

Amy smiled, sat down on the edge of the bed with a bounce, and said, "Sure thing!"

Rachel smiled, despite her exhaustion. Amy was so full of life. "I was just wondering why Beth seemed so interested in my Gift. Or rather, at this point, lack of a Gift."

Amy nodded to herself. "Beth is new here too. She hasn't been with us for very long, and she has been having a hard time figuring out how to sense her Gift. I think she was just trying to see if all of this was going to be easier for you than it has been for her. I think you made her feel better when you didn't know what your Gift was yet either. I assume she's been feeling a little frustrated."

Rachel asked, "Is two weeks an unusually long time for her to take to figure this out?"

"Not really. It's different for everyone, and some people know what they can do long before the Order ever finds them. Others can take a month or more to learn to feel what kinds of energy they are drawn to. Of course, once everything is ready for their Cleansing, they figure things out pretty quickly during the ritual. Robert has been working on Beth's Life Box and talisman for two weeks now, so it shouldn't be much longer before we are ready for her Cleansing. It's just that... well... I just *know* she'd feel better if she could start figuring this out ahead of time. I can see how it would be hard for her to be around all of these Gifted people and feel like she is the only one that doesn't get it. It will be good for her to watch you learn too."

Rachel smiled, and then stifled a yawn. "Good. I want us to be friends—like the two newbies. It should be fun."

Amy stood up, pulled back the covers, and indicated for Rachel to lie down. "I think I can help you sleep," Amy said with a wink.

Rachel snuggled down in the bed, and the next thing she knew she could hardly keep her eyes open. She was just barely aware of Amy saying, "Night-y, night," when she was suddenly waking up, feeling more rested than she had in days.

The light was streaming in through the lace curtains of the unfamiliar room. In a rush the events of last night all came back to her. Rachel smiled. It felt so good to sleep soundly. She luxuriously stretched her arms out over her head and wiggled her toes.

As she stood up, she could hear some of her joints popping. She walked over to the window, and was surprised by the height of the sun in the sky.

Astonished, she thought, "It must be the afternoon already! I can't believe I slept that long."

Actually, the more she thought about it, the more she *could* believe that she had slept so long. First of all, she had been dead tired.

Second, Rachel knew that Amy had used her power to knock her out. She would have to thank her when she saw her.

Rachel crossed the room and let her fingertips gently brush across the lace of the curtains while she gazed outside. The backyard was completely surrounded by tall leafy trees, making it a private oasis—completely blocked off from all the neighbors. The house itself sat on a larger-than-normal plot, and so it wasn't like the neighbors were that close anyway.

She saw plenty of shady areas, flowers, bushes, and a stone path that disappeared off into the distance. The college and this neighborhood were on the edge of town, and Rachel was pretty sure there was nothing but mountain range beyond the border of the trees in the backyard. Knowing what little she did of the Order, she could see why they might want to build a house close to campus, and yet as much on the outskirts of town as possible—privacy from other people, yet access to campus and the Gifted that might arrive there. She could see the mountain looming majestically above the tops of the trees.

There was a garden plot off to one side of the porch that looked freshly maintained and a gazebo covered in vines in the middle of the yard that housed a couple of benches. She thought it looked like the perfect place to sip lemonade and read a book.

Her thoughts wandered, "Everything is so beautiful. What a lovely place to go on a nice long walk with Donavon."

At that thought, Rachel's heart fluttered; she needed to get ready! Keenly aware that her chances of seeing Donavon today were pretty high, she didn't want to waste a moment.

As she started to turn around to find the bathroom, a cold dread stopped her.

What if the Voice came back today? What if she wasn't ready? What would happen?

Taking a steadying breath, she straightened her shoulders and thought, "At least I won't be alone when it happens again. When... not if..."

Rachel shuddered; she could almost feel the Evil's presence on the fringes of her mind, just waiting for the opportune moment to strike.

She crossed the hallway to the bathroom and closed the door behind her. The bathroom was well stocked for a visitor with soaps, towels and other necessities. Someone had also taken the time between last night and today to go to her apartment and pick up some of Rachel's personal items. She found her own toothbrush, make-up kit, and several other things. On the countertop there was a neatly folded pile of clothing. Sitting on top was a note written in scrawling handwriting. It said, "Got these for you—Amy." She couldn't help but smile. It was almost like she had found a long-lost sister in this energetic new friend.

After showering, she took her time to get ready, applying make-up and dabbing perfume on her neck. As she brushed out her freshly washed and dried hair, she kept telling herself that she was doing what she did every day. But as images of Donavon flashed through her mind, she knew she was kidding herself. She was taking extra special care getting ready for him. She knew that last night she must have looked horribly scary, and she was hoping to erase some of those first impressions.

Giving herself one final look-over, Rachel packed up her toiletries and left the bathroom. She wasn't sure if she should put her things back into the guest bedroom, or if she should take them with her downstairs. Part of her was hoping that she was going to become a permanent resident in the house, but she hadn't exactly been invited... yet. She felt like she was home here, and the idea of going back to her apartment—and her interesting neighbor—was not appealing.

Rachel finally decided it was best to think positively, so she placed all of her belongings on the desk in the guestroom. Then she made her way downstairs to the kitchen. She had slept through breakfast and lunch, so it was time for a late afternoon meal. Again, she wasn't sure if she should expect to be allowed to eat the food in the kitchen because she didn't really live here... but she figured she would take a chance.

One sandwich hardly seemed worth worrying about when faced with life and death.

Before she even entered the room, Rachel could feel that someone was already in there. As she rounded the corner, she saw Peter lounging at the table. He had textbooks open around him, and seemed absorbed in his work. At her entrance, he looked up.

His face lit up with a smile. "Good morning, sleepyhead."

Rachel laughed, "Morning? By the looks of the sky, I'd say it's more like afternoon."

Peter chuckled too, "Right you are." He glanced at his watch, "It's actually two-thirty, give or take."

Rachel's stomach took that opportunity to voice its discomfort with a loud gurgle. She blushed, but Peter was immediately on his feet apologizing, "Here! Let me get you something to eat. You have to be starved."

"I am a little hungry." Rachel admitted. She took a seat at the table and watched Peter dash around the kitchen.

Maybe feeling the need to fill the silence with conversation, he chatted as he prepared a plate. "Amy made some enchiladas for lunch. They might even still be warm. She's a pretty good cook. I think you'll like them."

He filled a plate with more than Rachel thought she could eat. After it was steamy and hot from the microwave, he placed the offering in front of her. It smelled wonderful. Her stomach growled again before she could blow on her first bite to cool it. Peter was happy to continue to chat with her while she ate.

She inquired about the homework he seemed to be working on, and Rachel discovered that Peter was continually taking first semester courses so he could find things in common with any Gifted that might suddenly appear at the college. Right now, he was trying to study first-year Spanish.

"In some ways, it's a lot like the other first-year languages I have taken, so it's not too bad, so long as I can keep it all straight." Peter laughed. "It's embarrassing when they ask me a question and I answer in French."

"So, you must be able to speak a lot of languages then."

Peter leaned back in his chair, crossing his arms. "Not really. Since I only take the first-year classes, I never get that in-depth. But, if you need someone who can ask where the bathroom is in six different languages, then I'm your man."

It was so easy and comfortable to speak to Peter. Rachel could really feel herself opening up to him, and she was confident that he wasn't even trying to use his Gift on her.

She genuinely liked him.

She felt like he was a large part of why she felt so at home here. They chatted the entire time it took Rachel to eat her lunch. She was surprised at how hungry she had been, and cleared the entire plate that Peter had prepared for her.

Finally, she asked, "So, what am I supposed to do now? You guys said you could help me."

Peter replied, "Well, we know that all of this must seem kind of sudden to you, but we have found that it is easiest for us to help if you hang around us as much as possible. You are going to need someone to help guide you and show you how to fight against the Evil until we can have your Cleansing." Seeming to not want to overwhelm her, he almost hesitantly added, "We hope to start teaching you this afternoon actually. Normally we would assign you a single teacher. But with what we saw last night, it might be best if everyone pitches in as much as they can." Peter looked very serious as he continued, "We're concerned you might not have a lot of time left. That was some serious darkness in your apartment yesterday."

Dread crept back into Rachel's stomach as she remembered the oily Voice.

Peter ran his fingers through his hair, "I've never felt anything quite like it. I spoke with my father this morning. He's a Locator as well. He was actually calling to answer some questions I had about Beth, but he was very interested in hearing about you as well."

Rachel was curious, "Is Beth okay?"

Peter frowned, "I think so. It's hard to say for sure. Her aura seems to be a little unstable. Usually it feels pretty weak, but then it will suddenly spike. My father had heard of one other case like hers, and so he went to investigate. The Order that he has been assigned to as Locator also had a few new recruits these last two weeks." Peter smiled at Rachel, "It seems it's a busy time for us." Then he continued, "He was having a hard time getting away, but he finally found a day to make a trip to the Council's Library."

"The Council?"

Peter clarified, "Oh, yeah. The members of the Council are kind of the ultimate leaders of the Gifted. They oversee all the Orders and Locators and make sure that we are organized and helping as many people as we can. They also have a huge library, full of records compiled from some of the Gifted that have come before us. It's important that we write down our experiences, especially if they are unique, so that others can learn from us." Laughing, he added, "It's not like we come with instruction manuals.

"Some of the Gifted dedicate their lives to collecting and storing these records. As you can imagine, these documents are very important to us, and it's hard to gain access to them. Locators are kind of the exception. We can go visit the Library any time we need information to help our Order.

"Dad spent several years working at the Library. He is passionate about learning. At one point, he thought he was going to be one of those Gifted that would spend their entire lives in the Library, learning and studying so he could help those around him. But then he met my mother and plans changed." Peter had a faraway look in his eyes as he thought about his family. "It was probably for the best anyway. The Council was not very happy having a Locator working in the Library as it was. There are so few Locators that they want every single one of us in the field. Of course, if my father had wanted to stay and study, the Council would never have forced him to leave. I think only my mother had the power to do that.

"Anyway, Dad knew he had read some document about a case like Beth's when he had studied at the Library years ago, but he couldn't remember exactly what it had said. He said it took him all day, but he finally found what he was looking for."

Rachel was finding herself captivated by this new world she was part of. She wanted to know more. "What did he find out?"

"Well, the document he remembered studying was very old. We are actually lucky that he had ever seen it at all. There are so many records to go through, but this particular one he had helped to copy the contents of to a computer file."

Rachel interrupted, "Computer file?"

Peter smiled, "Well, this is the twenty-first century. Musty old papers are too easy to lose or burn. The Gifted at the Library these days spend a great deal of their time transferring everything onto computers and making digital backups. Someday, Locators won't have to go to the library anymore. They will simply be able to access everything they need through the Internet."

At Rachel's incredulous look, he added, "Lives are too important to lose just because the information to save them is locked away in some library a hundred miles from here."

What Peter was describing didn't gel well with the romanticized version that Rachel had been briefly picturing in her head. She was envisioning an antique library, full of leather-bound volumes and stacks of papers so old and delicate that they crumbled under the slightest touch. She imagined the Gifted using ladders to climb to the higher shelves, dramatically blowing off the dust from their latest treasure, and retiring to some far corner of the library to savor every word.

What Peter was describing sounded far too realistic and sensible. Of course, an old antiquated library wouldn't serve this modern world as well as was needed. Rachel admitted, "I guess that makes sense. I wouldn't want something that could help me to be written on some crumbling piece of paper somewhere that people couldn't find it."

Peter frowned, "I'm sure that won't happen to you."

Rachel couldn't help but be touched by Peter's concern. To change the subject from herself and his worry, she pushed, "So, what did he find out about Beth?"

Peter shook his head, as if suddenly remembering what this conversation was originally about. "Umm… he said it wasn't a very clear manuscript. Parts were missing from the original, but, from what he was able to save all those years ago, it told the story of a Locator who found a woman who had similar issues with her aura. In her case, she had some kind of link to another Gifted man in her Order.

"The Locator in the story described how this link was visible to him with his Locator Eyes. It was as if their auras were connected to each other and the energy they each had individually would combine and feed off the energy of the other person. When the woman was away from this other man, her aura would fade, like Beth's does. But when they were together, it was brilliant."

Rachel thought it would be amazing to see the things that Peter could see through his eyes as a Locator. She thought the world must be a very beautiful place to him, when there was no Evil around. Peter had tried the night before to describe to Rachel what it was like to see things the way he did. She imagined it might look something like the aurora borealis.

"So, is that what is happening to Beth?"

Peter looked a little frustrated when he replied, "I'm not sure. My father kept saying that the record was not very detailed in its description, so it's hard to know. We don't know if the link that this other woman developed with the man happened gradually over time, or if it was present from the first day they met. The history doesn't say. The first time I felt Beth's aura spike was around Donavon, but that doesn't seem to be a consistent thing. It's hard to know if her power will eventually develop into a similar link or if this is completely different."

Rachel couldn't help but feel a little stab of jealousy at this revelation about Beth and Donavon.

Again, she felt the need to chastise herself for thinking that Donavon didn't already have ties to another person. She was being unrealistic to hope that he was completely unattached and just waiting for her to arrive. The dream of Donavon from yesterday seemed so far away, sitting in the kitchen here during the day with Peter. Rachel began to wonder if maybe her feelings from yesterday were some kind of figment of her imagination. Perhaps when she saw Donavon today things would be completely different.

Perhaps…

Besides it wasn't as simple as Donavon and Beth liking each other. They might have some kind of supernatural link. How was she supposed to compete with *that*?

She suddenly felt very foolish for spending so much time primping in the mirror for a man who might already be destined for someone else.

Just then, Rachel felt the distinct impression of someone using the Gift around her. Just like yesterday with Peter, she wasn't sure how she knew what was going on, but she could feel it. Her skin felt tingly and alive, and she knew that something was happening. She turned a questioning look on Peter, "What's going on?"

Peter eyes widened in surprise, "That's amazing that you can sense that already." Laughing softly to himself, he added, "I sure hope that means this will be easy for you." As if something had just occurred to him, he turned to her and hesitantly asked, "Can you feel anything, even when people are not using their powers?" Rachel wasn't sure exactly what Peter meant. At her frown, he continued, "Like, could you tell that I was in the kitchen before you actually saw me. Could you *feel* me in here even though I wasn't using any energy?"

Not knowing if the answer would be good news or bad news, Rachel worded her answer very carefully, "I could tell that someone was already in here, but I didn't know it was you specifically."

Peter seemed to take a moment to chew on what she said. "Maybe you are a Locator, like me. Hmm..."

He got up and walked over to the back door. "It looks like Donavon and Beth are outside practicing. That's probably what you are feeling."

Rachel stood up to join Peter and followed him as he stepped out onto the back porch. She could make out Donavon and Beth sitting in the gazebo. They sat on opposite benches, facing each other. Rachel didn't know exactly what Donavon was trying to do, but she could feel a tingling in the air as he used his power.

Beth smiled happily as she exclaimed, "I can feel that!"

Rachel's heart ached as she saw Donavon's radiant smile in return.

She wished she could be the one out there working with him—to have him smile at her when she could obviously already do what Beth was trying so hard to do. Feeling foolish again, she looked away in frustration.

No, I won't let him make you feel the fool.

The power of the Voice turned Rachel's veins to ice.

I can take care of her—of him—of everything. You will see. You will be mine, and mine alone.

CHAPTER 14: DESPERATION

Rachel felt the world start to spin.

It was too soon! Less than twenty-four hours had passed since her last attack. She started to turn to Peter in a panic.

If you tell him, I'll hurt him.

Rachel froze.

"I'll hurt him"—the same words the Voice used with Stu. Instead of looking at his face, she glanced at Peter's ring. She knew it was supposed to protect him from the Evil. Could he really be in danger with his ring on?

Her heart began beating rapidly. She didn't know how to fight yet! She didn't know what to do! Panic continued to well up as her hands started to shake.

Barely perceptible through the fog of terror in her mind, she could hear Donavon in the distance. He was telling Beth to take what she felt him doing and try to focus her energy in a similar way. She seemed unsure, but willing to try. Beth closed her eyes in concentration, and Rachel did the same but for very different reasons.

A breeze began to blow, and the leaves on the gazebo started to flutter and stir.

Rachel shut her eyes tighter. She was afraid to open them—to look at Peter—in case the Voice would make good on its threat. She gripped the railing on the porch to stop her hands from shaking; the wood sent little splinters into her palms.

She wanted to shout at the Voice in her head, "You can't hurt him! He's protected! He's safe!"

I have ways. I can accomplish anything, I promise you. I can make you hurt him for me. Wouldn't that be nice? Should we do it together, my love?

Rachel trembled against the force of the Evil in her mind. She didn't want to believe it. She would never hurt Peter. But then she remembered Stu and how he had been injured by something she had done.

She couldn't let that happen again.

Rachel chanted in her head, "I can fight this. I can fight this. I can fight!"

Don't resist. I just want to love you. To hold you. Let me into your mind, and I can give you unimagined pleasure.

Her thoughts were locking up with fear and revulsion as she tried to think of what she could do to protect herself. She could feel the energy around Donavon. She was sure she could feel Beth using some kind of energy as well, even if Beth didn't realize it herself. Rachel thought she should be able to figure out how to use her own power too. It was so easy for her to feel everyone else after all. Maybe she could use her energy to fight back.

Her thoughts were frantic, "Why can't I figure this out?! There has to be some way to fight back."

She tried to sense something within herself.

Straining and reaching, she thought that perhaps there was something there, on the edge of her senses, but she was too scared to focus like she wanted to.

I can help you find your power. I can show you what you are capable of. Just let me in. Together, we could do anything.

Rachel didn't want to know what she was capable of, not with the help of the Evil.

Beth sat, focused, concentrating hard as she worked with Donavon, and Rachel could feel Beth's power increase. It wasn't like the spike in energy that Peter had described, but she was definitely getting stronger. Digging deep inside herself, Rachel thought that she too was sensing something more, but now it frightened her that she was only sensing what the Evil wanted her to. If she was able to harness this power inside her, would it be for the Evil's purposes? How would she know if what she was about to unleash would help or hurt?

The wind was starting to pick up, and Rachel could feel her hair whipping around her back. She could feel the oppressiveness that comes from a storm approaching. The clouds were gathering and starting to block out the sun. Rachel kept her eyes closed, but she could still sense through her eyelids that the sun was disappearing, making her feel colder, and she wondered if she could unlock her limbs long enough to get back inside—back where she felt safe and loved.

However, terror had her rooted to the spot, and all she had the strength to do was open her eyes and stare at Donavon and Beth.

Look at them together. He doesn't want you, love. Nobody wants you. Not like I do. You are mine, only mine. I won't let anyone else have you. If you resist, I'll hurt them all. I'll make you wish you hadn't denied me.

Only seconds had passed, but it felt like an eternity to Rachel. Hopelessness began to swell within her chest as she wondered if the Voice was right. Why would anyone want someone who was so tainted by something so vile?

She watched as Beth continued to work, concentrating harder. The strength of the wind continued to grow and a light rain began to fall. Donavon and Beth were sheltered under the gazebo and didn't seem to notice, but Rachel watched everything as if in slow motion. She could see their hair moving in the wind and the leaves trembling in the lattice.

She wanted to call out to Donavon. She needed him to come and be her guardian, but she was also torn by doubt. By being near him, would she only be putting him in danger from the Evil as well? He looked so strong and confident. Rachel could try to make herself believe that nothing could touch him. That he could defeat any obstacle in his path.

No one can defeat me. Killing him would feel as smooth as a scalpel through flesh. Slice, slice, slice...

Rachel used all the strength she had not to moan. She needed to get out of here. She needed to get away from everyone. It was too late for her. She was only going to bring harm to those around her. These new friends, already like family to her, would be in so much danger if she stayed. How could she harm them when she felt such love and connection to them all? How could she hurt Peter? How could she hurt Donavon—this man she felt such a strange connection with?

Slice, slice, slice... watch the blood trickle out. Dance in the hot stickiness. Bathe and laugh. You can hear him screaming in pain, can't you? Listen, my love. Ahh...

Rachel felt like she was going to throw up. Her throat burned where the bile involuntarily rose.

Unaware, Peter commented, "I can feel Beth getting stronger." Then, wrinkling his forehead, he glanced up at the sky and then down at the patterns the rain drops were forming on the stepping stones. "Something doesn't feel right. You don't suppose Beth is making it rain, do you?"

Rachel couldn't respond. She was afraid that her voice would betray what she was so desperately trying to hide. She couldn't let him know what was going on.

I'll hurt him, I'll hurt him, I'll hurt him.

The blood was pounding in her ears and her knees felt weak.

When she didn't respond right away, Peter looked over and noticed how tense she was. "Are you okay?" He reached out to put an arm around her.

The Voice hissed in response to Peter's gesture. The sound seemed to be possessive in nature.

Afraid for his safety, Rachel gently sidestepped his embrace and tried to smile at him. "I'm fine."

Outwardly, Peter looked exactly the same, but Rachel could feel a change in the air around him, and she knew he was looking at her with his Locator eyes.

Peter gave a sharp intake of breath. "You're not okay." He moved forward, closer, trying desperately to get his hands on her. "I can see the Evil all around us now."

No! Move away. Make him leave you alone, or you will regret it. Don't let him touch you. You are mine. Mine!

The Evil was screeching in her head. Her heartbeat dramatically picked up in tempo, as the weight and violence in the Voice increased. She could feel her desperation multiplying. She could see the determination in Peter's face to help her, yet she could also feel the deep need of the Voice to hurt someone—anyone. Rachel backed up, working her way towards the steps on the other side of the porch. She had her hands raised to fend Peter off. In a whimper she said, "No. Please don't touch me."

Pain and confusion crossed Peter's face as he continued to advance on her. "I'm not going to hurt you. I want to help." Looking at the space around Rachel, Peter added, "It's so thick. I can't believe I didn't feel it sooner."

Peter continued to move forward despite the anxiety on her face. Her body began to tremble and she was afraid that if she made it to the stairs that she would be unable to go down them without falling. The look of anguish on his face at her continued retreat cut at Rachel's heart like a knife. Rachel worried that Peter might think she didn't trust him.

Something seemed to dawn on Peter, and he abruptly halted in his tracks and put his hands up in a placating way. In a very low and steady voice, he said, "Don't listen to it, Rachel. It's telling you lies. There is good in you. There is power in that good to fight this. You just need to find it." Desperately looking over her shoulder, Peter yelled in earnest, "Donavon!"

Rachel had made it to the edge of the stairs. With her hands still held up in front of her body, she turned in time to see Donavon's head whip up. His eyes locked on hers as he instantly started to rise. She was vaguely aware of Beth coming as well before she turned her eyes back to Peter.

Now with Donavon coming to her, Rachel didn't think it was possible, but her panic doubled, practically crippling her and causing tears to stream down her cheeks. In a voice that was thick and full of agony, Rachel pleaded, "No. Please don't. I don't want to hurt you. It will hurt all of you if you don't stay away from me."

The Voice was snarling incoherently inside of her skull. Vicious. Cruel.

Peter continued to move forward, slowly, and Rachel stumbled, moving backwards on the path under her feet. He pleaded, "It's going to be okay. It can't hurt us. Don't believe what it is saying."

He's wrong. So horribly, wrong. I can make their hearts stop beating, just like your father's heart.

She couldn't see anything through the tears that were trickling down her face now. Her lips trembled and her voice cracked as she whimpered, "It hurt Stu. I know it can hurt you. Please, no. Just let me leave."

Suddenly, there were arms around her. Donavon had crossed the entire distance between them in a matter of seconds. At his touch, the Voice roared in her head in frustration.

No!

Sensing the danger, Rachel's desperation turned into an almost unthinking animal frenzy. She tried to fight his grip and tear herself away.

Slice, slice, slice... I will enjoy seeing pieces of him fly. I'll start with those hands that dare to touch what doesn't belong to them. He'll never touch you again.

A wail of despair tore from her throat as she continued to fight Donavon's grasp. Her tears and her screams seemed to be unending.

Slice, slice...

"Please no, please no!"

Peter continued to look at the space around all of them. With urgency in his voice, he said, "Hurry Donavon! It's getting thicker. It's everywhere."

Donavon's grip was unyielding, and she could barely make out that he was trying to talk to her. Using her last shreds of sanity, she fought to listen to his voice. He whispered in her ear, "Rachel, use my strength. Feel my power. Let the good from me protect you. Use this energy to fight. Let me help you." His voice was low and steady, yet full of urgency. The rain now slashed the ground in torrents.

He lies! No one can save you. Only I can release you.

Donavon tried to hold her thrashing body closer to himself. He continued to speak in her ear, gentle and pleading. "You can fight this. You can beat it. I know you can. I can feel it within you. Take my energy. Use it to fight." His arms were strong enough to hold her despite her struggles, yet his embrace was tender and sheltering. There was a desperate note in his voice as he tried to calm her whimpers. "Shh... it will be okay. Hold on. I'm here."

Her mind felt like it would split in two, but she tried to force her panic to subside enough that she could attempt to feel Donavon's energy. In her struggle and fear, she had lost her connection to the flows of energy that he and Beth had been using. She was hardly aware of the rain that drenched her to the skin.

She wanted to curl her body up into a ball and hide. The pain was just too great. She felt trapped—destined to hurt those around her yet unable to escape. She tried to cry, "No, no, no…" but the sounds that came from her throat were not distinguishable as words.

She clamped her teeth to control her cries, and she concentrated on regaining her connection with the power around her. Her mind was in such a panic that it was practically impossible to focus on one single thing. Her thoughts were bouncing around so frantically that she could hardly grasp one thought before it was gone in a fresh wave of terror.

Finally, she was able to get her body to stop fighting Donavon's grasp, although she did not relax. Instead, she held all her muscles rigid and tense, waiting for her mind to focus.

Somewhere, on the fringes of her consciousness, she became aware of a sense of good, of calm, of peace—of Donavon's power. It felt very far away, and it kept skidding away like it was being repulsed by the dark power surrounding her. The Evil was battling in her head against Donavon's presence, and Rachel was not sure if it was a war that she could help Donavon win. Just as in her dream, she could feel the warmth of the place that she wanted to be in, and yet the drag and pull of the Evil was like some unstoppable force that was going to suck her into the darkness. It was like a black hole, consuming everything that dared get too close.

Rachel could feel Beth's presence nearby. Beth seemed to be channeling her energy in some way, possibly trying to help Rachel as well, although it was harder for her to feel Beth's energy next to Donavon's overpowering presence.

The ground began to tremble and shake. The wind was howling and Rachel heard a loud snap and crash as huge limbs from the trees started to break off and fall into the yard. One of them landed dangerously close to all of them.

That's right. Watch as the tree impales them. See their bodies twitch as I take the life from them. Then it will just be you and I. Alone.

Frantically, desperately, she reached out with her aura to pull Donavon's energy into her. She needed his strength to fight back. It was like swimming against the pull of a riptide. For every stroke she made towards the shore, she was pulled back three. She was afraid her efforts would not be enough, and that she would be swept away.

Join me. Let me have you. Caress you. I will never give up. I will always be here. You can't leave me!

She heard Donavon groan with the effort he was putting into sending all of his power to her. He was becoming tired from the exertion, and Rachel knew he wouldn't last much longer. With the last bit of strength that she had left, Rachel lunged with her aura towards Donavon's energy. She screamed with the effort. The static charge in the air made all the hair on her arms stand on end. The earth shook more violently, almost knocking them to their knees. The sky, which had turned black, suddenly lit up with multiple strikes of lightning all around. Rachel's eyes flew open and she was momentarily blinded by the brightness. As her sight returned, her gaze locked on Beth, who was concentrating intensely.

Rachel could feel the power of Donavon all around her. His energy had finally broken through and she could feel it force the Evil out of her like a giant shock wave. The blast from the conflicting energies felt like an atomic bomb. Peter flinched away from them and shielded his eyes, as if trying to protect them from a blinding light.

The earth ceased to shake, and her knees sagged in response as she tried to fall forward.

Then, there was silence.

CHAPTER 15: NEW HOPE

Rachel could feel her body gently swaying as she was carried into the living room. Everything sounded like it was under water, but she could tell that Peter was calling for someone—or something. She felt herself being placed on a soft surface.

She thought she could hear voices speaking to each other in hushed tones of anger. She couldn't imagine who would be mad at anyone else but her. Wasn't *she* the one bringing all of this Evil down on them? She was a walking curse, hurting and destroying everything and everyone in her path.

Slowly Rachel began to feel the other energies around her again as the last vestiges of the Evil's black tendrils loosened from her mind. She realized that someone else had joined them. This new person was using the Gift on her, pulling her back towards the surface of her consciousness. Again, she wasn't sure she wanted to resurface. Life was getting so complicated and dangerous. She felt safer wrapped in this cocoon of numbness. But the power was unrelenting, and she felt herself coming around against her will.

"I think it's working." Amy's voice was the first intelligible thing that Rachel could discern.

"Thank you." Donavon's strong, deep voice was like a soothing balm on her nerves. Rachel felt her skin tingle with excitement as she realized that he was still there with her. Then she mentally scolded herself. Hadn't she just put him on the Evil's hit list? He would be safer if she left him alone with Beth—as much as that would hurt and break her heart.

"I called for you the instant I knew what was going on..." That was Peter. Rachel felt confused as she realized that Peter and Donavon were the ones who were fighting. Peter sounded like he was being defensive.

She heard Donavon's sigh: "I know." He sounded annoyed, yet resigned. By the proximity of his voice, she knew he had to be right next her.

She could feel herself becoming more and more awake as the seconds passed. She finally felt able to open her eyes and struggled to sit up. Immediately, Donavon's hands were on her arms, helping her to push herself up. His hands were warm compared to her cold, wet skin. Rachel was acutely aware of the chill left behind when he took his hands away. Her skin felt electric where Donavon's hands had been. She crossed her arms over her body and rubbed the now sensitive area with her palms to keep from shivering.

This felt like déjà vu from last night. Rachel found herself back on the couch, soaking wet, and in the living room for the second time in less than twenty-four hours. In fact, the couch smelled slightly like damp fabric that hadn't had time to completely dry.

Rachel's eyes found Donavon's. He looked tired and drained. His eyebrows were drawn together in worry, making a wrinkle just above his nose. She didn't like to see him so unhappy. Unthinkingly, she reached out and tried to smooth away the wrinkle with the tips of her fingers. Just like his hands, the skin on his face was hot under her touch, almost feverish. He briefly closed his eyes at her caress, and some of the tension in his face disappeared.

Amy leaned in over Donavon's shoulder and asked, "Are you feeling better?"

Surprisingly enough, Rachel did feel better. Her voice was still rough when she answered, "I think so." She coughed to clear her throat.

Amy beamed, "Good." Seeing that Rachel was fully awake now, she stopped using the flows of her energy to stimulate her.

Rachel could see Peter standing behind Amy. He had his arms tightly folded across his chest, and if Rachel wasn't mistaken, he seemed upset.

She could imagine what the scene outside had looked like—the way she had screamed, fought and cried while pushing Peter away when he had tried to help.

Feeling the lowest she had ever felt, she thought, "He must think that I hate him."

Her voice broke with emotion as she wept, "Oh, Peter! I'm so sorry."

Peter seemed to instantly respond to her apology. His face got visibly softer and he ran a hand through his wet hair and took an involuntary step toward her. His faced seemed to change to a look of guilt as he replied, "Hey, I should be apologizing to you. I don't know how I didn't sense sooner that you were in danger." In a gesture of frustration, he slammed his fist rhythmically into his palm to emphasize his next words, "I mean, I was standing *right next to you!*"

Donavon gave Peter a knowing look.

Apparently, this is what the argument had been about.

Rachel tried to stand up and walk to Peter, but her legs were still too wobbly to hold her up. As her balance teetered and she fell back to the couch, Donavon's hands were instantly there to ease her back down. He whispered, "Maybe you should sit a little longer."

Rachel smiled weakly at Donavon, embarrassed by her unsteady display.

Peter snapped, "She can come see me if she wants to."

Her head whipped up to look at Peter. His tone surprised her. She didn't exactly understand the situation, but she wanted to diffuse the tension she had obviously created between these two friends. She laughed nervously, "I guess I'm not ready to stand up yet."

Peter crossed the space between them and stood over the arm of the couch by her head. He reached out and touched her hair, "Are you sure you are feeling okay?"

She tried to look up at Peter and smile, but the angle was difficult because of where Peter was standing, "Sure thing. I guess I just need a minute."

She wanted everyone to stop worrying about her and place the blame where it was due.

On her... not Peter.

During the entire exchange, Donavon kept his hand on her arm. It was comforting and not restraining in anyway. His voice was calm and soothing as he asked, "What can you tell us about what just happened?"

The small knot of fear that had been dissolving in her stomach lurched as she involuntarily started to recall the attack outside. Her pulse picked up speed as she remembered.

They were in danger.

They were all in danger because of her.

Seeing the panic in her eyes, Donavon added, "You don't have to think about it now if it's too much. Take your time."

Peter's hand slipped from her hair to her shoulder and squeezed reassuringly.

Rachel felt like she was surrounded by two people who deeply cared about her. She didn't know what she had done to deserve it in such a short period of time. In fact, if anything she felt like she should have earned the exact opposite reaction from Peter and Donavon. She needed to tell them what was going on, and she needed to get away from them as quickly as possible, before she hurt them or their friendship anymore.

Clearing her throat, and trying to put on a brave face, Rachel said, "It's okay. You need to know." Her mind recoiled at the memories, but she forced herself to speak. "I was on the porch with Peter, watching you and Beth work. Suddenly the Voice was there, and it told me that if I told Peter what was going on that it would hurt him." Panic crept back into her eyes and she glanced at Peter. She could feel tears welling up, so she turned her face to stare at the ceiling and blink the tears back into her eyes before they could betray her and spill down her cheeks. Despite her efforts, Rachel heard Peter's intake of breath at her words and expression.

Donavon gently pushed, "And then what?"

"And then, the Voice said it wanted me and would hurt all of you if I denied it." Her voice started to rise in pitch as she continued. "It said it would make *me* hurt you." Her voice cracked on the words, and the hot tears she had been fighting back started to spill down her cheeks anyway. She could feel the panic taking over again as her words came out faster and faster. "It said you weren't safe. You're not safe from me. It will make me hurt you. I can feel it!" Her hands were shaking and she brought them up to hide her face.

Donavon uncoiled from his crouch next to her and slipped onto the couch to cradle her in his arms. Gently rocking her back and forth, he cooed, "It's okay. Shh… It's okay. It can't hurt us. It lies. Shh… You'd never hurt us."

After a moment, Rachel finally regained her composure and Amy handed her a box of tissues. She smiled gratefully, and took several to wipe her hands and face. She took a few deep steadying breaths and looked back at the ceiling for strength.

Donavon kept her cradled in his side as Peter moved to stand in front of her. He squatted down and put his hands on her knees.

Peter's expression was trusting as he said, "We have protection, Rachel. Our rings protect us from the Evil." She looked down at Peter's hand on her knee and saw the beautiful sapphire ring he wore. The gems sparkled in the light, and she wanted to believe what Peter said was true. He smiled at her, "It can't hurt us."

Rachel trembled. They might be safe from the Evil itself. But could it protect them from her? She could, at that very moment, reach out and claw Peter's face. He wouldn't expect it. He wouldn't have time to stop her. Is this the sort of thing that the Evil saw her capable of doing?

That, and so much worse.

How could Rachel voice something so terrible about herself? Everyone would probably just laugh at her and tell her she was being ridiculous. Maybe it was better to just leave them all without explaining why. If they wouldn't understand, then she might as well save her breath.

Amy's cell phone started to chime, "Hello?... Ah, okay. Just a second." She offered her phone to Donavon.

Donavon reluctantly released his hold on Rachel to stand up and move into the hall to take the call. At Peter's questioning stare, Amy added, "It's Robert."

All Rachel could make out from the one-sided conversation in the hallway was a series of agreements from Donavon's end. Amy had followed Donavon into the hall, leaving Rachel and Peter semi-alone.

Rachel jumped at her chance to talk to Peter without an audience.

Placing her hands over his on her knees, she said, "I'm sorry I couldn't tell you what was going on out there. Please don't feel guilty that you didn't know." Sensing that Donavon was wrapping things up on the phone, she quickly added, "Don't fight with Donavon. You all mean too much to me. I don't like to see you hurting."

Peter seemed pleased with her words. He lowered his voice and smiled, "Donavon can be a little... presumptuous at times. He can assume he knows more about what's going on than anyone else. But don't worry. It will all be okay."

Rachel was glad that Peter didn't seem to be feeling too put out by Donavon's accusations. She knew Peter had been trying to do everything he could to help her outside. She was the one who had resisted help.

Rachel heard the beep the phone made as the called was disconnected. Donavon strode back into the room looking determined and powerful—almost exactly like Peter had just described—like he had a plan. Rachel's heart skipped a few beats at the sight. It was hard to believe that he could be in any kind of danger. He looked so confident and his ambiance was alluring.

Leaving him with Beth was going to be one of the hardest things she would ever have to do.

She swallowed back the lump in her throat.

"Okay, it's settled then." Donavon came to stand near Rachel.

Peter stood up to move slightly out of the way. He smiled and winked at Rachel, as if they were sharing a secret. Donavon didn't seem to notice as he stated, "Robert is going to have a Life Box ready for you by tonight."

Rachel was stunned. "How is that possible?" She had been told it would take weeks for Robert to complete her box.

Just then, Beth entered the room with Blake and Nancy. Blake looked at Rachel, and seeing that she was alive and well, plopped down on the loveseat and asked, "So, what did I miss?"

Beth looked apologetically at Donavon. She whispered, "I found them as quick as I could." Blushing, she looked down.

Donavon reached out and placed a hand on her shoulder, "You did great, Beth. You are just in time. This involves you, too." Donavon lowered his hand and looked back at Rachel. "Robert and I both can see that there is little time to help you, so we need to act quickly. It's never been done before, but Robert is going to try to take the box he was creating for Beth and turn it into yours."

Beth's voice gasped, "Oh."

Rachel could see the hurt and fear in Beth's eyes. They were going to take away the box that was supposed to protect Beth and give it to Rachel instead. Now Rachel was putting Beth in more danger as well. It would take Robert weeks to have another box ready for Beth.

Blake was the first to state the obvious, "But isn't that bad news for Beth?"

Donavon matter-of-factly stated, "She doesn't seem to be in any real danger at the moment. She hasn't had a single attack yet, and she doesn't even seem to be displaying symptoms of headaches. Robert and I both feel confident that he can create another box for Beth in plenty of time."

Not cowed by Donavon's certainty, Blake continued, "Not to play the devil's advocate here, or anything, but what if you are wrong and there isn't enough time?"

Donavon turned to Beth, "If you feel you are in too much danger, we can proceed with your Cleansing first. It's your choice, of course."

Rachel heard Peter scoff. Granted, she didn't know Peter and Donavon's relationship that well, but she was still surprised by Peter's harsh attitude today.

Beth meekly looked at Rachel and then Donavon. "It's all right. You can use it. I trust you," was her simple reply.

Rachel didn't think she could stand any more guilt. She suddenly burst out, "No, it's *not* all right. I can't let you be in more danger just to save my own skin! It's not right. It's not fair."

Amy tried to comfort Rachel, too, "It's okay, Rach! Donavon would never suggest anything that would hurt anyone. If Robert says he can do it all before Beth is in danger, then I believe him. He is amazing at what he does, after all."

Nancy spoke up, "I am not usually in favor of anything rash, but I have to agree with Amy. Robert knows his limits. If he says he can build a box for both of you in time, then I bet my money on Robert."

Rachel shook her head. If anything happened to Beth before Robert finished her Life Box, she would carry the burden on her shoulders for the rest of her life.

Her mind was screaming at her, "I can't believe this! I should just run away right now."

But Rachel couldn't run away. If there was even the slightest hope that they could save her, then she had to see this through. Her survival instincts had started to kick in.

If they could cleanse the Evil from her, then she wouldn't be a danger to anyone anymore. She would be safe with her new family.

She would be home and everyone would be safe from her— safe *with* her.

It would also mean that she wouldn't have to part with Donavon.

That was a bittersweet victory. She couldn't explain her sudden attraction to him. Maybe it was like they said—love at first sight did exist. But if she stayed with her new friends, she might have to stand by and watch Beth take him from her.

Was gaining an entire family worth it? Would it be harder to lose him from afar if she left, or be up close and personal while he slipped through her fingers?

With anguish, she thought, "He was never mine to begin with. This makes no sense. And yet, why do I feel like my heart is being ripped in two?"

All her life, Rachel had made fun of the flighty and flirty girls who only dreamed of the day they would fall in love. Rachel felt like she had a pretty good head on her shoulders, and never thought that she would be swept away by silly emotions.

Yet, here she was—mourning the loss of a love that she had not even experienced.

She felt silly and small.

But her choice was simple. She would take the risk and stay. She would see if these incredible new friends could save her life. She would stay and see if the man from her dreams could ever really be hers.

Or she would take them all down as the Evil claimed her soul.

CHAPTER 16: DONAVON

Robert crafted Life Boxes and talismans in a workshop of sorts hidden among the trees several miles up the mountainside. There was a solid tree-line at the back of the property that kept a private rocky road obscured from view. At the start of the road—which was no more than two dirt ruts with grass growing in the middle—was a gate with a "private property" sign hanging on the front. Rachel looked towards the trees and wondered how long it would take to get up there. Almost immediately, the path twisted out of view and there was no way to see anything that lay much farther ahead than a few feet.

Donavon had told her that they needed to go immediately so she could help Robert complete his work. They crossed the backyard together, headed towards a large garage that was also hidden from view just before the gate. Parked inside were several gleaming vehicles—cars, SUVs, Hummers and motorcycles. And while Rachel wasn't up on her knowledge of cars, but she was willing to bet that these cars were worth more money than she had seen in her entire lifetime.

Donavon walked her over to a black sport utility vehicle. She was pretty sure the symbol on the front grill was for a Mercedes Benz. The tailgate said GL 550, but that didn't mean much to her. However, she could appreciate that it was a beautiful machine. The onyx exterior was so polished she could perfectly see the entire garage reflected in its glossy depths. Donavon stood, holding the door open for her, and she could see the lush leather interior. She raised an eyebrow at him and inquired, "Is this your car?"

Donavon smiled, "One of them." His eyes had a mischievous glint to them—like a child in a candy store. "We share all of them, but we each have our favorites." He gestured towards the dark green

Hummer in the corner. "That's Blake's favorite. And that yellow Mini Cooper convertible over there is Amy's baby."

Rachel shook her head in awe. If she did end up living with these people, it was going to be quite the adjustment from her microwave burrito college days. She quietly slipped into the passenger seat and buckled her seatbelt. She deeply inhaled the mixed smell of new car and leather—a luxurious combination.

Rachel sat perfectly straight in her seat, tense and aware of the fact that this would be the first time that she and Donavon would be alone together. Her tongue suddenly felt thick and heavy as she tried to think of what she could possibly say. Sweat broke out over her palms, which she quickly wiped off on her jeans.

She didn't want to make a fool of herself by saying things she would regret later. There was no way Donavon knew of her feelings for him—sudden and irrational as they were. She needed to keep it light and casual.

Rachel took a deep breath and waited for Donavon to come around the side of the car and get in the driver's seat. Keenly aware of the amount of opulence surrounding her, Rachel couldn't help but take stock in her own appearance compared to Donavon's. She hadn't paid that much attention to his wardrobe before, but now she could tell that his jeans looked expensive; tailored to fit him exactly. His untucked shirt was a stylish button-down with the top few buttons left open. The sleeves were rolled up, revealing strong forearms. One wrist held an expensive looking watch, and the other had a leather bracelet with braided strands woven together. Everything was tasteful and sophisticated, yet with undeniable sexy undertones. Rachel felt a little out of place and self-conscious wearing her big-box-store specials.

The tint of the windows made it feel like evening inside the car, but Rachel knew it was still the middle of the afternoon. Donavon started the engine and pulled out of the garage. The gentle pulsing of the ventilation system flooded the air with the scent of Donavon's skin. He smelled incredible—like aftershave and fresh soap.

As they drove, Rachel marveled at the gorgeous scenery. Being autumn, the trees were wonderful shades of red, yellow, orange and brown. Like a painting. For being no more than two dirt tire paths in the ground, the road was remarkably smooth to drive, with no holes or pits.

Turning back to Donavon, Rachel decided to start the conversation with a safe topic: "So, how am I supposed to help Robert with my box?"

Donavon looked relaxed, more so than Rachel had ever seen him, with one hand on the wheel and the other arm draped along the open window door frame. His face was open and inviting now that the tension and worry had left his features. When he didn't appear to have the weight of the world on his shoulders, she thought he could pass for an Armani model.

He was watching the road as he replied, "You won't really have to do anything at all. Robert's the one who has to do all the work. He just needs to be around you and get a feel for your aura." Rachel felt a little relieved. If all she had to do was stand there, it was going to be hard to mess that up. She desperately didn't want to do anything to embarrass herself in front of Donavon.

He continued, "Only Robert really knows how his Gift works. It's similar with all of us, I suppose. No one can describe exactly what it's like to do what each of us can. It's sort of a private, personal experience. That is why it's so hard for some people to detect their abilities accurately for the first time. It can also make it difficult for them to figure out how to control their talent, or even use it at all, for that matter."

"Like Beth..." The words were out of Rachel's mouth before she could stop them. She wasn't really ready to bring up Beth yet. Just saying her name was like inviting her into the car with them—an invisible Beth, making sure that Rachel wasn't putting the moves on her man.

Donavon sighed. It was hard to tell if it was from tenderness or frustration. Selfishly, Rachel would hope the latter. "Yes, like Beth. She is getting much closer to figuring out her Gift. Just today she was able to sense her power and control it a little bit. That's a big step for her." Donavon looked over at Rachel as he continued. "Sometimes it's hard for me to be patient." He held her gaze for just a moment and then, looking away, he added, "As her teacher, it can be frustrating when I suspect that I am not helping her as much or as quickly as someone else could."

Rachel couldn't imagine that Donavon was not giving one hundred percent to help Beth. He seemed like an all-or-nothing kind of guy. During his practice session with Beth earlier, he had acted both engaged and focused on his work.

Thinking about earlier in the day, Rachel also remembered being able to feel Beth discovering her power. Rachel couldn't tell what exactly Beth had been trying to do, but she could tell that she was doing something, and getting much stronger at it all the time.

"Do you have any guess as to what her Gift might be?"

Donavon's face clouded as he responded. He obviously did not like his answer and Rachel could see a bit of tension return to his jaw. "I'm not sure. She isn't sure of it herself at this point, and there are so many things she could be slightly manipulating that we aren't even aware of." He shrugged his shoulders, "When a picture frame suddenly and unexpectedly falls from the wall, is it the result of someone using the power of their Gift, or is it just random luck that the nail gave out at that exact moment? Only the person using their power would know for sure, and sometimes not even then if they are new."

Rachel thought back to what she had seen and felt before the Voice started to attack her. "Well, when Peter and I went out on the porch I could feel the energy you were using around her." Before she could continue with her description of the events, Donavon cut her off.

"Wait a minute. You could feel what I was doing?" Donavon seemed as surprised by this information as Peter had.

Rachel was hesitant to answer. She never knew if her answer was going to be good news or bad news. Lately, there had been so much bad news that she had become a little gun shy. However, she trusted Donavon, and she knew that he might have the most power of anyone to help her.

Rachel admitted, "Yes. I could feel the change in the air. When I told Peter, he said that maybe I was going to turn out to be a Locator like him."

Donavon's face was unreadable but serious. "Interesting. What else did you notice?"

Rachel took a deep breath, unable to shake her feeling of uncertainty. "Well, eventually I could feel that Beth was able to harness her power as well, only it wasn't nearly as powerful as yours." She knew he was waiting for more of an answer than that, but Rachel couldn't help but stall by asking, "I know that you can manipulate a person's sense of touch. What were you doing to her anyway?"

Donavon seemed a little surprised by her question, or maybe by the shift in conversation. "Well, I wasn't doing anything *to* her, exactly. I was more focusing my energy around her, hoping that she could find a way to feel it. If I had been using my power directly on her, then she would have immediately been able to feel whatever change I was trying to create—tingling, warmth, pressure—that sort of thing. I can stimulate those kinds of feelings in anyone, not just the Gifted, so that would have been useless to her. What I was trying to do was to help her sense my power indirectly, and in effect learn how to sense her own.

"If she hadn't been able to feel anything, I might have tried using a combination of both sending my energy around her and also using it on her in some way. That sort of thing has helped her in the past."

Rachel wasn't very happy trying to picture Donavon and Beth alone together, working, while Donavon was trying to manipulate Beth's sense of touch. It seemed reasonable to assume that if Donavon could make someone feel any sensation he wanted, that would include both pleasant and unpleasant sensations. Right now, the pleasant sensations were the ones that bothered her—the *very pleasant* ones. It made her think about his power in a completely different light—in a light that made her blush, quite frankly.

Now her palms were sweating for an entirely different reason. Shoving those thoughts from her mind, Rachel shook her head; she needed to focus.

First, Peter was shocked that she could feel him manipulating her when she woke up in their house the first time. Then, he had been surprised when she could tell he was in the kitchen before she entered the room. Now, Donavon was surprised that she could sense when he was using his power, even though he was trying to get Beth to do that exact same thing. Why was it so shocking that *she* could do it? Was there something inherently wrong with her?

She voiced her concerns, "For me, isn't it a good thing that I can sense these things already?"

Donavon flashed his radiant smile and Rachel's heart skipped a beat. "Oh, it's a very good thing."

Relief flooded her as she thought, "At least I'm not damaged goods or anything."

He continued, "It's just astonishing in a number of ways. First of all, it's remarkable that you can so quickly and easily sense when someone is using their Gift around you."

It obviously was not so easy for Beth.

"Also, it's unexpected that you can sense when someone is using their Gift on *someone else*." Donavon seemed greatly amused, like he had that first time when Peter had been manipulating her in the living room. The mirth in his voice was almost tangible.

After a moment, seeing that Rachel was still confused, he went on in a slightly more subdued fashion, "When the Gifted use their power on a normal person, typically that person is completely unaware of what is going on. They don't have the higher awareness that we have to sense the change around them. Although, when the Gifted use their power on another Gifted, that person can typically tell that something is happening. It can be difficult though. Not everyone can detect the use of energy around them as easily as others.

"That is what I was trying to do with Beth. I was directing my energy towards her—around her—to see if she could feel it and recognize it.

"But, coming back to you, while it's easy for another Gifted to sense when someone is using their power directly on them, it's much harder to sense when the flows of energy are being used on someone or something else. That is, unless, of course, you are in extremely close proximity to what is happening." He turned to peer at Rachel's face. "For you to be able to feel those flows from halfway across the expanse of our back yard... that is extraordinary. Even a Locator couldn't accurately tell what was going on from that distance, although they would be able to see it if they were looking with their Locator eyes."

Donavon still looked pleased with this news. Staring questioningly at his face, Rachel asked, "And that's... a... good thing?"

He laughed softly to himself. The resonant tones of his voice filled the car. "In my opinion, yes. I surprised a number of people with my abilities in the beginning, too." He turned again to look at Rachel. She noticed for the first time that his eyes were a deep brown color, almost like richly polished wood. She could feel them pulling her in. His voice was low and sincere as he added, "Finding you is like finding a kindred spirit."

Quickly looking away, her breath caught in her throat and she felt a thrill of excitement. She wanted so badly for there to be a deeper meaning to his words, but she would not allow herself to get carried away. Stubbornly, she reminded herself, "He belongs to someone else."

Or does he?

Looking back to the road, he added, "Like I said yesterday, we need to be careful not to underestimate you."

As they continued along the road, his words echoed in her mind; kindred spirits.

Rachel couldn't help but be excited by this. Maybe Beth wasn't the only one with a connection to Donavon after all. She could hardly wipe the smile off her face as he spoke again. "It's also remarkable that you can sense people with a Gift even if they aren't using it at the moment, like you did when you sensed Peter in the kitchen. He might be right. That sounds exactly like what a Locator can do. But there are two things I can't understand."

Rachel squirmed in her seat, afraid that there might be some unpleasant news coming. She whispered, "There are a lot of things I don't understand."

Donavon smiled, yet gave Rachel a sympathetic look. He whispered back, "It's okay. You're going to be all right now." He reached over and took Rachel's hand. The unexpectedness of it stunned her, and her stomach burst into butterflies. An intensity entered his eyes as he added, "I'll do everything I can to make sure you are safe. I promise."

Rachel could tell that Donavon wasn't using his power on her, but the way her skin reacted to his touch was electrifying. Again, it was far too easy to imagine what he could do to her if he tried. The thought made a blush creep up her neck again, which she was sure he noticed.

Donavon had to place his hand back on the steering wheel to make a sharp turn. Like before, Rachel was extremely aware of the chill left from the absence of his touch. Suddenly remembering that he had left his last thought unfinished, she prompted, "So what don't you understand about me?" Her voice was husky in a way that betrayed her thoughts.

As if he had been thinking about something else entirely, Donavon cleared his throat, "Ah, yes. Well, many things. But for starters, the Gift of being a Locator is usually something passed down in a family line. Parents typically watch for the signs in their children and help them through their Trial. That doesn't seem to be the case with you."

Rachel was pretty sure that neither of her parents belonged to this surreal world of the Gifted. She could hardly believe it herself. If they had known what she was going to go through, they hadn't let on. Her parents both seemed so ordinary.

"Are there ever Locators that don't get their powers from their heritage?"

Donavon nodded, "Yes, but it is very rare." Flashing his heart-melting smile again, he added, "But you seem to be full of surprises."

Rachel smiled back.

He continued, "Also, Locators tend to be drawn to the Gifted. It would have made more sense for you to have been drawn to us long before now. You might not have known what you were doing, but somehow you should have ended up on our doorstep weeks ago. It just doesn't seem to fit."

What he said made sense. Rachel hadn't felt drawn or compelled to go anywhere in particular or do anything that would have led her to the new family in those first few weeks of school. Mostly she just felt like Grayson was where she was meant to be. She almost wished she had found them like a Locator would have. If she had been mysteriously drawn to these people sooner, she might have found Donavon before Beth had shown up. It was hard to swallow that Beth had only beat her to Donavon by two weeks.

But, if he and Beth did share a mystical link to each other, would it have made any difference if she'd gotten there sooner?

Rachel just needed to find out how much they each cared for one another. From what little Rachel had seen, it was obvious that Beth wanted to please Donavon more than anything. She was sure that Beth was trying her hardest to do exactly what Donavon wanted her to do.

Donavon was harder to read. He seemed fond of Beth, but she hadn't witnessed anything that would suggest they were a serious couple—no hand holding, or secret stolen kisses. Maybe it wasn't too late.

Thinking so much about Beth made Rachel feel like the invisible Beth was back in the car with them, listening to Rachel's every word.

Donavon changed the subject back to the original topic. "Anyway, you were telling me about what you noticed this afternoon."

It was like Rachel's mind just didn't want to think about the horrible attack. She had completely forgotten that she was supposed to be answering Donavon's questions, instead of interrogating him herself.

Rachel backpedaled her thoughts, "Well, like I said, I felt Beth using her power, but it wasn't nearly as strong as yours. She was finding it though and focusing it more all the time. Even when you came to my rescue, she followed and was trying to do something with her energy as well."

Donavon frowned, "That was dangerous of her. If she isn't even sure what she is doing, she could have hurt someone."

Rachel replied, "I couldn't tell that anything she did was hurting me. I know the storm was raging and the ground started to shake, like an earthquake." Remembering the weather also reminded her of Peter's comment. "Right before the Voice started talking to me Peter said something about maybe Beth was controlling the weather. Do you think she could have been making it rain?"

Donavon continued to frown as he thought. "I have heard of others who can manipulate the weather, or at least part of it. To cause a storm of that magnitude would require a great deal of energy— enough that I should have been able to sense it in her, especially since I was sitting right next to her."

Rachel was curious. "Are *you* strong enough to do something like that?"

He paused, as if giving the question serious thought. "Possibly… I'm not sure I can make a fair comparison because my Gift is different from controlling the weather. But I think I would definitely have a better chance at it than some."

When Rachel felt Beth using her Gift, it hadn't felt nearly as powerful as Donavon's. Using that as a gauge, it seemed unlikely that Beth could create the savage storms that had been thrashing the area in the last two days.

He added, "She could have been contributing to part of it, but I couldn't say which part. It will be interesting to watch her now and see if Peter is right."

His comment about being able to feel Beth's power because he was sitting right next to her got Rachel thinking. She was a little afraid to ask, because it might sound silly or presumptuous, but she asked anyway, "Well, I'm right here. Can you tell at all how powerful I will be?"

Donavon didn't seem to be bothered by her question at all. "Well, I'm not like you. I can't feel someone's power when they aren't using it." He went on, "But earlier today when you were in danger," his face seemed to darken at the memory, "I could feel a great deal of energy once I was right next to you. How much of that was you and how much of that was the Evil, again, is hard to say."

Rachel felt a little foolish for having asked. "I see…" she said quietly. Another thought occurred to her, "Could the Evil have been causing the storms or the ground to shake?"

Taking another moment to think, Donavon seemed intrigued by the idea. "I have only heard of the Evil talking to and manipulating people—not physical things. Some have *suggested* that it could control objects around them, usually with the intent to harm someone—sort of like a poltergeist. Upon further study, though, it usually becomes apparent that the object being used is actually being controlled by the Gifted under the influence of the Evil. Things like that are speculative, though, because most often those involved in such an advanced attack don't survive, leaving others to piece together the clues later." This new grisly topic left the atmosphere in the car feeling cold and uncomfortable.

Donavon turned the car off the dirt road they had been following. It almost appeared like he randomly turned into the trees, but once they got going in the new direction Rachel could see the well-concealed path that he was taking to another distant part of the mountain. It required either a steady vehicle like Donavon's SUV, or something small and nimble like a motorcycle. Other people would never find it if they didn't know what to look for. Donavon changed the subject. "It's not safe to try it right now, but in a protected place at another time, do you think you could focus your power like you felt Beth and I doing today?"

The power within her felt like such an intangible thing to find. Sure, she could feel it when there was power being used around her—like static electricity in the air. But to be able to create that static on her own, out of thin air… Rachel wasn't sure what would happen if she tried.

Cold fear started to seep into her mind as she remembered that the Evil had suggested her power could be used as a horrible weapon to hurt those around her, just like Donavon had described. The words of the Voice rang in her head, "*I can make* you *hurt him for me. Wouldn't that be nice?*"

Her voice was small as she answered, "I don't know." To herself, she thought, "I think I'm too scared to even try."

Rachel sighed and sat back, "What was all of this like for you?"

She could see that it wasn't easy for Donavon to talk about his past—his Trial. He took several moments before he answered.

When he did, his voice was quiet and somber. "It was difficult... and unusually fast. One day I was just a normal guy, going to college and trying to find my place in the world. The next day I was in incredible danger."

That sounded very familiar.

Some of the color had drained from his face. "It didn't start for me by being found by a Locator, or even simply having headaches. It started with the Voice in my head. My first attack paralyzed me and knocked me to the ground. I was fortunate to have had three very powerful Gifted around me. They helped me find myself again, instead of being completely pulled under by the Evil."

Rachel could see Donavon's knuckles turning white as he gripped the steering wheel. He continued, "It took all three of them pouring all of their energy into me to dispel the Evil enough that I could claw my way back. At first, I couldn't even sense their power and the good in it. When the energy finally broke through, it was the most beautiful feeling. I felt like a prisoner who had been locked away in a room with no windows finally getting to see the sun again."

He shut his mouth into a small thin line and Rachel could tell this was really hard for Donavon to talk about. It seemed too personal for her to pry into further. It wasn't like he knew her very well, after all.

"Ok, we're here." He said suddenly, and Rachel could see, just ahead of them on the road, a building camouflaged in the trees.

Rachel steeled herself. It was time to see her Life Box and she hoped against hope that it would live up to its name and save her life.

CHAPTER 17: LIFE BOXES

As Rachel stepped out of the car, she scanned her surroundings. It would be easy to miss this small and unimpressive building if someone didn't know what they were looking for. The forest had literally taken over every surface of what looked like an abandoned one-room cabin, moss growing on the outer walls and plants forcing their way between the boards of the porch.

Donavon came around to her side of the car and walked with her up to the partially open front door. It was falling off its hinges, and the two of them more or less stepped around it without touching it.

The room they entered was in stark contrast to the luxury that Rachel had just been enjoying in Donavon's SUV. All or most of the windows were broken, with shards of glass scattered around. The floor was dirty and covered with litter from the forest. There was an old fireplace in the corner, but the stones that made up the hearth were falling off. A broken chair was leaning awkwardly in another corner. One of its legs had been broken off and was sitting on the floor next to it. There didn't appear to be any plumbing or electricity.

Looking up at the ceiling, the beams were exposed and there were holes in the roof. Rachel could see the leaves on the trees swaying and the sun peeking through. Apart from a small white motorized scooter parked in the corner, nowhere did Rachel see any signs of Robert, Life Boxes, or another living soul. It was hardly even a shelter. If some lost person stumbled upon this wreck, Rachel was sure they would hesitate to even enter, let alone stay the night.

Maybe that's the point.

Concentrating, Rachel tried to see if she could find Robert's aura. Unless something funny was going on, he should be close by— at least she assumed so. However, there was nothing she could feel.

Rachel could only sense Donavon's overwhelming presence and the empty forest.

Seeming unconcerned by his surroundings, Donavon walked right over to the middle of the room. Kneeling down on the floor, he appeared to be feeling for something. With one swift movement, he lifted a concealed trapdoor.

Rachel took a surprised breath. The floorboards looked to be long and solid, but in reality, this door had been cut out of the middle. The pieces fit together so perfectly that when the door was closed, it was impossible to tell that it even existed. Someone could walk over it, and even crawl across it on their hands and knees examining it, and never know there was a door there until it was opened.

Donavon pulled a flashlight out of his pocket and extended his hand toward Rachel. She couldn't help but get butterflies in her stomach as she reached out to accept his hand and was led down into the darkness. The stairs were also dirty and covered in spider webs and leaves. The concrete was old, chipped and crumbling away in places.

They only went down about one flight before they came to dead end. There was a cement wall directly in their path, which Donavon slide aside to reveal another door. This one looked high tech and sturdy. It appeared to be made of thick, heavy metal and had a keypad next to it. Quickly, Donavon punched in a series of numbers and Rachel heard the soft click as the door lock released. Still holding hands, they entered a passageway. The door softly closed behind them, and Rachel could hear a slight sucking of air, like they were being vacuum-sealed.

Suddenly everything was very clean and industrial looking—much more like what she would expect from the Order. Donavon switched off his flashlight because there was no need for it now. There were florescent lights every few feet above their heads lining a stark hallway. The air lost its woodsy smell and instead smelled stringently climate controlled.

Several doors sat on either side of the passageway, but Donavon took her all the way to the end and stopped in front of another heavy-looking metal door. This time there was a hand plate on the wall onto which Donavon placed his hand, palm down. Rachel saw several green lasers flash across under his skin before a light above the door turned green and the digital display above the hand plate registered, "Welcome, Donavon."

Slightly under her breath, Rachel muttered, "Wow."

She thought she saw the corners of Donavon's mouth turn up in a smile as he continued to grasp her hand to lead her beyond the final door. Robert was inside waiting for them, and Rachel could suddenly feel his electric aura mixing and mingling with Donavon's. Until the door had opened, she hadn't even known that Robert was nearby. It made her wonder what kind of material those doors were made of.

This room looked more like the work area that Rachel had been expecting to see all along. There were several long tables covered with various tools and supplies—most of which she was unable to identify. Most of the room was pitch black, and where there was light, it seemed extra dim. Robert was sitting on a tall stool, bent over something small. One extremely bright work light shone down on himself and whatever it was that he was working on. The contrast from the darkness of the room compared to the extra bright work light made Robert the sole focus of attention. She could hear a radio playing in the background—classical music.

Without looking up from his work, Robert remarked, "Glad you made it. You are j-just in time."

Donavon didn't reply, so Rachel filled the silence, "In time for what?"

Robert looked up at her and pushed some of his floppy brown hair out of his face. He smiled in a boyish way, and Rachel noticed again how much younger he seemed than the rest of the Order. He was incredibly thin. He held his hand out to her, and she could see how delicate his wrists were and how long his fingers seemed. Held between those fingers was a ring.

Rachel gasped.

It was beautiful. The band was silver in color, but Robert explained that it was actually white gold. It was thin and elegant. Overlaid on the top of the band was a braided and curving s-shaped piece that was entirely made up of alternating white and blue diamonds. Rachel had never heard of blue diamonds before, but apparently diamonds came in all sorts of colors. She had never seen anything like it.

"Try it on." Robert's eyes looked excited and eager. "I had to guess on the size, but…" giving Donavon a knowing look he continued, "I'm p-pretty good at this sort of thing."

Rachel was a little hesitant to take the ring. First of all, it would require her to let go of Donavon's hand. It was silly, but she enjoyed having the connection with him. But more than that, Rachel had never owned a single piece of expensive jewelry in her life, and the idea of holding that ring and possibly hurting or losing it was enough to make her uneasy.

However, knowing that this is what she had come for, Rachel unclasped Donavon's hand and took the ring from Robert. She slipped it on to her righthand ring finger. It fit perfectly. The singular bright overhead light in the room made the diamonds sparkle and twinkle as if they were alive. The facets threw rainbows of glittering light around the skin of her finger where the ring sat.

It felt like it was meant to be there—on her hand.

Now that it was on, she wasn't sure she wanted to take it off. Just like the women in jewelry commercials, Rachel held her hand up to the light, turning her wrist from side to side to inspect the work of art adorning her finger.

"Do you like it?" Robert's voice was strangely timid and yet confident at the same time.

Rachel smiled and her voice was breathy, "Oh yes. Very much." She couldn't have come up with a more perfect ring for herself if she had tried.

Suddenly, an unpleasant thought occurred to her. "Was this supposed to be for Beth, too?" Rachel didn't like the idea that this ring had been constructed originally for someone else. She had already intruded so much on Beth's life—taking her Life Box and in essence putting her life in danger. It tinged some of her happiness to think that this ring was another small part of that.

Robert's answer was a relief. "Oh no. I have a separate piece in mind for her. I had started it, but it isn't f-finished yet because I have been working on your ring instead." Robert had turned away and was tinkering with some things on the workbench—tidying up, she supposed. He seemed more comfortable talking to Rachel when he wasn't looking directly at her. "I should have Beth's d-done in another day or so." Turning to Donavon, he added, "Her Life Box is going to take at least a week or more to recreate."

Donavon looked grim, but still determined. "I think we have plenty of time. She still wasn't displaying any obvious symptoms today."

Robert nodded, "That's good."

During their exchange, Rachel had been glancing around the room. It was amazing to her that this place existed in the middle of nowhere. In her wildest dreams, looking around at the serene forest, she never would have guessed that this high-tech facility was below the surface.

She asked, "So, where did this place come from?"

Talking was obviously not Robert's strong suit, and he appeared relieved when Donavon decided to answer her question. "The cabin was owned by a member of an Order a long time ago. They donated it as a cover so we could build this facility in secret. It took a lot of work to carve this out of the mountain without drawing attention to ourselves."

Rachel asked, "What kind of cover story did they tell the people who worked on the construction?"

Donavon continued, "Oh, they were all Gifted. There was no need to come up with a story. People who are good at metal, rock, electricity, and anything else needed to build a structure came together to help create this and many of the other buildings that the Gifted use all over the world." He added, "There aren't a lot of us out there when you compare numbers to the rest of mankind, but there are enough to get the job done. And it doesn't take as long as you might expect when you have the right people with the right Gifts."

Robert walked over to the far wall in the room. There appeared be to a giant safe or vault embedded there. Next to it was another hand scanner. Robert scanned his palm and then opened the door. Inside, Rachel could just make out an inner chamber large enough for Robert to walk inside of. His small frame almost completely blocked Rachel's view. However, she did make out shelves lining the walls in the vault.

Robert returned carrying a small box. It was about a foot wide and less than a foot deep and high, respectively. Rachel thought it looked a lot like the shape and size of a jewelry box that she used to play with as a child, only this box didn't seem to have a lid or hinge on it.

It was also not made of wood. It appeared to be made entirely of cut crystal. Inlaid in the top of the box was a pattern that looked reminiscent of Rachel's ring. There was a braided piece of white gold spanning across the middle of the length of the top. Curving in that delicate s-shape around the braid were more white and blue diamonds. It was just like her ring, only much larger.

Rachel's trepidation at the wealth currently wrapped around her finger seemed silly as she gazed at the jewels embedded in the top.

"This is your box." Robert said simply, as he placed it in front of Rachel on the table. The bright work-light had a similar effect on the crystal, making all the colors of the rainbow dance and gleam like the diamonds in her ring.

The Order seemed to have no limit when it came to money, jewels and the finer things in life. She couldn't help but comment, "How can you afford all of this?"

Robert met her gaze, "When your talent is with rocks and minerals, it's not too hard to come by whatever you need for a Life Box." He added, "It is important enough w-work that many are happy to help. I guess you could say that we have suppliers."

Rachel shook her head, stunned by what she was looking at. The box seemed alive and glowing. She could see the patterns of light it was making on Donavon and Robert's faces. It reminded her of being in a large aquarium, the way the light from the fish displays will dance and play around the people standing in the dark observing area.

The amount of money invested in the box was stunning to Rachel. She hadn't grown up poor by any means, but money just seemed to be flowing around the Order. She couldn't resist asking, "But does everything have to be covered in diamonds? Wouldn't something like… colored glass look just as nice?"

Robert crinkled his face up in disgust. "Colored glass!" Rachel could see that the artist in him was completely turned off by the idea.

Rachel didn't think it was possible for Robert to show any strong emotion—other than shyness—so his outburst surprised her. He continued, "Everything has to be natural, and just right. You can't possibly use synthetic colored glass to make a Life Box. People's lives are at stake! You have to have the purest elements with the highest energy capacity to house the Evil. Glass isn't strong enough." Robert impatiently brushed his hair off his forehead again. He wasn't really talking to Rachel anymore as he said, "No, no, no. Impossible." As an afterthought, he added, "And so ugly!"

It dawned on her that Robert hadn't stuttered at all during his little rant just now. Apparently being completely focused on his passion in life helped Robert forget that he was talking to a woman. His nerves and shyness seemed to melt away as he began to tell Rachel about his Gift and how Life Boxes work.

"The Evil is made of dark energy. You see, that energy has to be able to flow freely and be channeled from the talisman into the Life Box." Robert continued instructing as his hands began to work on some other project on the table. He didn't even appear to need to concentrate very hard on what he was working on, his hands moving of their own accord. "The box has to be strong, and full of energy. It has to last a lifetime and contain the Evil forever. The longer a person lives, or the stronger their Gift, the more of the dark energy the box will have to contain."

Rachel wasn't bothered by Robert's lecturing tone at all. She was actually pleased that he was opening up. She prompted, "So, do you have a bunch of boxes in that vault just waiting to be used?"

Again, Robert looked taken aback by such a suggestion, "Of course not. What good would that do? People with my Gift have to be around the person we are making the box for. It's as if we have to…" he hesitated over the choice of word, "…sample your aura to be able to use our Gift in the right way to create the box.

"After we have a sense of your aura with your unique flavor, we can then use our energy in a way that will create the perfect box for you." Noting the music in the room, he continued, "It's almost like being a composer, but *you* have to supply the melody line for us before we can fill in all the harmony parts to create a symphony.

Everyone's melody is personal and distinctive, unlike any other. Until those with the Life Box Gift have met someone and felt their aura, we can't make a box for them. In fact, we can't even start a box until we meet someone new who needs it."

"Oh, really?" Rachel smiled at Donavon, pleased that Robert was still talking so openly and freely with her. Donavon eyes twinkled as he watched Robert work.

"Yes. I am sure you can see the benefit of being able to make a box quicker than the usual two weeks or more that it can sometimes take. In your case, for example, since there is not much time it would be helpful to already have some of the work done ahead of time to move the process along that much faster. But the flows of energy that we use to create the box only work while they are fresh and strong. If a box sits uncompleted for any period of time, waiting for the owner to be found by a Locator, the energy will fade away, and we would be left sitting around with a bunch of useless boxes on our hands." Wrinkling up his forehead again, he added, "What a waste that would be."

Robert suddenly looked around, as if remembering where he was. His eyes locked on Rachel's, and suddenly his cheeks and neck flushed red in a blush. "It's all v-very complicated."

Rachel found Robert's energy and enthusiasm to be charming and endearing. He was a little like the nutty professor and a little brother all wrapped up in one. She also noticed that Robert didn't seem to stutter when he spoke to Donavon—only to women.

Donavon gestured towards the pattern on the top of the box. "The pattern on the top matches the pattern of your ring, connecting the two together—sort of like identifying marks. If you are familiar enough with someone's talisman, then you can identify their Life Box when you see it."

Just like the craftsmanship of the floor in the cabin, the pieces of the Life Box fit together so perfectly that Rachel couldn't tell that the box had a lid until Robert removed it and placed it off to one side. Inside was revealed a small sphere that fit perfectly against the sides of the box. It was clear like glass, and therefore was not detectable from the outside of the clear box. Robert informed her that it was also made of crystal, but it looked like glass because it was smooth all the way around.

Robert held the sphere delicately in his hands. His voice was almost reverent as he explained, "This is the heart of the Life Box. The heart will actually be what draws the Evil from you." As if trying to find the best way to explain this, Robert reiterated, "The heart draws the Evil away, but the box contains it."

Robert indicated that Rachel should sit on the stool by the workbench. As she did so, he carefully handed her the heart. As if she needed the warning, he softly cautioned, 'D-don't drop it." He smiled shyly at her.

Donavon looked at Robert and said, "So, are we ready then?"

Robert nodded, and Rachel knew that it was time to do whatever it was that she had come to do today.

The heart was oddly heavy. Rachel was worried that her hands would start to sweat and she *might* actually drop it. The sudden tension in the air was not helping the situation either, and she had to suppress the urge to giggle as she thought, "I could literally break my own heart."

With Donavon standing on one side and Robert on the other, both men put their hands on Rachel's shoulders. Donavon's voice was low and gentle as he said, "Now, you don't have to do anything but relax. Concentrate on the sphere. Robert is going to use his Gift to link your aura with the heart. To speed up the process, I am going to lend my energy to the mix."

Rachel turned her eyes to the heart she held in her hands. Both Robert and Donavon closed their eyes and took deep breaths. Rachel could feel the air around her start to tingle, and the lights in the room dimmed and faded completely away—almost as if Robert was drawing on all the energy in the room, including the electricity in the lights.

For a moment, Rachel thought they would end up sitting in the dark, but the sphere in her hands suddenly began to glow. It was pale at first, but gradually began to increase in intensity. Rachel wasn't sure what Robert and Donavon were doing, but she could feel the intense amount of energy that was being used around her. The light emanating from the sphere glowed—brilliant and beautiful.

It was hard for her to describe exactly what she was seeing, but it was almost as if clouds began to form and swirl around inside the sphere. There were sudden small flashes of light from within the swirling cloud, almost like lightning. Rachel felt like she was holding a storm in her hands. All the hairs on her neck and arms wanted to stand on end. Then, the diamonds on her ring and the diamonds on the lid of the box started to glow in response to the heart of the Life Box. She looked up at Donavon and Robert, but they both had their eyes closed, concentrating.

All too soon, it was over. Donavon and Robert removed their hands from Rachel's shoulders, and the dim lighting in the room returned to normal. The light coming from her ring and the lid of the Life Box disappeared. However, even though the heart of the Life Box stopped glowing so fiercely, its power and radiance did not disappear completely. The storm clouds continued to churn and swirl in the sphere, but the lightning stopped flashing, and the sphere continued to give off a soft glow that seemed to pulse slightly.

This time, when Rachel searched their faces, both Donavon and Robert had their eyes open and were staring at the heart. She asked, "Why is it pulsing like that?"

Robert reached his hands out to take the sphere from her and return it to the Life Box. "It is in sync w-with your heartbeat." He returned the lid to the box, and the lid magically fused with the sides, making an unbreakable seam.

Donavon added, "It is connected to your life force now. As long as you are strong and alive, it will stay strong and alive as well." He locked eyes with Rachel, "It's beautiful."

Rachel smiled. "Thank you." He hadn't really given her a compliment personally, but the way he said it made her feel like he really had been complimenting her in some way.

She had another question, "So, will it protect me now?"

Donavon's said, "No, not yet. You are connected, but it won't be able to draw all of the Evil out of you until we perform your Cleansing."

Donavon continued, "Every time the Evil attacks you, it takes a stronger hold on you. We need to break that hold and force the Evil into your Life Box instead. Once that happens, you will be safe from any future attacks, no matter how close you get to any source of Evil. But it takes a great deal of energy to accomplish that. We need the entire Order together to have the best chance possible of dispelling the Evil."

It sounded frightening to her. To think of everyone using all of that energy to battle the Evil that was trying to take hold inside her— it made Rachel feel nervous and intimidated. Trying to reassure herself that she had made the right decision to stay, she thought, "There is no way I can fight this by myself."

Donavon motioned for Rachel to stand up; it was time to leave. Robert had safely placed her Life Box back into the vault. She was actually sad to see it go. There was something very comforting about having it near her. Rachel reached down to take the ring off her finger and leave it with Robert.

As she did so, suddenly the ring would not come off, as if her knuckle were suddenly too large for the ring to pass over, although she was sure that couldn't be. "Oh no! I think it's stuck. Maybe it was too small after all."

Robert chuckled and Donavon put a gentle restraining hand over her attempts to remove the ring.

Smiling, Donavon explained, "You can't take it off… not unless Robert wants you to." At Rachel's startled expression, he added, "It's a safety precaution. That way you can't lose the ring and no one can steal it from you."

Robert was already tinkering away at some other project on his bench, but he chimed in almost absent-mindedly, "It's the same principle as the lid on your Life Box, or the trapdoor in the cabin. It's a strange q-quirk of my Gift. That's why it's so important that you like it. You w-will be w-wearing it for a very long time."

Rachel asked, "What if someone cuts my finger off?"

Donavon grimaced, but replied smoothly, "That would work. But let's hope a thief is not that desperate."

Rachel felt satisfied. Donavon walked to the door and called to Robert over his shoulder. "Don't be too long. We are going to move a few of Rachel's things over to the house, and then we will all meet for the Cleansing tonight." He turned to Rachel, "As long as that is all right with you, of course."

Looking into his warm brown eyes, she wasn't sure if Donavon was referring to her sudden invitation to live at the house or his reference to having her Cleansing as early as tonight. Either way, it was all perfectly fine with Rachel. As long as she was going to be by his side, she felt ready to face anything.

CHAPTER 18: MOVING OUT

Peter anxiously paced his room. Donavon and Rachel had been gone for a couple of hours and he felt empty without her around. He had wanted to take Rachel to see Robert, but Donavon's cool logic had put an abrupt end to that.

His thoughts were irritated, "Donavon is stronger, so he needs to be the one to help Robert make the link to the Life Box. Blah, blah, blah…"

Peter's mind seethed with jealousy. His entire life, Peter sat by and watched as females swooned over Donavon and then would turn a sisterly kind of affection onto himself. This time was going to be different though. He had never felt this way about anyone before Rachel, and he was not going to let Donavon mess it up—not without a fight at least.

His thoughts continued to churn, "He already has Beth worked up into knots! What more does he need?"

Peter thought back to the passionate kiss he saw between Donavon and Beth. People don't just sit next to someone else and suddenly trip and find themselves in a lip lock. If Donavon wanted to play games with women, that was his business. But Peter was going to protect Rachel from him if it was the last thing he did.

He and Rachel obviously shared a connection.

Peter remembered her words right before she left to see Robert, "Don't fight with Donavon. You mean too much to me. I don't like to see you hurting."

Peter smiled at the memory.

She didn't want him to fight with Donavon, so Peter was determined to try and keep his cool when they got home. Sure, he and Donavon had fought before. They'd been friends for a long time, so a few fights were inevitable. However, this time things just seemed to annoy Peter worse than they ever had.

Donavon just seemed so cocky—so overprotective. His mind raced, "And possessive! What gives him the right? You would think that when she woke up that first time that she'd said *his* name instead of mine!"

Peter paced over to one of his sneakers and kicked it against the wall. He couldn't imagine what was taking so long. They should have been able to drive up to the cabin, link Rachel to her box, and then drive home by now. Donavon was probably trying to put the moves on her. He should never have let her go with him.

Peter tried to take a deep breath, "Calm down, man. Calm down."

But then there was the way Donavon tried to blame Peter for Rachel's most recent attack. Peter still didn't understand how he had been able to stand right next to her on the porch and not realize what was happening sooner. The guilt was eating him up inside and he already felt awful. He didn't need Donavon's righteous indignation on top of everything else. He would have given anything to help Rachel—anything!

The more Peter thought about it, the more upset he got.

He almost couldn't breathe quite right when Rachel was gone. His skin felt like it was crawling and he had so much nervous energy he thought he might burst. Amy, with her Gift, often appeared that way. She had so much energy at times that Peter was sure she was going to blow some kind of gasket.

Maybe he just needed some time alone. A good brisk walk in the crisp autumn air seemed to be a good idea. He wouldn't go too far, because they could return any minute.

Peter bounded down the stairs and grabbed his jacket off the hook near the door. He slung it over his shoulder and headed out.

The sky was overcast and the leaves almost glowed in beautiful fall colors. Peter didn't quite need his jacket yet, but it could get cold if the wind picked up. The leaves under his feet gave satisfying little crunches as he pounded his way up the street. He even succumbed to the urge to kick a big pile, sending them scattering in a shower of colors. It was soothing. It reminded him of walking through the woods behind his house back home—of going to the abandoned car... with Donavon.

Peter halted in his tracks.

The fresh air was doing him good. He felt like his brain was clearing and he could think more rationally than he had for some time.

Donavon was his best friend. They had seen each other through so many hard times that it was impossible to count. He was being too hard on the guy. That kiss with Beth was hard to explain, but maybe he wasn't being as possessive of Rachel as Peter thought.

At any rate, he hadn't seen Rachel responding to Donavon.

Peter just needed to up the charm a bit. She had already said some encouraging things to him; he just needed to be patient.

Peter sighed and turned around to head back to the house. His brain felt tired and he didn't want to think about things anymore. He just wanted to get back to Rachel and make sure everything was still okay.

He'd never been able to stay mad at Donavon for very long anyway.

As Peter entered the house, he could tell immediately that Rachel was back. Her aura was clear and obvious to him as a Locator. He could have closed his eyes and walked right up to her with no difficulty. He thought, "How did I wander around for weeks and not know she was here? How did I not feel this sooner?"

She was in the living room with everyone else in the house—only Robert was missing. As soon as Peter walked in, it was like walking into a brick wall. He was stopped dead in his tracks by two things. The first thing he noticed was how beautiful Rachel looked. His heart skipped a few beats. It was almost as if he had started to forget how incredible she was until he could see it with his own eyes again.

The second thing he noticed was the way Donavon was sitting next to her on the couch. There was far too much intimacy and familiarity in the way he was hovering over her. Donavon's arm was slung across the back of the couch. Although he wasn't technically touching her, his arm appeared to be possessively curved around Rachel's form at the same time.

Peter's lighter mood suddenly took a dark turn, "Maybe I was wrong about him. What kind of game is he up to anyway?"

All of the anger—all of the annoyance and hatred—that Peter had been trying to suppress bubbled back up to the surface.

Suddenly Peter was annoyed by Donavon's perfectly tailored clothes and dark handsome looks. It also made him feel defeated by comparison as he thought, "Who was I fooling anyway?"

Peter glanced at Beth, and he could see the pain on her face as she was watching Rachel and Donavon sit together.

He was about to storm over and tell Donavon to take his hands off Rachel, when Amy came bouncing over to Peter and exclaimed, "Robert is ready! Isn't that great? We can do the Cleansing tonight, just as soon as we move Rachel over to the house." Amy was jumping up and down just a tiny bit, "We will have another roommate!"

In spite of himself, Peter felt his heart lift. Rachel would be living there with him. It was almost enough to cool some of his fury. That was, until he remembered that Donavon lived there too.

Rachel took that moment to cross the room to Peter. She had a look of concern on her face as she approached him, "Are you okay, Peter? I don't have to move in if it bothers you." Her bright blue eyes were so clear and earnest that it pulled at Peter's heartstrings.

He shook his head and immediately tried to rearrange the features of his face. Of course, by the look on his face, she would think he didn't want her here. His rage must have been so easy to read, and she was misinterpreting it. Peter was a little pleased that she was so concerned about his feelings and approval.

He put on his most winning smile and said, "Oh, I'm fine. I was just out for a little walk thinking about things. I think it's great that you are moving in!" He put his hands on her shoulders and looked her right in the eye. "You are very welcome to live here."

Her smile in return was radiant. Peter couldn't help but note how much happier she looked now that she was out from under Donavon. He was going to have to work harder to make sure that she was getting the space that she needed.

He mentally noted, "Maybe Donavon needs a little talking to."

Peter tried to casually slip his hands off her shoulders, down her arms, and finally clasp her hands. Still smiling he added, "I will even help you pack."

Rachel looked down at their hands, and Peter took that opportunity to gauge Donavon's reaction. He was always so hard to read that Peter wasn't sure he saw much of a reaction there. But he also knew Donavon like a brother, and Peter could tell that Donavon didn't like what he saw.

Pleased, Peter thought, "Good! Deal with it, man."

Peter let go of one of her hands. Gesturing to the door with his free hand and pulling her along with him, he said, "Should we go now? I've got boxes you can borrow."

Rachel smiled and laughed, but she pulled her hand away from Peter. "Not so fast there, cowboy. We were just talking about that."

Peter didn't take the rejection hard. He had obviously walked in during the middle of things. Rachel was just being responsible and trying to get the plan straightened out.

She continued, "Beth was just saying that she thought she could use some more help from Donavon tonight before the Cleansing."

Amy was somber as she added, "Beth had her first bad headache while they were with Robert."

Peter noticed Beth did look a little shaken up and upset. "Are you okay?"

Beth nodded weakly. "I think so." She looked pleadingly at Donavon, "I would just feel better if I could get a little more help tonight."

Donavon nodded his head, "Of course. We have plenty of time before Robert is completely ready. We will work as long as we can, and then you will be coming with us, so you will never be alone."

Beth smiled slightly, and seemed to be happy with Donavon's answer. Peter was also pleased that Donavon would be busy with Beth all evening, and that would mean that he could be alone with Rachel.

The plans were set.

Before long, Peter found himself following Rachel up the staircase to her apartment. It was a completely different experience from the last time Peter had been there. There was no crushing Evil, no swirling black mist—and no Donavon.

Rachel reached in the pocket of her jacket to get her keys. Fitting them into the lock, she tried to open her broken door. It immediately came off of the busted hinge, and Peter had to reach out and grab it before it crashed to the floor. The movement put him directly against Rachel, with his arms practically wrapped around her to reach the door.

Just then the next-door neighbor opened her door and peered out into the hall.

Rachel, frantically trying to help Peter catch the door, called over her shoulder, "Hi, Tiffany."

Tiffany took one look at the broken door and Peter's apparent embrace and she snickered, "Hey, don't mind me. I like it rough, too."

Making some obscene gesture with her hand, she disappeared back into her apartment.

With the door steady, Peter moved one of his arms, allowing Rachel to move away and into the apartment. Blushing, she turned back to him and said, "There are definitely going to be some things about this place that I won't miss."

Peter smiled, "Oh come on. She seems... charming."

Rachel laughed and then motioned for everyone to come inside. It didn't take long to pack up all of her stuff. The apartment had come furnished, so all of the larger things didn't belong to Rachel anyway. Peter assured her that they would send someone in to clean things, and it would be like she had never even lived there.

In no time at all, everyone was back at the house, and Peter was bringing the last box up to Rachel's new room. It was his moment to be alone with her, and he was going to take advantage of it. As inconspicuously as he could, Peter placed the last box on the floor before he sat down on the bed. Rachel was looking tired as she glanced around the room.

"I have so pathetically little, don't I?" She wiped tired a hand across her forehead.

Peter chuckled, "Well, my packing legs are glad for the light load. Besides, it just shows that you are practical and that you don't hoard things."

Realization dawned on Rachel, and she quickly pulled her cell phone out as she explained, "I completely forgot! I promised to call Stu today." She dialed the number and placed the phone to her ear. "Hi there stranger... no, I'm still alive and kicking. I did sleep in pretty late today, though... Thanks for worrying about me." With a grimace, she added, "How's your hand?... Uh huh.. Well, that's good. Hey, look. I was just calling to let you know not to swing by the apartment if you want to see me... No, no, everything's okay." She looked up at Peter as she replied, "I think I am going to stay in the house for a while with my family." Peter and Rachel smiled conspiratorially at each other. "I feel safer here... yeah, okay... thanks... bye." With that, she hung up.

Rachel walked over to the window and touched her finger tips to the curtains. Almost as if talking to herself, she said, "Donavon and Beth are out there working, again."

Peter stood up and crossed the room to her, also looking out the window. Now that Donavon was not a hovering threat, it was easier for Peter to be less paranoid about him. He admitted to her and to himself, "Donavon is a good teacher. Beth is lucky to have him."

Something about his words made Rachel look up. Searching his face, she asked, "She seems to really trust him. She seems to like him a lot."

Peter looked out the window. He could see Donavon and Beth sitting on the grass working. Beth looked so peaceful and content out there. Peter couldn't believe that his friend would hurt her and play with her emotions. He sighed, "Yeah. She likes him a lot..." As an afterthought, he added, "...if that kiss was any indication."

Rachel looked startled. "Kiss?!"

Peter looked down, embarrassed. He mentally berated himself, "It wasn't my place to tell. Stupid, stupid!"

Oh well.

The cat was out of the bag, so to speak. Peter took a deep breath, "I walked in on Beth and Donavon kissing the other night."

He glanced up at Rachel, but she was looking back out the window, and her expression was unreadable. All she said was, "Well, she seems very nice."

Peter wasn't sure what to make of her expression. Maybe she was trying not to pry and didn't want to appear over interested in the gossip of the house. Maybe she was trying to figure out what kind of game Donavon had been playing all along. Peter would have given anything to know what had happened earlier during the car ride to see Robert.

One thing was certain though. Rachel now knew that Donavon had another side, and whatever kind of advances he had been making couldn't have been that serious in light of the situation with Beth.

Rachel didn't appear as upset about it as Peter had feared she might be. That was a good sign. It gave him courage that he had been reading her signals correctly. She obviously must feel the connection that she and Peter shared, and maybe she was as uncomfortable with Donavon's advances as Peter had interpreted.

Steeling his nerves, Peter thought, "Carpe diem. It's now or never."

Peter took another deep breath and turned to Rachel. "You know, I am really glad that you are going to be living here." He reached out with his hand, and cupping her chin he gently turned her face so their eyes could meet. She had the most beautiful eyes—blue like the sky. He reached with his other arm and took her hand. His skin tingled in anticipation as he caressed her fingers.

Rachel blinked and then softly said, "Peter…"

He loved the sound of his name wrapped in her voice. He removed his hand from her chin and pressed one finger to her lips. The connection of their skin felt electric to him and he whispered, "Shh… we have a connection you know."

Rachel's brow seemed to pull down in confusion, "Well, you are a Locator…"

Peter almost laughed out loud as he thought, "How could she possibly think that I am talking about that connection right now?"

Sometimes the best way to make a point is by showing someone.

Peter could feel the butterflies in his stomach take a wild leap as he leaned in closer to Rachel's face. His hands felt hot and he thought the expectation of the moment was going to be enough to make his heart stop.

But what a happy way to die!

Her breath was intoxicating on his face—like mint and strawberries. He leaned in and let his lips brush across hers in the gentlest of kisses. He tried not to let it turn into something too strong. He wasn't going to be like Donavon and rush ahead in wild abandon.

As his heart started to slow, Peter pulled back and opened his eyes. That's when he saw that Rachel hadn't moved a muscle.

Suddenly fear stabbed at his heart. Even with their connection, perhaps that gentlest of kisses had been too much too soon.

It was possible that Rachel wasn't as aware of their bond as Peter was. He pulled back to give her some space, and hastily added, "I'm sorry. Was that too fast?"

Rachel stuttered, "Peter... I... I'm very fond of you."

His world started to spin. He couldn't possibly be getting the "you are like a brother to me" speech from Rachel. But he had seen that look on other girl's faces, and he could guess what was coming next.

Maybe she just needed it explained to her.

Before she could continue, Peter rushed on, "Can't you feel this connection between us? It's more than just an illusion. It's more than just some Locator thing." Doubt was rushing in. He had to state the obvious and make her understand what he knew. "When you woke up yesterday, you said my name without even being told what it was. You knew it. You know me!" Sounding like a pitiful broken record, he added, "We have a connection."

As Peter watched, it was as if he could see things were clicking into place in Rachel's mind.

Relief started to swell in his heart as he thought, "She gets it now!"

Rachel went to sit on the edge of the bed. She put both hands up to her head and leaned down to put her elbows on her legs. Her fingers were tangled in her long blonde hair. Peter gently sat down next to her. He wanted desperately to reach out and put his arm around her, but instead he was determined to give her the space she seemed to need. His mind warned, "I won't be like Donavon!"

Finally, Rachel straightened up and turned to look Peter in the eye. Her voice was soft and shaky as she said, "Peter, I have a confession to make."

Okay…?

He waited for her to continue.

"I was there when you met Beth for the first time. I was behind the tree that day when you offered to walk her to class. I heard you say your name then."

Disbelief flowed through his veins.

It was impossible.

It couldn't be.

But obviously it was true.

However, this little detail didn't have to ruin everything. Peter was confident their bond ran deeper than that. He wasn't willing to give up yet.

Something else occurred to him in that moment, "That's why Beth's aura seemed to fade as I walked away with her. It's because I was leaving you behind."

Mentally, Peter considered, "Maybe my Gift hasn't been as messed up lately as I thought."

But Peter couldn't be sidetracked right now. He tried to reach out and take Rachel's hands again, "But it doesn't matter how you know my name. Can't you feel what we have together?"

Rachel avoided his grasp and quickly stood up to move away. She was obviously reluctant to cause Peter any pain. Her next words were quiet, scared, and yet determined, "I know you said that

Donavon and Beth are together. That doesn't make any difference." She turned to face Peter, and her eyes burned into his with passionate intensity as she continued, "I had a dream and I saw Donavon before I ever met him." Stubbornly, she continued, "My connection is with *him*. I know it. It has to be. I may never have him because of Beth, but I will just have to live with that." She sighed softly.

Peter felt the room tilt and everything seemed to shatter around him. He couldn't imagine what kind of expression he had on his face, but it couldn't have been good.

Rachel rushed to his side. "I am so sorry, Peter. I really wish things could be different for us. I never meant to hurt you like this."

A terrible new reality was settling around him.

He had to move.

He stood to leave the room. His legs felt numb and he wasn't even sure how he was going to make it to the door. One leaden foot after the other was slowly taking him away. Before he departed, he turned to Rachel and admitted the truth, "From the moment you opened your eyes that day, you were already gone. I was too late."

Tears welled up in Rachel's eyes and spilled down her cheeks. Biting her lip, she nodded her head. Her voice was choked-up as she replied, "I was already gone."

Peter left the room without another word. He couldn't remember how he had gotten to his room, but he suddenly found himself on his back, staring up at the ceiling from the bed.

Donavon had won before Peter even had a chance. In a dream—Donavon had won in a dream. There was nothing Peter could have done. The kiss with Beth didn't even matter. Rachel was going to choose Donavon anyway. It was like Donavon had become some unstoppable force and Peter was just foolish for getting in his path.

The anger and frustration that Peter had been trying to suppress all day began to overflow. His hands started to shake, and he had to grab fistfuls of his bedspread to keep them steady.

He had to get out. He had to get away. Before he could think about it twice, Peter rushed from the house, not even bothering to stop and grab his jacket on the way out.

***

Down the hall, Rachel was also staring at the ceiling in her room. Her mind was a dizzying mess of emotions. She couldn't believe that she had hurt Peter so badly in such a short time. She hadn't even been able to respond fast enough to spare him the memory of the kiss he had given her. Why couldn't she have at least been able to save him the memory of *that*?

All she wanted was to be accepted into this new family and to be able to protect herself from the Evil.

And she wanted Donavon…

But Donavon was with Beth, and Rachel was fooling herself if she had thought any different.

It was a horrible day for both her and Peter.

Suddenly, ice cold fear stabbed her in the heart as a voice dripping in cruelty and malice whispered in her mind.

See, my love. Didn't I tell you that I would make you hurt them for me? No one can have you but me. I love you, Sunshine.

Rachel's blood-chilling scream pierced the air.

CHAPTER 19: THE CAVE

The cave was unfamiliar. The earthy path was hard-packed and well-used, twisting down through the darkness. The air was crisp, dank, and stale. Rachel wondered how many had come this way before her to be Cleansed.

And how many had never returned.

When everyone thought she was too far gone to hear anymore, she had heard them whisper about the dangers still ahead. Apparently, many things could go wrong tonight before they could save her, especially with Peter missing. No one had ever done a Cleansing without a Locator present.

They weren't even sure if it could be done.

Besides that, the amount of energy required to do the Cleansing could easily destroy her as much as help her. One little mistake and everything could go wrong—deadly wrong.

Blake was also not going to be able to help. The details of that were fuzzy for Rachel.

After her scream, she lost track of time. It seemed like forever, and yet only moments, before most of the house had assembled in her room. Donavon was first one to arrive. He had pulled her into his arms and was yelling for the others to come and help. Beth had been standing in the hallway in her yellow jacket, looking ashen and afraid. Amy showed up, only to be sent away to call Robert and tell him to take everything to the cave.

Nancy had come next. Most of what she said had been hard for Rachel to hear. The Evil was in her mind causing pain—excruciating pain—while it whispered words dripping with foul sweetness.

Come to me… I am here waiting for you. I will have you. I need you. I can make the pain stop, but only if you learn. Only if you surrender.

The Evil in her head was stronger now. With every passing minute, every passing step, it grew stronger.

She caught enough of what Nancy had been saying to piece together that her scream had startled Blake while he was helping with dishes in the kitchen. He had dropped a knife and it stabbed him in the foot. He was wrapping it up as best he could, but it was bleeding badly and needed stitches.

Pretty blood, hot and flowing. Look! I did it for you. All for you, my love. I love the pretty colors I make for you.

Everything had happened in such a rush after that. Donavon was scooping her up and running out to the garage behind the house. He gently placed her in the back seat of his SUV, and Rachel found her head being cradled by Amy, who was sitting beside her.

The motion of the car irritated Rachel. She tried to squeeze her eyes closed to block out as much of the movement as she could. The pain in her head was nauseating and she was sure she was going to throw up all over Donavon's beautiful car.

As much as Rachel tried to clench her teeth to keep her screams in, moans continually escaped as the agony racked her body. She wanted release, and was almost willing to accept it in any form that was offered.

Amy stroked her hair and tried to comfort her as best she could. Rachel knew that Donavon was in the front seat speaking angrily to someone, but she was too far gone at the moment to even attempt to understand what he was saying or who he was talking to.

Next, Rachel was aware of the SUV stopping. She had hoped the lack of motion would ease her discomfort, but the pain in her head as so intense that there was no relief to be found. She could barely hear other car doors slamming as she was being carried into the mouth of a giant cave—where she was now. The wind and rain had begun again, and Rachel was glad for the shelter.

Donavon quietly swore under his breath. "Amy, I forgot the lights. Blake, are you sure you can walk all the way down?"

I can make it stop. Just let me in, my love. Let me take over your mind. Don't resist. It hurts us both when you fight me.

She didn't want to die like this. She wasn't going to be some helpless creature that simply gave in when things got hard. She needed to fight back.

Struggling, she tried to push away from Donavon to stand on her own two feet. In a shaky voice, but with as much strength as she could muster, Rachel said, "Please, Donavon. I think I can walk. Let me try to walk."

Begrudgingly, he set her down and took a lamp from Amy to light the way. "Let me go first and make sure it's safe." Donavon's voice was strong, yet Rachel could hear the fear.

With Nancy and Amy on either side, Rachel started to follow Donavon deeper into the cave. Every step took more focus than she had ever used in her life. Blake came at the rear, an expression of severe pain on his face. Even his dark skin was pale with the pain and effort.

Another bolt of agony seared through Rachel's brain. She stumbled.

You are mine. No one else can save you. Come to me...

She could feel her eyes glossing over as the Evil cooed inside her brain.

Perceptive, Donavon glanced back, a crease of worry on his brow as if he could hear the voice too. His dark hair was damp from the moisture in the air. A sheen of water glistened on his skin. While others would be uncomfortable in the moist underground tunnel, Donavon didn't even seem to notice—his worried thoughts consumed with the task ahead.

The footsteps of the group echoed off the walls with a steady beat that felt like a funeral procession. The dark path wound down for an eternity. Nancy and Amy supported her body when the Evil would strike.

Beth followed behind everyone, looking scared and frail, her yellow jacket oddly bright in the darkness.

Finally… mercifully… they reached the end, arriving at a spacious cavern that housed a small beach and a large underground pool. Off in the distance, she could make out the sounds of water trickling down the rock face.

Illuminated by the lantern in his hand, Donavon strode over to the large man-made circle of rocks in the dirt. The women gently guided her to the center and helped her to kneel.

"We need to begin soon. There isn't much time left. Where *is* Peter?" Donavon, usually so calm and cool, had to stop for a moment to contain his rising agitation. His eyes narrowed dangerously as he scanned the dim cavern for the Locator.

Rachel hadn't known that anyone had found Peter. Off to the side in the shadows, a slight movement caught her eye. It looked as if Peter was slowly rising from his seated position. He began an unhurried tread over to the group. To the Order. She hadn't been expecting him to be here, but obviously someone had told him what was going on. After their last encounter, she couldn't blame him if he refused to come to her rescue… again.

With equal hostility in his voice Peter sarcastically sneered, "Sorry to keep you waiting." Anger, frustrations, and possibly even hatred burned like embers in Peter's eyes. A dark, sick terror crept into her heart, as she wondered if he would rather let her die than try to save her.

The voice spoke again.

Peter is with me… You know it… You can SEE IT! Come to me. Be with Peter. Wouldn't that make him happy? You want Peter to be happy. No pain. No fear.

Rachel tried to block out the Voice. She knew it would tell her anything to control her mind—even lies. But every good lie contains a grain of truth, and what she heard next was enough to freeze her heart.

Look in Peter's eyes. I am there.

The voice mimicked a soothing quality, yet bile rose up in her throat as she felt dark fingers twisting inside her brain, manipulating her thoughts. Reaching up, she absentmindedly rubbed her temples. The throbbing in her skull began to be overwhelming. She mumbled, "Get out, get out…" Unconsciously, her voice grew louder and more desperate. "Get out, get out… GET OUT!" Her screams echoed off the surface of the water before coming back to the quiet crowd.

She crumpled to the ground holding her head. Rocking back and forth, she weakly moaned, "Out, out, out, out…"

Peter glanced at her aching form. Sympathy and tenderness overshadowed the fury in his eyes for just a moment. Then, stone-faced, he took his place in the Order.

Robert took out the Life Box and set it in front of him. Donavon, being the most powerful of the group, would take the lead and begin the ceremony to Cleanse her.

With a savage intensity, he turned to Peter and spat, "Can you do this?" Donavon's face was tormented, but he spoke softer as he added, "I know you are upset with me. But I *need* to know if you can put your feelings aside." His voice waivered with emotion. "Help us save her."

She watched as Peter glared back—the fervor in his eyes intensifying. He stated simply, "Time is running out." His face was torn with anger. Hurt. Possibly jealousy. Or betrayal? Her heart wanted to break.

Her whole body shuddered violently, but not from the cold of the cave or the agony in her mind.

From fear.

Her fate rested in Peter's hands, and she was helpless except to wait and watch.

**

Peter glanced around the circle at his friends—his family. Directly across from him in the circle was his best friend, Donavon. But in this moment, after all that had happened today, Peter could hardly make himself recognize his friend standing there.

After leaving the house earlier, Peter had blindly walked wherever his feet had taken him. When he finally felt the urge to look up, he was standing in front of Rachel's old apartment building. Until that point, he had been blocking out all of his emotions and feelings, simply trying to escape. Seeing where his subconscious had brought him, Peter groaned as the memories flooded in.

Like a drowning man trying to break free from the ocean's pull, Peter fought the pain that was searing his chest. He sat down heavily on the curb and dropped his head into his hands.

How had things gotten so out of control? He had been so sure that he and Rachel were meant to be together. All the signs had been there! Every phrase she had spoken made him believe that she felt the connection too.

Or had she?

Every doubt, every insecurity he had ever felt—about his Gift and his purpose in life—came rushing to the surface to join in the fray. Is this where he was meant to be? Is this what he was meant to be doing? Would he spend his entire life manipulating people's feelings with his Gift, and always stand on the sidelines while his wants and desires passed him by?

Peter had never tried to make Rachel return his feelings by way of using his talent on her. The idea repulsed him. If she was going to love him, it was going to be of her own free will.

But maybe that was how things were for Locators. Was it really unfair to use the natural ability given to him to find happiness?

Guilt and rage fought in his mind as he though, "Yes. And you know it."

Peter stood up in disgust and started to walk again. Thoughts of Rachel were swimming around in his head—her blue eyes like the sky, her blonde hair like the sun, her smile and warmth.

And the kiss…

Peter could feel his pulse throbbing loudly in his ears as he remembered that one wonderful moment before his entire world fell apart. Even the purity of that heartfelt kiss had not been enough to make a difference.

Donavon had won.

Without even trying, Donavon had stolen her heart in a dream, right out from under Peter before he even had a chance to fight. Like an all-powerful Greek god, Donavon simply had to exist and the world was his oyster. Peter cursed his best friend, with his perfect looks and cool demeanor that women found so attractive. Peter would always be second best—the buddy—in comparison.

He knew he was mostly feeling self-pity. But he also felt like he had earned the right to wallow in a little pity—for the moment at least.

His thoughts rushed ahead.

He'd even told Rachel about the kiss with Beth. Why didn't that at least count as a few points in Peter's favor? It was not as if he had been locking lips with some other girl just a couple days ago!

Peter found himself back outside his home. He was not ready to go back inside and face reality yet. Instead, he jogged around the side of the house and headed up the mountainside. Nature was soothing, and he felt like he could use all the calming vibes he could find.

Peter was not a stupid guy. He was willing to admit that maybe Donavon's over-possessive nature around Rachel had mostly been in his head. Love can make a man see things that aren't there.

But Peter *knew* he had seen Beth and Donavon in a passionate embrace. Why was Rachel still willing to choose Donavon over himself with Beth in the equation?

If Donavon was truly a good guy, then maybe he only had feelings for Beth, and Rachel was simply wasting her time.

Inspiration and hope started to emerge in Peter's mind. All he needed to do was be patient, and maybe Rachel would come around. Maybe she would see that Donavon had chosen Beth, and that the connection she thought she had with Donavon was something on a different level—a student-teacher connection, perhaps.

Just as these thoughts were circling around in Peter's brain, he heard the familiar sound of his cell phone ringtone. Absentmindedly, he answered his phone and said hello without checking the display to see who was calling. He instantly regretted his decision as Donavon's familiar voice began to fill his ear.

"Peter, where are you?" Donavon sounded upset and frantic.

Peter's mind instantly rebelled as he thought, "I am so not ready to talk to you yet, buddy. Deep breath."

As Peter took that steadying breath, he answered, "I'm in the woods."

"We need you back here right away. Rachel is having another attack and we are taking her to the cave right now."

Rachel was in trouble and Peter hadn't been there to help her! He had failed her again.

Donavon added forcefully, "Why weren't you watching her? You were supposed to be with her."

Peter's growing concern for Rachel was immediately replaced by anger at Donavon's accusations. He growled into the phone, "Don't you try to blame this on me again. You're the super powerful one. Maybe if you hadn't been fraternizing with your girlfriend in the backyard then *you* might have noticed what was going on."

Donavon voice was equally harsh as he replied, "What is wrong with you? What are you talking about?"

Peter snapped, "Beth! I'm talking about Beth! If you weren't trying to move in on every girl in our house, maybe you could focus better."

Donavon sounded annoyed and his voice was angry and authoritative as he continued, "You are out of line Peter. I don't know what you think is going on with Beth and me, but you are wrong. I don't have time to argue with you about this. Rachel needs me."

"Ha!" Peter snorted. "Don't you pretend to care about Rachel!"

Donavon's next words were dead serious and cold, "I'm not pretending."

The weight of those words brought Peter up short.

His brain couldn't find the right words to argue back, so he simply seethed on his end of the phone.

Donavon's voice was like steel. "Get to the cave right now. I am not going to lose her because you are having some kind of misguided delusion." The threat in his final words was unmistakable, "Don't test me right now, Peter."

He could have cared less about Donavon's threat. Peter wasn't about to be intimidated or bullied. However, there was a piece of his brain that was surprised by the strength of Donavon's reaction. He had never known Donavon to be so fierce with him before. Could he really care that much about Rachel?

The small hope he had been trying to build moments earlier was crushed. It didn't matter that Peter could be as patient and unmoving as stone. Donavon was not going to choose Beth, leaving Rachel to find comfort in Peter's arms. The conversation on the phone had made that clear enough.

All of that was beside the point.

Rachel was in danger. Peter loved her too much to let her suffer, and so he found himself running as fast as he could towards the cave. He had to help her, even if he would then have to let her go.

So, Peter had arrived slightly ahead of the rest of the Order, and was waiting in the cavern when Donavon snapped, "Where *is* Peter?" He could feel his anger and annoyance build even further when Donavon had dared to ask—in that authoritative way that Peter was coming to think of as being oh-so-Donavon, "Can you do this?"

Oh, he could do it, all right! But he was doing it for her, and not because their great leader Donavon had demanded it.

Peter didn't know if he could return to the house after all of this was over, but for now he was going to remain a part of this Order. He was going to do his duty, and he was going to help save the woman he loved.

Again, Peter made himself look across the circle towards his best friend. He didn't know what the rest of the night was going to bring, but he knew nothing was ever going to be the same.

CHAPTER 20: THE CLEANSING

By Donavon's unseen command, the Order took their places in the circle. Blake looked particularly shaky and unstable. Rachel wondered if he could handle what was about to take place in his weakened condition. Everyone looked at Donavon, waiting for the ritual to begin, when her fears were suddenly realized as Blake collapsed to one knee with a groan.

Nancy was immediately at his side. Her voice was higher pitched that Rachel had ever heard it before, and there was an edge of hysteria to it as she commanded, "Look at his foot! Look at all the blood. Someone help him!" Then she turned her pleas to Blake himself. "You need to get off it. You have to sit down!"

A small sob escaped Nancy's lips. It surprised Rachel, who had always thought of Nancy as being so strong and tough. If there had been any doubt about Blake and Nancy's relationship, there were no questions now. Her obvious distress over his wellbeing, and Blake's attempts to reassure her were those of a couple.

Rachel's head was pounding mercilessly, and she was grateful to be kneeling in the middle of the circle. As Amy and Robert tried to help Blake move away and sit down, she could just make out his protest over the blood pounding in her ears, "No, you need me. You can't do the Cleansing without a complete Order. It's too dangerous."

Donavon left his place in the circle and helped Amy and Robert move Blake. His voice was sympathetic yet still confident. "Blake, you are in no condition to even stand, let alone participate in a Cleansing. We have Beth here." Donavon paused to look Beth in the eye. "I know you are still new at all of this, but we were making some great progress earlier today and I think you are in better shape for this at the moment than Blake. If you are willing, you can take his place in the circle."

Rachel looked up long enough to see the worried glances being exchanged by everyone standing around Blake.

Amy spoke up, "Are you sure that's a good idea? Beth has never done anything like this before."

Donavon's voice was desperate. "What choice do we have? Rachel needs help *now*, and Blake is in no condition to complete the circle." Turning to Beth, he added, "You are getting stronger. I felt it. Just remember what you've learned."

Beth's voice was timid, but she said, "If you think I can help, I'll do it."

Everything was settled, and the members of the Order took their places around the circle again with Beth in Blake's spot. Robert knelt down to open Rachel's Life Box, and he reverently took the heart in his hands and walked toward the center of the circle.

Rachel could hear the Evil hiss inside her mind at the sight of the heart.

You think that can stop me? Have you learned nothing? They will never Cleanse you! I will take you with me and we will be together, forever. In death I will have victory, my love. Tonight, we will die together, Sunshine.

Another stab of pain shot through Rachel, and she whimpered, yet extended her hands towards the heart and took it from Robert. He returned to his place in the circle.

At Donavon's command, the Order closed their eyes— everyone except Peter who had to look on with the eyes of a Locator.

Despite the pain coursing through Rachel's body, Donavon's voice rang out loud and clear in the chamber of the cave. She could hear it perfectly. "Now, extend your hands towards each other, stretching out with your energy and link the circle as one. Draw all the good you can sense in your aura and focus it. Channel it."

Rachel could feel the sudden build in the energy flowing around her. As the Order concentrated and increased their focus,

Rachel's pain also grew. Her limbs began to shake, and she was afraid she would drop the sphere, which had started to glow. The storm cloud from earlier had returned, but compared to what she saw the first time, this storm swirled like a hurricane inside the heart.

The heart's glow almost pierced her eyes. Sweat was beading on her forehead, and Rachel closed her eyes against the brightness of the sphere. However, even closing her eyes, nothing could stop the tears flowing down her cheeks.

Donavon's voice surrounded her. It was everywhere. "Now, focus your power and good on Rachel and our minds will link and allow us to force the Evil out."

Suddenly, all the power that Rachel had felt building around her was slicing right through her body.

Too many things happened at once for her to really comprehend what was going on. Her mind linked with those around her, but the Evil was snarling and screeching inside her skull so she couldn't make out any coherent thoughts. The pain reached a level that she never knew could exist. Rachel's back involuntarily arched, and a scream of agony ripped from the depths of her throat. The ground began to shake, and pieces of the cave ceiling began to rain down around the outside of the circle.

Rachel was aware of other screams and sounds of distress— one in particular more bloodcurdling than the rest. The heart tumbled away from her trembling hands as she was violently struck by something. The last thing she remembered was something hot, wet and sticky running down her face as the light from her heart began to fade and everything went black.

***

Peter wasn't sure how he had ended up on the ground, but he was suddenly flat on his back, choking and gagging on the dust and debris in the air, his talisman burning into the flesh of his finger from the power of the Evil. He had been absorbed in the power and beauty of the Order using all their energy as one. He had seen the flows of energy swirling around the circle, building and connecting everyone to each other. When it had reached its peak, he had heard Donavon explain how they were supposed to focus the massive amount of energy on Rachel and link their minds to hers.

As he felt that link begin to develop, not only with Rachel, but with everyone in the Order, something had gone terribly wrong. Peter had felt his mind connect with the already familiar auras of his family. Then as the last connections were being made, suddenly there was a taint.

The Evil was there in their minds.

Peter had expected this from the link with Rachel. They were trying to find the Evil that was going to take a hold of her mind and force it out. But this was different. The Evil was coming at them from two places—from the center and also the edge of the circle. And even more disturbing than this, the Evil was more powerful coming from somewhere on the edge than from Rachel.

With their minds all linked, everyone in the Order came to the same realization at the exact same moment.

It was Beth.

Beth was in far more danger than anyone ever suspected.

She hadn't been displaying any outward symptoms, but the Evil was by far stronger in her than in Rachel—and she didn't even know it herself. Peter expected some small pull from the Evil because Beth was Uncleansed, but it should have been minimal—insignificant given her symptoms.

Beth's scream of terror echoed around the cavern and everything began to shake. Pieces of the ceiling began to fall, and their connection with the energy was immediately broken. The force of the break was so powerful that it drove Peter backwards and pinned him to the ground.

Now, as he tried to stand up, so many things were suddenly clear. The mental link had born its fruits, and Peter knew—as did everyone else—what had really been going on.

First of all, Beth's Gift was earth. She was the one who had made the ground shake and the cave ceiling crumble. In fact, she had made the ground shake earlier that afternoon during Rachel's previous attack, only Beth herself had been unaware of what she was doing.

More than that, she had more than one Gift.

Beth's *other* talent was manipulating the energy of the mind.

A Gift comes from an energy source, but energy is everywhere—in the air, the earth, fire, electricity, water, sound… and also in brain waves. As a Locator, Peter now easily recognized this power in Beth through the link. He supposed it was similar to his Gift to befriend those around him. His talent was a manipulation of the energy waves in the brain to some degree as well.

But Beth was far more powerful.

And dangerous.

She didn't even know what she was doing, and she had no control. Memories flashed in Peter's mind rapidly as all the pieces fell together to make a terrifying picture. They had all been so blind to what was really happening.

That first day of school, Peter remembered having a nagging feeling in the student union that he had looked at Beth several times, but his focus would slip past her.

Beth had been hiding.

Naturally shy, she was able to use her Gift to make those around her ignore her presence, turning her into the perfect wallflower.

Later that day, in their home when he had felt Beth's energy surge in response to seeing Donavon for the first time, she had let her guard drop for just a split second out of shock. The tremendous surge in power Peter had felt was Beth's true ability. She wasn't as powerful as Donavon, but she possessed an incredibly strong Gift.

And the kiss... suddenly seeing all of these memories through the clarity of the link's revelation, Peter had been able to see what was behind the kiss between Beth and Donavon.

Donavon had been trying so desperately to help Beth while they were working together that he had completely opened himself up to her, making himself vulnerable to her Gift. Beth had been in love with Donavon. Her feelings became so strong for him, that as Donavon kept working with her and things got more intense, Beth unconsciously started to manipulate the situation. Without either of them even knowing what was really going on, they suddenly kissed.

Peter now also saw into Donavon's mind. He saw the shock and remorse in the moment that followed. Of course, Donavon blamed himself. He was the man and should be in control of his feelings. Donavon didn't know why he had done it, but he knew it had happened and he needed to take responsibility.

Beth's actions hadn't been vicious in any way, but she had still been using a power that she didn't understand and couldn't control. No one in the Order was familiar with this kind of situation—with a Gift like Beth's—and they had all been helpless to intervene.

Beth had fooled them all.

She hadn't been displaying any of the usual symptoms of suffering from the Evil because she was able to mask them with her ability—her ability to be unnoticed. Regardless, the Evil had been present the entire time, silently manipulating and poisoning her thoughts.

And the greatest treachery had been with Peter himself.

As pieces of the puzzle continued to slide into place, he and Beth had realized at the same moment that she had been unconsciously pushing Peter into loving Rachel all this time. From the very moment Beth had seen Donavon carry Rachel into the house and place her on the couch, from the second she could tell that he was protecting her and caring for her, Beth's mind had searched for a way to get Rachel out of the equation. Her eyes had landed on Peter, and the solution had been simple.

If Rachel was with Peter, then Beth could be with Donavon.

Beth's mind hadn't even been sure of her course while Rachel was unconscious on the couch. It wasn't until after her conversation with Peter on the porch that she had decided what she wanted. Then, when Peter went back to check on Rachel, and Rachel opened her eyes and said his name, it was all a done-deal.

Beth's influence was too strong for Peter to resist.

But that wasn't entirely true.

Deep down inside, Peter knew that he would have loved Rachel anyway. His breaking heart was real, and Beth had only expedited the entire process. It was true that the few moments Peter had been able to get away from Beth—going for walks, or Beth leaving the house—he had been able to think more clearly. His rage would subside, along with his jealousy of Donavon and uncontrollable love for Rachel. But even then, he had always still loved Rachel in his own way.

The Evil had been playing the most dangerous and powerful of games. It had been playing the game of love, and they had all been unknowing pawns.

In the moment immediately before the link with the Order had been shattered, Peter had felt something else shatter with Beth's horrible scream—her mind.

The Evil had won, and Beth was never going to be the same again.

Peter pushed himself back up to a standing position. The dust in the air was starting to settle, and he could hear groans of pain around him from his family. He called out into the blackness, "Is everyone all right? Robert? Where are the lights?"

It was amazing how much clearer in thought Peter had become in just the few moments that Beth had withdrawn her compulsion. The lanterns flickered back to life—thanks to Robert—and Peter was able to get his first glimpses of the destruction and chaos that Beth had surrounded them in.

The chamber was unrecognizable. Enormous chucks of the ceiling were scattered around, along with smaller bits and pieces. The circle was completely littered with debris, and heavy dirt clouds were still filtering out of the air. Nancy had a large gash across her right arm, and she was protectively huddled over Blake who was now nursing the wound in his foot along with a nasty cut that was bleeding all over the leg of his pants. Amy appeared to be unhurt and simply covered in a heavy coating of dust and dirt. Robert was squatting down by Rachel's Life Box. He had a thin scratch down the left side of his face.

Peter called out, "Where is Beth?" She needed to be contained immediately, before any more damage was done. However, using his Locator skills, Peter knew that Beth was gone. In the middle of the chaos, she had run away.

Continuing to scan the cavern, Peter noticed that Donavon wasn't anywhere near his original position. Instead, he was sitting in the middle of the circle with his back to Peter. He appeared to be rocking back and forth and his head was bent over something.

Rachel.

Peter ran over to his friend, dodging the boulders and rocks in his path. When he knelt down next to Donavon, he could see his friend's face contorted in pain and covered in tears. He had blood all over his chest, completely soaking the front of his shirt.

Peter gasped, "You're hurt."

Donavon simply shook his head. His voice was so full of anguish that Peter could hardly recognize it. "It's not me. It's her." Donavon lifted his gaze to stare unseeing at the ceiling. His voice ripped from his throat, "Oh God! There is so much blood… so much blood!" He looked back down at Rachel and continued to rock her back and forth. He leaned his face down to her ear and whispered, "Shh… it will be all right. It's all going to be okay. Shh…"

Rachel's body was limp and lifeless, but Peter could just make out the shallow rise and fall of her chest. The heart of her Life Box was weakly pulsing next to her body, and fading slightly with each passing moment.

Donavon was right. There was far too much blood. She had been struck on the back of the head by a large jagged rock. She would bleed out in a matter of minutes, and they were miles from any kind of medical help.

Hopelessness and helplessness washed over Peter. There was nothing any of them could do. Amy and Robert joined them, both with terrified looks on their faces. Robert whispered, "Donavon… I am so sorry."

Amy pushed her way over to Donavon and placed a hand on his shoulder. She spoke in the most serious tones, "You have to help her Donavon. There isn't much time left."

Donavon looked up at Amy, his eyes burning with emotion, "I'm easing her pain as much as I can. I don't think she can feel anything right now."

Peter was grateful to Donavon in that moment. He was doing more than any of the rest of them could for Rachel.

"That is not what I mean." Peter glanced at Amy as she continued. "When we were linked, I think I discovered something that we never knew about you."

Amy knelt down beside Donavon and Rachel. As if to emphasize the weight of her words, she put both of her hands on Donavon's shoulders and forced him to look her directly in the eye. Smiling, she said, "I think you can heal her."

Donavon turned his head up to look at the ceiling again. Taking a deep breath, he squeezed his eyes closed as more tears streamed down his face. His voice was shaky, "Amy, we don't have time for this. If you had discovered something, we would all know about it through the link. What are you talking about?" He sounded hopeless, and acted as if he just wanted to be left alone in his final remaining moments with Rachel.

Amy gently tilted his head back down and continued to look him straight in the eye with a smile on her face. "You didn't know about the connection I made because I didn't figure it out until after the link was broken. My Gift is with the physical energy that people possess—manipulating the physical body. Deep inside you, untapped, I could feel that same energy—only different in some way." Amy's eyes were sparkling with excitement. "And then I remembered Peter's scar."

Amy stood up, walked to Peter and slid his sleeve up. There, visible even in the dim light, was the scar that Donavon had given Peter the day he was first attacked by the Evil. It was a scar in the identical shape of Donavon's hand. Amy continued, "My Gift works two ways. I can give someone more energy or I can take it away. Your Gift has to be the same way. If you can hurt Peter then you can also heal him. You can heal Rachel!"

The logic made sense. Peter could feel the beginnings of hope starting to return. It was almost too much to believe that Donavon might have the power to save the woman they both loved—that he could heal and never knew it.

Conflicting emotions raged across Donavon's face. Cautiously, he asked, "If that's true, then I had this ability all along. Why didn't anyone discover this about me during my Cleansing?"

Logically, Amy answered, "Probably because no one else in your circle had the same Gift I do and so they didn't notice the difference. They could tell about your talent with the sense of touch, but dismissed anything else. They could have misinterpreted Peter's scar and why he got it." For further clarification, she added, "You know, this is the first time I've ever been linked with you."

It was true. While Robert had been the youngest in the house for a long time now, Amy was still the newest before Beth and Rachel came along. As far as Peter knew, this was the first Cleansing Amy had participated in since her own which had been done by a completely different Order.

Hope continued to blossom in Peter's heart. Maybe Donavon could do this. Before Peter could get too excited, Amy sobered a little. "There is one catch that I am afraid of."

Peter wanted to scream, "What now?!" He felt like he was on an emotional rollercoaster. Just when things started to look up, everything would suddenly take a turn south.

Amy continued, "You don't have any training in using this new ability, and there isn't time for me to help you figure it out. So, we are going to need to recreate things, as much as we can, to resemble the last time you used this Gift."

Donavon's voice was bleak as he finished for her, "My Trial... I have to take off my ring."

Nancy had been listening from across the cavern while helping Blake. Peter heard her hiss in response to Donavon's statement.

Amy looked pleadingly at Nancy for understanding. "It's the only way. Donavon called on this particular ability to defend himself when he was being attacked by the Evil. It was before his Cleansing. If he removes his ring now, he will be susceptible to the influences of the Evil again and he might be able to recreate his use of the power."

Turning to look at Donavon, she added, "But this time you know what you are doing, and you can use it to heal instead of hurt. You are the strongest among us. If anyone can do this, it's you."

Nancy snapped, "It's too dangerous."

Nobody had suffered as greatly at the hands of the Evil as Donavon had. During the years that he had been protected by his ring, Peter was sure Donavon had continued to grow in power, and would therefore be even more susceptible to the Evil's influence—the stronger the Gift, the stronger the Evil. Donavon had barely survived the first time with his life and sanity intact. There was every likelihood that this time, the Evil would win.

Amy said softly, "Without trying, Rachel will die."

Donavon looked grim, yet there was hope in his voice as he said, "I'll do it." Quietly, as if speaking only to Rachel, he added, "Without you, I'm already gone anyway."

The memory of Rachel's voice echoed in Peter's mind, "I was already gone."

Peter closed his eyes and clenched his fist at the stabbing pain in his heart.

Amy softly corrected, "No, *we'll* do it—together. You won't be alone. We can all link again, and we can use our energy to try and protect you both while you heal her."

Blake's voice was strong as he added, "If this thing takes you, man… it will take all of us with it too."

Peter suddenly noticed that Nancy and Blake had joined their little circle. Everyone was huddled around Donavon and Rachel now. They were all in this together.

Like family…

This was it, the beginning of the end. They were all going to leave this place together, or they were all going to die.

And they were ready.

Everyone sat down around Donavon and Rachel to join hands and reform the circle. Blake was in no condition to stand, so sitting was going to have to do. Rachel's breathing was still shallow and her sphere flicked dimly. Everyone knew that when the light went out, she would be gone.

Peter looked at his family through the eyes of a Locator. He wanted to memorize the colors and brilliance of their auras. He wanted to remember this moment forever, as they joined and used their energy together. Only he could see their talismans' glowing, sparkling with the red of rubies, blue of sapphires, white of diamonds and green of emeralds.

And yet there was also a darkness still hovering around Rachel and her almost lifeless body. The Evil was waiting, ready to attack.

Donavon spoke, "Then let's do this—together." He made eye contact with every member of the Order. "When I take my ring off, we will have very little time. Be ready."

He then looked at Robert, needing Robert to allow him to remove the ring from his finger.

Robert looked back and said, "Now."

Donavon slipped the ring from his finger, and there was a flash of light as everyone poured their energy into protecting him and Rachel. Their minds linked, and through Amy's awareness, everyone, including Donavon, was able to feel the new Gift lying dormant inside him. Peter could feel him desperately grasp for it, but the Evil was much faster.

Suddenly, darkness was everywhere. The swirling black mist grew, and voices of pain and torture started to emanate from within the dark cloud. Peter could feel it seeping into his brain. It was so much more potent and powerful than what he remembered from before his own Cleansing. Every fiber of his being called out in terror and agony.

Peter could hear the struggles of everyone around him, working as hard as they could to push the Evil away with their combined strength. Peter concentrated on the pulsing light coming from Rachel's sphere, and he pushed with all the strength he could find.

The darkness screamed in protest. A horrible voice filled the air.

I will take them. I will kill you all and take Donavon and Rachel's power with me.

Peter fought even harder. Rachel's sphere was like a beacon of light in the middle of a raging black storm. Peter could feel the air whipping past his face. Rocks and dirt felt like sand paper as they scraped his skin raw. It was getting hard to breathe, and everyone was rapidly growing tired. The Evil was beginning to overtaking them.

Donavon's mind reached out to everyone. The words he sent to their minds were pure and confident. "I have to let the Evil in."

Peter could feel Donavon's confidence in the link. He knew it was the only way to save Rachel and rest of them. He was going to sacrifice himself to save everyone else.

He was going to stop resisting the Evil and focus entirely on saving Rachel.

"No!" The word ripped from Peter's throat. He could feel the panic of those around him as well, but it was too late. Donavon had dropped his defenses. Peter could feel the intensity of Donavon's pain as the Evil seeped into every cell of his body.

But he could feel something else too.

He could feel Donavon stirring the dormant power that was within him. He could also feel Amy guiding him, helping him discover what was hidden inside. Blake, Nancy, Robert, and Peter were all struggling to shield them from the darkness as best they could, but it was an impossible task with Donavon inviting it in.

As the battle raged, Peter felt a weak presence start to contribute to the fray. Even though she hadn't moved a muscle, Rachel was drawing strength from those around her, and in turn she was beginning to fight back the Evil as well. Peter could see the distinct impression of her aura joining with the others. Her feeble presence was weakly linked to the rest of them, and Peter could tell that she was trying in her desperation to help protect Donavon. Donavon was growing weaker and weaker, and Rachel only had moments left before she would be too drained to do anything further.

But something strange was happening…

Donavon and Rachel's auras were growing and connecting to each other.

In that instant, Peter had another sudden revelation. Something his father had told him, along with the memory of racing to Rachel's apartment to save her, suddenly clicked together. That day, as Donavon had rushed to Rachel's side for the first time, their auras had connected in a sudden burst of light.

Donavon and Rachel were bonded, just like in the story Peter's father had told him. He could see it now with his Locator eyes. He thought, "They really are meant to be together."

Peter felt the quiet, peaceful confirmation from both Rachel and Donavon in his mind.

Suddenly, he knew what they had to do. With one mind, Peter allowed the rest of the Order to see through his Locator eyes. Everyone focused on the visible bond between Donavon and Rachel that they could now see as well. They poured their energy into that connection, which started to grow and light up the room, in a myriad of dazzling rainbow colors. The bond continued to expand. Its power was self-feeding and becoming stronger by the second.

Donavon took that power, and he focused his pain, his anger, his desperation and his love into using his new Gift—into healing. Through his eyes, everyone could see the wound on Rachel begin to knit back together. The bleeding slowed, and then stopped completely.

The power intensified as they all concentrated harder. The wind continued to whip around the cavern, and the terrible voices in the darkness howled in pain and rage. They were finally getting the upper hand, and the Evil was being pushed back.

With the thrill and adrenaline of this sudden turn of events, Peter, along with the rest of the Order, dug down into the last reserves of strength they possessed, and reached inside Rachel and Donavon to rip the Evil from their minds—from their souls.

Suddenly there was an explosion of light, and then everything was calm.

Peter blinked.

It was over.

Everyone took a moment to stare at each other as they sat in the circle. Nancy and Blake fell back on one another, and Robert's pale face looked almost translucent. Everyone's breathing came in gasps, and they all sat exhausted.

And yet disbelief began to give way to smiles and then finally weak laughter.

Rachel's eyes fluttered open and searched Donavon's face. Despite Peter's relief and happiness at the outcome of this terrible night, there fluttered a sweet pain in his heart as he watched his best friend and the woman they both loved. He glanced over at her heart, it glowed with a throbbing yet pure intensity that mirrored her own heart.

Carefully Donavon slipped his ring back on his finger and he and Rachel stared at one another, reflecting each other's deep love. Their bond had overcome the Evil.

Somehow it was the key that they needed to fight back.

And with everyone's combined strength, they had won.

EPILOGUE: AFTER

Much of her Cleansing remained hazy in Rachel's mind. When she tried to recall the events a few days later, she mostly remembered overwhelming feelings of pain and terror.

No one had located Beth yet. When Rachel had asked what would happen to her, they sadly told her that Beth probably wouldn't survive. Not every Gifted person was found by an Order, and many of them were not found in time to be saved from the mind-shattering effects of the Evil. In those cases, they would usually go insane, and eventually the body would shut down without the mind. Sometimes the victim would rampage around the world causing unspeakable horrors—reports of mass killings, schools burning with children inside, suicide bombings—and sometimes they would end up locked away for the rest of their lives.

While no news outlets reported any unusual events in the area or a mentally deranged person wandering the streets, the Order was convinced that Beth's mind had shattered during the events in the cave. The break had been felt by everyone. They assumed that she had wandered off in the woods and would probably starve to death, huddled underneath some tree.

Rachel shuddered. She had liked Beth. It wasn't her fault that the Evil had targeted her. And Rachel had been so close to breaking herself.

For the last three days Blake, Robert, or Donavon covered different sections of the woods surrounding the cave, searching for Beth. Blake came back yesterday afternoon with the yellow jacket that Beth had worn that night, but that was it.

Rachel wondered why the talismans had not protected everyone from the Evil's influence through Beth's mind control. Donavon explained later that the talisman would only protect them from direct attacks from the Evil itself. Beth's mind control came from inside herself. It was no different than Donavon's ability to manipulate touch. The Gifted could choose to use their talents for good or for ill, but it was a personal choice and completely separate from the direct influence of the Evil. Beth, unknowingly, had been using her powers against those she cared about.

With such great power and the potential for danger hidden in Beth… It was a reminder of why it was so important to find the Gifted and Cleanse them quickly.

Rachel again could not believe that she had made it through. And she had the Order to thank for that.

Thinking about everyone in the Order made her sad because Peter was gone now too.

The morning after they returned from the cave, Rachel lay resting in bed, trying to recover her strength. Physically, she was as good as new. Donavon's power had been so strong in those last moments that he had actually reached out and healed the injuries of everyone in the cave. Even Peter's scar on his arm had disappeared.

But emotionally, Rachel felt wrung out and tired. She wanted to lie in bed for a long time, just to gather her thoughts and figure out what life had in store for her now.

A gentle knock on the door was quickly followed by Peter making his entrance. He smiled a warm smile at her, and softly announced, "I've come to say goodbye."

Rachel had bolted upright in bed and looked at him with huge innocent eyes. All she could do was gasp, "Why?"

Peter frowned slightly, but came to sit on the bed next to her. He gently took her hand and smiled again. There was no awkwardness for her in his touch now. Everything between them was going be friendship. There was no other way around it. After the mind link in the cave, everyone knew exactly how each of them felt about the other. Peter was intimately aware her feelings for Donavon.

That had been one of the few good things about the entire experience. Rachel saw inside Donavon's mind, and he into hers, and there was no doubt about the depth and breadth of their connection and love. They knew each other perfectly now.

She also saw inside Peter's mind, and he in hers, and they had both discovered a deep friendship. Peter's was a confusing mix of friendship and a more intense romantic love, but Rachel's heart had been pure, and Peter knew that she had a deep affection for him that was greater than anyone else in the house.

In an odd twist of fate, they had ended up with a connection too—a deep and lasting friendship unlike any she had ever known.

However, Peter also knew that he needed to move on, and that was what he had come to do.

Looking deeply into her eyes, his voice was husky with emotion as he explained, "I have to go. I need to clear my head and figure some things out." Rachel began to protest. Her heart was breaking for her friend, but he silenced her with a finger to her lips, "Beth might have made me go crazy, out of my head, madly in love with you," he smiled, "But she didn't have to work very hard at it. That love was already inside of me, and I need to deal with that."

He stood up to pace around the room as he continued, "You don't know what it's like to have someone messing around in your head the way she was in mine."

One surprising factor of Rachel's immediate bond with Donavon was that, once it had been established between them that very first day, it had counteracted Beth's ability to influence their minds. From that point on, no matter how much Beth unconsciously tried, she could not change the feelings that Rachel and Donavon had for each other. It was like they had become immune.

So, it was true. Rachel didn't know what it was like to have Beth in her head.

"Will you be coming back?" She was a little scared to ask.

Peter stopped pacing and looked at her again. "I don't know." Then, a little more light-hearted, he added, "I hope so."

Suddenly, there was a knock at her door.

Peter and Rachel looked at one another.

"Come in," she called.

The smiling face of Stu poked around the door. "Hey there, Sunshine! Hey, Peter!" He came in and immediately could feel the tension in the air. "Did I interrupt something?"

Peter shook his head, "I was just leaving." He walked over to Rachel's side and leaned down to give her a kiss on the forehead. "Goodbye, sweetie."

Rachel and Peter exchanged one last tender look.

Stu cleared his throat, "Are you sure you guys are related?"

Peter chuckled softly. Making his way to the door, he told Stu, "I said we were *like* family." And with that, he left.

Later, Rachel went into Peter's room, only to discover that he had spent the entire night packing.

Rachel was racked with guilt, and she had curled up on Peter's old bed. Over the course of the next few days, she often found herself in Peter's room.

That was where Donavon found her today. He quietly slipped into the room and gently lay down on the bed beside her. Peter had been gone for three days, and Rachel acutely felt the lack of his presence in the house.

Donavon cradled her in his arms, and his lips were next to her ear, sending shivers down her spine, when he whispered, "It's not your fault, you know."

Rachel felt her eyes start to sting and she fought to control the tears. "It's all my fault." Donavon squeezed her tighter, and she continued, "Maybe if we had tried to Cleanse Beth first, instead of using her box for me, maybe she would have made it. If I had never shown up, maybe Peter would still be here and I wouldn't be ripping our family apart."

Donavon's voice was kind, "That's an awful lot of maybes, my dear." He gently started to rub his hand up and down her arm in comforting strokes. "And it wouldn't be 'our' family if you weren't here."

Rachel knew there was no way she could stay away from Donavon now. She suspected that would remain true, even if it meant she could fix all the wrongs of the last month. The thought made her guilt deepen. She couldn't change the past, but she still felt the need to try and fix things now.

An idea occurred to her, and she propped herself up on one elbow to look Donavon in the face. "Can I ask for something?"

Donavon's smile was lazy and pleased. He'd been so relaxed and comfortable around Rachel ever since the link in the cave. The only time Rachel saw him unhappy was when they talked about Beth or Peter. She could tell that he missed his friend deeply, and he too felt some guilt towards Peter's pain.

But right now, he was like a content cat stretched out on the bed. He laughed, "You can ask for anything."

"Can I come with you to look for Beth today? I know it's your last day trying to find her." Rachel had to get out of the house and do something—anything—and this was her last chance to try and make a difference for Beth.

Donavon reached up to pull her back into his arms, "Sure. I was going to leave in just a few minutes." She could hear the more serious turn his voice began to take. "I don't have a lot of hope that we will find anything, but maybe with your special awareness of the auras around people, you can help us find anything we may have missed."

It was strange for Rachel to think of herself as Gifted. As promised, the Cleansing in the cave had uncovered what her unique talents were. She had a few, it turned out, which was unusual.

Then again, it seemed like Donavon, Beth and Robert all had multiple Gifts. Maybe it wasn't as unusual as everyone had once believed. Or, maybe there was something extra special about *this* Order.

Robert had a Gift with both Life Boxes, metal, and electricity. Donavon could manipulate sense of touch, and now he had his newly found ability to heal. Beth could use the energy in the earth and change brain waves.

Rachel liked to think of her talents as being in two categories.

First, she could manipulate the weather. Apparently, she had been the one causing all the storms during her attacks. She hadn't really put together that the weather had been bad every time the Evil appeared in her mind, and when she had noticed, she assumed the Evil was causing it.

Included with her ability to control the weather, there were smaller Gifts consisting of air, water, and fire. The most frustrating thing was that Rachel had no idea how to use or control any of these Gifts. Donavon assured her that with training she would figure it out. She had gotten glimpses through the link of how it might work, but she was too scared to practice yet.

The second category of Gifts was her unusual talent to sense Gifted people when they were nearby. Just recently, in the last day or so, that Gift had developed even further. If Rachel concentrated hard enough when she was sensing someone, she could actually see a picture in her head of where that person was, and what they were doing. It only worked over very short distances, and it was sporadic at best, but Rachel was excited by the possibilities.

She thought, "Maybe I can help find Beth, if she's even still out there."

The idea of Beth alone in the woods for days made Rachel shiver. Even worse was the idea of Beth's dead body somewhere in the forest. Donavon, misinterpreting her shiver, held her tighter.

It was time to go.

This time Blake was coming along with them. They had divided the mountain side into quadrants, and today's section was the last to be searched. The weather had made a turn for the worse, and it was getting uncomfortably chilly. Winter was coming, and Rachel suspected by nightfall she would be able to see her breath in the cold air.

She mused, "Maybe when I learn how to control my Gift, it can be Spring all the time."

Rachel had to laugh at the idea. No one was that powerful.

As they hiked, the hours slipped by. Rachel fell into a kind of a trance from the rhythmic crunching of the dead leaves under their feet. The sun was rapidly disappearing behind the trees, and it was still a long walk back home. They hadn't seen any signs of Beth, and Rachel hadn't felt a glimmer of any other presence besides Donavon and Blake.

She hadn't actually expected to find Beth, but she had hoped that coming out to look for her would somehow ease the pain in her heart and the guilt in her chest.

Rachel was so disappointed that she now felt guiltier than ever.

Holding hands with Donavon, they walked all the way to the end of the deer path they had been following. It stopped on the bank of a shallow swift stream. Everyone agreed it was time to turn around and head back, but Blake wanted to stop by the stream for just a minute to wash his face.

That was when Rachel finally felt it. So far away that she almost missed it, she picked up on something—a presence.

Beth…

Rachel reached out and clutched Donavon's arm. He immediately turned and looked at her with serious eyes, "What do you feel?"

Rachel was shaky with the sudden adrenaline. She whispered, "It's her."

Blake whipped his head up, "Are you sure? Where is she?"

Rachel tried to focus, but it was difficult to control this new awareness. "I know it's her for sure, but she's far away."

Blake smiled in his boyish way, "That's one awesome power you got there, Rach."

She was focusing so hard she couldn't even offer Blake a smile for his comment.

A vision was coming to her.

Rachel was terrified it would slip away before she could figure out where Beth was, so she closed her eyes and concentrated even harder.

Beth was under a tree that looked like every other tree they had passed today. Her surroundings gave no clue as to where she was. Her clothes were muddy, and she looked exactly like someone who had been lost in the woods for three days. She seemed weak, and Rachel was sure Beth's life was going to slip away soon if no one found her.

Rachel wanted to reach into her mind and pluck Beth to safety, but that was frustratingly impossible.

Suddenly, there was movement next to Beth. Something was coming out of the bushes. Rachel grabbed Donavon's arm even harder as she watched a man step out of the leaves and kneel down by Beth.

When he spoke, Rachel thought her heart would stop beating. His voice was exactly like the Voice she heard in her nightmares. It dripped with the same nauseating darkness that kept her up at nights, too afraid to sleep.

Rachel could hardly hold back the scream that rose in her throat as the man's words rang in her ears.

I've come for you, Beth, my love.

ABOUT THE AUTHOR

Marsha graduated from Utah State University in Music Education, but then got the crazy idea to write a novel. She currently resides in Utah with her husband, sons and dog. She loves music, family, friends and reading (or writing) a good book.

For more information on *The Order Saga*, visit the website at:
http://sites.google.com/site/theordersaga/

Or the blog at:
http://theordersaga.blogspot.com/

Or become a fan on Facebook at:
http://www.facebook.com/ordersaga

Or follow Marsha on Twitter:
http://twitter.com/TheOrderSaga

SPECIAL THANKS

November, 2020: Nothing takes more time, energy, and favors than creating your first novel. Looking back, years later, I cannot even begin to remember all the people who helped me on my journey, but I am going to give it a try. (If I miss someone, let me know and as long as I am able to update and edit my own manuscripts, I will be sure to correct it!)

A very special thanks, all those years ago, to Julie Gardner and Emily Jensen for doing the most professional job a friend could ask for in helping me edit my very first creation. They each took hours and hours of their personal time to help me and support me. For that, I will always be grateful.

Thank you to some of my very first readers and editors. My husband, Scott Stokes… my sister, Krystal Hall… one of my best friends from college, Nicole Oksness… You guys were the ones who kept my secret for Christmas, read my manuscript chapter by chapter as they were written, and encouraged me all along the way. I will always remember the excitement of those months, watching my story unfold, and being the most surprised of anyone when I actually finished it.

Thank you to Angela Tomlinson for sharing my work with MK McClintock, who then graciously helped me set up a virtual book tour. I learned so much from MK, and continue to follow her and be inspired by her work. One of my favorite stops on the tour was A Novel Idea Live and their interview. I felt like a real celebrity!

And thank you to any of my readers who reached out and told me how much you enjoyed my work. I know I have left you hanging for years and year, but good things come to those who wait, and your words of praised have continued to keep me inspired over the years to never give up on writing more of my characters' stories. Love you all!